2

Dislocation

Dislocation

STORIES FROM A NEW IRELAND

Edited with an Introduction by

Caroline Walsh

CARROLL & GRAF PUBLISHERS
NEW YORK

Dislocation
Stories from a New Ireland

Carroll & Graf Publishers
An Imprint of Avalon Publishing Group Inc.
161 William Street, 16th Floor
New York, NY 10038

First Carroll & Graf edition 2003

First published in Great Britain by Scribner/Townhouse in 2002

Library of Congress Cataloging-in-Publication Data is available.

ISBN: 0-7867-1206-6

Printed in the United States of America
Distributed by Publishers Group West

Contents

Introduction

by Caroline Walsh

The opportunity to edit a collection of contemporary Irish short stories couldn't have come at a better time. A new century, a new generation of writers, a radically changed Ireland – the prospect was exciting. However, as the dust settled, challenges began to emerge. What, for instance, constitutes Irishness in 2002? Irish forebears? An Irish passport? Are there stratas of Irishness or is it now more a perspective, a state of mind? Opting for the broadest possible definition – inclusiveness – seemed the best way to proceed: Irish born and bred, Irish in England, Irish American, the net is wide.

As Ireland grew in confidence in the past century the novel form, as had been anticipated, became more established, but happily not at the expense of what Richard Ford once memorably called Ireland's national art form – the short story. There are lots of fine short story writers working in Ireland today. The challenge was not so much to identify them as to select which of them to include. Restricting the field to those whose work has come to prominence over the past ten to fifteen years made this somewhat easier, though it still entailed difficult decisions. Interestingly, several of those included are novelists as well, belying the notion that the short story is just a stepping stone, an apprenticeship, to the longer form.

Another challenge was whether or not to select from the established canon, go the safe road as it were, or take a chance and commission new stories. Ultimately the prospect of calling original short stories into being proved too tempting. Asking writers for new work meant that the character of the collection would be defined by what they produced rather than by any framework an editor might impose. Several contributors asked if there was a theme, to which the answer was no. Theme collections, like theme parks, rarely shake off the cloak of contrivance.

The result is a very diverse collection, diverse in a whole range of ways. Set in contemporary urban Ireland, London, Manhattan, the west coast of the US, Scandinavia, Mitteleuropa, rural Ireland, airborne over the Atlantic and beyond, the stories would seem to mirror the 'frantic, globalized, dislocated Ireland' identified by Fintan O'Toole in 'Writing the boom', an essay on contemporary fiction which appeared in *The Irish Times* in 2001. Several of the observations made by O'Toole are borne out by this collection, notably his contention that, 'These days, it is by no means clear what the big story of Ireland actually is, or indeed that the whole notion of "Ireland" as a single framework has any validity'. But diversity of geographical setting is only part of the tableau to emerge. The time zones these stories inhabit range from an era steeped in folklore and pishoguery to a world of virtual reality fantasies, surreal, drug-induced hallucinations, sheer speed and even eternal space. Equally, while some of the stories, be it wistfully or wryly, hark back to a more familiar Ireland, others aren't concerned with Ireland, good, bad or indifferent. Ireland and Irishness feature prominently in this collection alright, but not as the defining forces they were in the past.

It is no longer possible to offer a single artistic version of the nation, nor indeed is it even desirable. Key cultural, historical, reference points – the Catholic Church, the violent birth pangs of a new state – have receded so rapidly in the last decade or so as to be now almost invisible.

Despite all that diversity, however, there are a number of common themes worth considering. Ironically, these themes – alienation, isolation, disaffection – can be seen as stemming from the same root as that divergence. Several characters in these stories have what the narrator in Molly McCloskey's *A Nuclear Adam and Eve*, calls 'the appetite for meaninglessness that would come to mark our generation'. Here is a world in which people in grocery stores wander the aisles alone facing 'a grotesquerie of choice', a world marked by an 'exponential increase of everything unpleasant'. Matt, the narrator in Blánaid McKinney's *These Important Messages* is similarly at odds with the fast moving scenario into which he lands. He rails against the barrage of advertising to which he is constantly subjected. He is brought to breaking point, literally driven crazy by its 'flood of logo-effluent'. The avaricious, roller-coaster London world in which he finds himself is one which 'does not seek things out to salvage them; it seeks them out to destroy them'.

This same urban malaise, this estrangement, is at the heart of Sean O'Reilly's *Playboy*. This story, which confirms the often-expressed notion that the short story comes into its own when depicting the lives of the marginalized, is set in netherworld Dublin. It is a city of random assaults, drug-crazed odysseys and violent sex. It is a place of savage extremes, a city spinning frantically out of control. Here the quotidian is remarkable. On this squalid stage the workers, the breadwinners, who 'would be out of work in less than an hour' are the aliens, the freaks.

Through the musings of a 7' 2" tall very frequent flyer, Keith Ridgway, in *Grid Work*, depicts a world which, though not destructive in the same sense as that conjured by O'Reilly, is nonetheless closing in, slowly killing its narrator. References to Microsoft, to Enron, create a contemporary flavour, but it is fear, fear of the bomb in the hold or just fear itself, which is at the heart of this story. 'We are so close to chaos. You know? We are so close to collapse. It's in the air. It's in the fucking air. The whole thing is solid but it hangs by a thread in the air. The only currency worth anything is fear. It holds the grid. It holds the grid. It holds the grid.'

The way in which loneliness can fester is teased out by John MacKenna in *Maps*. This is a world of familiar touchstones, an ostensibly safe setting. And yet the forces which leave individuals confused and dislocated are as active here as in many other stories in the collection. The predicament which these forces create is succinctly voiced by Joseph O'Neill in *Ponchos*, 'How alone we are! William thought, with anguish.'

Irish fiction, as Colm Tóibín points out in his introduction to *The Penguin Book of Irish Fiction*, is full of dislocation and displacement. There is certainly plenty of both here.

In addition to being directly addressed in some of the stories, estrangement and disaffection take shape, in others, around a sense of loss for a more coherent world. This harking back to lost Edens is apparent in Claire Keegan's story,

Night of the Quicken Trees. Stack, the 49-year-old bachelor in this story, despairs of a younger generation. 'Young people couldn't catch a fish or skim cream off milk. They went around in cars they couldn't afford with small children who'd never tasted their mother's milk, committing adultery at the drop of a hat.' But while Stack can be regarded as a staunch defender of the past, that past is both threatening and treacherous for Margaret, the story's protagonist.

In Tom Humphries' story, *Australia Day*, the old and the new are also juxtaposed. Set in a rural, Irish town in boom time, the narrator frequently refers to how dislocated he is by the changes taking place around him. 'I couldn't draw you a map of where is where anymore. Lots of the good places that I grew up in died when the money came in.' Gone is the Eureka Cinema and Hank Moore's bookmaking shop, in has come the world of ISDN lines and satellite dishes, prerequisites of the weekenders who arrive in big cars from Dublin 'approaching like herds of buffalo driven across the plains'. It's a new, prosperous Ireland, but it's not to everyone's liking.

In spite of his troubled relationship with his father, the sheer pull of the homeplace takes the narrator in John MacKenna's story back there every Saturday. 'I called for the smell of heat from the range, the sizzle of the kettle, the warmth of the lino in the kitchen, the worn feel of the green paint on the banisters. I called for comfort.' The world of childhood, with its familiar touchstones and recognizable boundaries, has a similar allure for Molly McCloskey's narrator, Jane. 'Long ago, it was like living in a warm blue globe, a perfect circle of yes and no and there-but-no-further than.' This is the safe backdrop against which the ravages of the contemporary world are sketched. It is life before the

Unabomber and the anthrax scare, a time when being 'a mailman didn't yet mean being caught in the crossfire of American madness'. For Jane, who periodically has the sensation of being held by nothing, childhood looms large as a time when she was tethered to something limiting and solid, necessary and inevitable, before life opened up to 'too many possibilities, most of which we would never be equal to'.

In Blánaid McKinney's story, Matt, a priest, dwells on a 'world where we all knew our place, and where our place was the place to be'. What Matt is most afraid of is having to chart the course of his own life: '... the notion that the rest of my life might actually belong to me, is the most terrifying, loneliest thought I've had all day'. Having sex on the empty upper deck of a London bus may be a novel experience for him – he's not the only priest in this collection with a complex sex life – but that excitement notwithstanding, he ultimately rejects a world where doubt and forgiveness have no place.

In *Gracefully, Not Too Fast*, by Mary Morrissy, the backward glance is wry. The focus is on pre-garden-centre Ireland, when gardens were kept rather than cherished, a time when a neighbourhood of red-brick streets was not trendily dubbed the Jewish quarter, before its local school became loft apartments and its little bakery 'a place of pilgrimage for atheists to buy pastries on a Sunday morning'. The contradictions and juxtapositions of contemporary life are portrayed here and given a rhythm.

In Aidan Mathews' *Barber-Surgeons,* the entire narrative is anchored by its characters' shared understanding of their place in the scheme of things in a bygone era, a bygone Dublin. 'What sort of a fucked-up faraway place is Yankee Doodle Dandyland?' asks a waiting customer rhetorically in

Mr Bevan's barber shop. Here is a world in which two middle-aged men from different backgrounds can find commonality, even closeness, because they implicitly understand their place in the world.

That safety of the known – the familiar – is central, indeed is ultimately the epiphany, in Éilís Ní Dhuibhne's *It is a Miracle*. Finding herself at a librarian's conference in central Europe, Sara the narrator is irritated when her colleagues head off to visit a concentration camp. Here, the backward glance has very different consequences. *Schadenfreude* holds no appeal for Sara. To her there is something voyeuristic about contemplating the pain of the victims. 'Misery likes bedfellows; tasting true horror on a vast scale, in the safe confines of a museum, puts minor personal pain into perspective. Relativity. Healthy people make such comparisons without knowing it, weighing a divorce against execution in the gas chambers, arthritis against the Iron Maiden.' But then this is a contemporary, western world where, to quote another of Ní Dhuibhne's characters, 'It's ME- time'.

Not surprisingly, the plight of men in what is seen by many as a post-feminist era is centre stage in these stories. For the cast of Joseph O'Neill's characters in the 24-hour Starlight diner in Manhattan, 'men with no-shit, no-flies-on-him names such as Frank and Steve and Champ', the question is 'what about men's rights?' As one, Johnny, puts it: 'Women don't have the slightest fucking idea of what it's like for men, on a biology level. It's part of the conspiracy of silence, it's all about political correctness: nobody talks about the struggle we go through every fucking day.' The trials for William of fulfilling his 'monthly coital responsibilities' in a marriage beset by infertility with its endless trail of 'thermometers, ovulation charts, copulation schedules, ejaculatory precautions', are all explored here. From a man's side.

'You can spot the single men by their tell-tale meals-for-one. You could loiter in the no man's land between one sliding door and the other, where baskets are stacked and dogs wait shivering and a photo booth operates, and prey on them like they were runaways in a railway station. Because men alone are such sad beasts. They have a way of looking like they don't deserve their lives.' So writes Molly McCloskey, who makes no bones about identifying the syndrome as: 'the emasculation of modern man'. If women were once the ones who cried in fiction, now it's the men, like the Italian doctor in Éilís Ní Dhuibhne's story with tears rolling down 'his lovely bronze cheeks' as he discloses details of his emotional distress.

Frequently pitted against the vulnerable man is the assertive woman. Take Blánaid McKinney's Laura, for instance, a strident advertizing executive who will 'loot and ransack *anything*, all in the case of the brief. The brief, the concept, the client, the contract.': Woman as monster, as lethal at corporate games as many a man before her.

'A man was a nuisance and a necessity. If she'd a man she'd have to persuade him to take baths and use his knife and fork,' thinks Margaret Flusk, Claire Keegan's primitive, exultant heroine. 'If I could only cut out the man, Margaret thought, I might have a child.'

There is not a whole lot of redemption on offer in these stories. Some characters are left floundering in worlds which remain unremittingly brutal. Transforming realization, such as that experienced by Matt in Blánaid McKinney's *These Important Messages*, are the exception. There are, however, more than a few quiet epiphanies, more than a few of those subtle shifts in understanding, so much the hallmark of the form. Perhaps these might also be described as attempts – successful attempts – to impose coherence on an otherwise incoherent world. As such they would seem to bear out William Trevor's assertion, insightfully expanded upon by Declan Kiberd in a piece in *The London Review of Books*, that of all literary forms, the short story belongs most unequivocally to the modern age.

It would be possible to go on sifting through these stories indefinitely, identifying this or that linking thread. The above critique is simply offered as notes for the curious. It may or may not enhance a reading of the individual stories, each of which is, above all, complete in itself: the work of a distinctive, assured voice saying something original in a well-crafted way.

'Stories are what make our lives worth living,' writes Richard Kearney in *On Stories*. They have 'the power to bring a hush to a room, a catch to the breath, a leap to the curious heart, with the simple words "Once upon a time"'. There will, he says, always be someone there to say, 'tell me a story', and always someone to respond. So, the last word here must be one of thanks to the writers who answered that call, bringing this collection to life.

Caroline Walsh
June 2002

Dislocation

AIDAN MATHEWS

Barber-Surgeons

To begin with, they had nothing in common, the surgeon and the barber, although Mr Bevan was a great devourer of newspapers and could always find something in them, so long as it wasn't the sports page, to entertain a customer.

'I see,' he said, 'that Pope John has gone and excommunicated Castro.'

'Has he?' said the surgeon. He was staring at his hands in the mirror, and wondering if he should insure them. Look what had happened to the child's finger in the car window. Even across in London they could have done nothing.

'He has,' Mr Bevan said. 'It's not like Pope John to do that. Even Protestants think he's a pet. But I suppose the whole Cuba business is beyond the beyond.'

'Has he excommunicated Chairman Khrushchev?'

Mr Bevan thought about this for a while as he clipped briskly at the base of the skull where the surgeon's hair-oil had pollinated his shirt collar.

'Khrushchev,' he said, pronouncing the word as his client had, with the stress on the second syllable and not on the first, which was strange, 'may not be subject to Pope John's jurisdiction. Would he be a Russian Orthodox?'

'Quite.'

Then there was a silence for a space, and the surgeon stared in the mirror at the barber's girlish wrists, at the one recessed knuckle-bone from an old collision, and at the hands themselves then, which were quite middle class, really, for a cutter of hair; and the barber listened in turn to the vertical rain in the little street upstairs, the great crashing glasshouses of it that gave him always a queer pleasure. Something wonderful must have happened to him once in a downpour. That was it.

'And Eichmann is for the high jump,' he said. The man in the chair was wearing a cheap chain of some sort round his neck. Perhaps he was a Catholic after all, though you would not think it from the genteel things he did, such as taking off his chamois glove to shake hands or saying Quite where he might as easily have said Indeed. Good manners was always a giveaway.

'Eichmann,' the surgeon said. 'I imagine he's happy to be hanged. I imagine he's been waiting for this for almost twenty years now. He must be the most miserable person on the planet.'

'There's that. It would certainly make you think.'

Mr Bevan's breath whooshed loose small hairs from the doctor's neck. There was grey among the auburn and it served him right, too. In or out of a barber's chair it was discourteous to say something that was so paradoxical as to be unintelligible. But the barber let it pass. Better to lose the conflict than the custom.

'Mr Horngrad,' he said, 'who comes into me each and every month for a trim and a talk has a tattoo from the camps. Don't ask me which one. It's not Belsen. It's not Buchenwald. Anyhow. There's more hair on his arm than on his head, but you can see it. Now, sir!'

And he whisked the green gown away like a toreador's veronica, pedalled the chair down to the dismount level, and steadied the surgeon as he stepped out on to the magpie rug of hair on the new linoleum. It was a good day when he had to sweep that floor before lunchtime.

'I'm tired of the Second Vatican Council before it begins and I'm tired of the Second World War since it ended,' said his customer. 'But I never get tired of the cinema. I went to see a film the night Kennedy talked on TV about the missile sites. Had the whole place to myself too. Have you seen *Dr. No* at the Capitol?'

'Have I seen *Dr. No*?' Mr Bevan said. 'I've seen it twice. The queues!'

'The dialogue. Or at least the double entendres.'

'And the stunts,' said Mr Bevan. 'Lord above!'

'And the girls.'

'And the girls, God bless them,' Mr Bevan said.

'Bless them and breed them,' the surgeon said. 'We could do with a few.'

But that was the slightest bit off-colour, and Mr Bevan metabolized it slowly, putting the clippers away awkwardly among the sterilizers.

'And Connery, of course,' he said then. 'Cometh the hour, cometh the man.'

'Beautiful body,' said the other. 'If I had that body on my operating table, I think I'd call the College of Art instead of the College of Surgeons.'

It had stopped raining. Mr Bevan looked up the narrow stairs to the street. It was as if his ears had been syringed. The pond of his hearing quivered and cleared and became sky. Sun broke through.

'You're a doctor?'

'I'm a general surgeon,' he said. 'I work around the corner. I do mostly the throat to the privates. The odd one survives me. My name is Roper.'

'My name is Bevan, Dr Roper,' said the barber. He still had the gown in his hands too, with a long yellow nail on his index finger. Anyone would think he was a smoker or dirty. But it was only the strong rinses gave you the soggy, stained palps.

'Surgeons are never called doctors,' Mr Roper said. 'Don't know why. It's just a thing. Anyhow, I'll be your outpatient in future, Mr Bevan. I'll ask for you specially.'

'I'm the only one here,' the barber said. 'I inherited the second chair and the name of the shop. I wouldn't have chosen The Barber of Seville myself. It's a bit loud. I would have chosen something more subdued.'

'Why not the girl's name from *Dr. No*? Was it Honey Ryder?' And the surgeon hummed a few phrases from the film's theme as he sank into his saturated coat. Wet or not, it was as good looking a garment as any undertaker's.

'Goodbye now.'

'Goodbye, sir.'

Mr Bevan watched the consultant taking the rubbered steps two at a time. There was no price inked indelibly on those shoes. The handmade leather shoes from God knows where waited an instant on the mat at the metal door-saddle, and were gone.

*

After that it was mostly plain sailing.

'I'm wrong,' said a waiting customer from a bentwood chair in the tiled corner, and he coughed productively. His nose had been set by an intern at some stage and not by a registrar. It was still deflected, as if pressed against a tumbler. 'It's not two thousand. It's twenty thousand. Sure I'm wearing my brother's glasses. No wonder. Twenty thousand dead in a landslide. See for yourself. Page three, top of, right-hand side. What kind of a fucked-up faraway place is South America?'

But Mr Bevan and Mr Roper were gone off to other latitudes.

'How they get away with it is the question,' the barber said, slicing through a silver strand at the scalp. 'Pussy Galore, how are you? The censor must have been born in the bogs. Even I knew that much growing up in Stoneybatter.'

'Did you ever hear gobblejob?' said the surgeon.

'That's typical Liberties English for you,' Mr Bevan said. 'Stoneybatter set a higher tone to things.'

'I heard gobblejob on my ward rounds yesterday,' Mr Roper said. 'First sighting in twenty years. Thought it went out with Chaucer. None of my students cracked it. They're all from the suburbs, you see. Of course, they all knew Oddjob.'

Mr Bevan snipped considerately along the curve of the ear where the morning's razor had forgotten to. There was a pink linear indentation there. That, of course, was from the elastic of the mask he wore in surgery.

'Oddjob the Jap,' he said to the doctor. 'Oddjob and his bowler hat. I met a fellow who was a POW in I don't know where. Maybe Burma. He used to memorize a page of the Bible and then use it for cigarette paper. By the time he was freed he could have gone for the priesthood. But he wasn't able to sit through *Goldfinger*. He'd put up with beriberi and beatings, but the mere sight of a Nip was enough to make his hands sweat.'

Mr Roper looked at the large wall-mirror in front of him and saw in its reflection the further reflection of a small hand-mirror held behind his head for a customer's close inspection of results. The capillaries were definitely whitening like cradle-cap. His testicles would be snowy in ten years' time.

'Kennedy would have loved Pussy Galore,' he said to the barber. 'He was a genius and a great man, of course, but he was also what they call in the States a fraternity jock. He would have gone for Honor Blackman. He would have gone through Honor Blackman. In fact, I think he may have seen the movie at a private viewing before he went to Dallas.'

'Would you believe that it wasn't even made then?' said Mr Bevan. 'No, it was the earlier one with Robert Shaw as the gentleman caller from Spectre. That was *From Russia with Love* and JFK previewed it in the White House, only a week or ten days after I waved to him in Winetavern Street. I was so close, Mr Roper, I could almost smell his aftershave. Sure the bodyguards were hugging the kiddies. It was like a Corpus Christi procession gone mad.'

'He was my age exactly,' said the surgeon, standing on the footrest. 'Give or take a few weeks.'

'Me too,' Mr Bevan said, 'give or take a few months', and he stood on his toes to brush scintillating debris from the surgeon's shoulders. Was it destiny or the few quid that made the specialist's skin supple and his scaly? 'He was the only man you could stand up in public and say *I love him*, and get away with it.'

'Sometimes I loved him, sometimes I hated him,' Mr Roper said eventually. 'Role models have an awful way of turning into rivals. Today's outstanding examples become tomorrow's enemies. I prefer a world without Gods. A world without Gods is entirely human.'

'There's that,' said Mr Bevan. 'It would certainly make you think. I'll get your jacket.'

'Listen to this,' said the waiting customer with the deviated septum, and he looked up at them. 'Page four, middle of, left-hand side. The Supreme Court in America has banished prayer in the classroom. There you are in black and white. No more Our Fathers, no more Faith of our Fathers. What sort of a fucked-up faraway place is Yankee Doodle Dandyland?'

But Mr Bevan was noticing sweat stains on the lined armpit of Mr Roper's jacket; and Mr Roper in turn had seen the tremor in his hand as he reached up to the antlers of the coat-stand.

'Middle age,' said the general surgeon to the general barber, 'is neither one thing nor the other. You can't see the starting line; you can't see the finishing tape.'

They looked at each other briefly, the brown and the blue eyes.

'Old age thinks well of the half-way stage,' said the barber. 'A man in the Incurables said to me once he'd rather be sick and thirty-five than well and seventy.'

'You meet a wise class of patient in that place.'

'There was a lovely thing I saw in the *Reader's Digest*,' Mr Bevan said, although he had really been saving this for the next visit. 'It said that the sun itself is a middle-aged star, so perhaps we're in good company.'

And even when the doctor had gone, laughing his way up the stairs and out of earshot, into the lanes of prams and the glaring winter, and Mr Bevan was slapping stinging water on the sandpaper skin of the man with the concave face, he still loaded and reloaded that parting shot. It had been perfectly timed and thought through. It was almost worthy of 007.

★

Then the screen faded and the houselights came up and the barber in the back row under the projectionist's lens condensed again into Terylene trousers and a single sibilant denture. Why did they ruin it for everyone with an intermission? It was a terrible thing to step from the clarity of Caribbean waters, in the company of Dominique, and into the chlorine of a sterile public baths, from coral to parterre in the sunspot of an instant. It was a kind of death beside which dying itself could seem lively.

Thunderball, he thought. Even the title was stylish. Masculine and concise with a slipstream of slyness from its submarine innuendo. But how had Bond twigged that the wraith in widow's weeds was a lethal transvestite? Yet you couldn't really cavil: wit, killings, bikinis – they accomplished an infinite trinity. And there was a fifth film promised already, its première to be held in the Queen's presence. So much for the scoffers and sneerers. So much for the bald-headed bishop of the Church of Ireland who had cut him as he started small-talking Bond business the week before during a ten-minute tonsure. They could laugh their varsity hearts out at the daft plotlines and bedlinen, but that had not prevented *Goldfinger* and *Dr. No* from being tremendous and true, at least as much as the sagas of round towers and round tables.

It was that very truth which challenged Mr Bevan now. Why had he never considered the secret service? He was old enough to be entitled to a British passport. To be sure, he would slaughter more sparingly than James, and afford each foreign agent opportunities for prayer before the necessary ballistic climax. But it was all too late. There was too much water under the bridge. Indeed, there were too many bridges under water.

Would he chance a packet of Rolos? They had stuck in his plate last time.

When he angled his distance glasses on the bridge of his nose, he saw the doctor at once, a beige, slightly italicized figure, buying an ice-cream tub from a teenage girl with a tiered refreshments tray at the fire exit; and his first instinct was to stand, because his body had known no other relationship to the man. Then, because he was standing, he waved; felt foolish, hunched, and hid.

The chandeliers were going out again. It was just as well. Mr Roper might be with children or with their mother, if he had a wife, or with a housekeeper, even. The lack of a ring on his wedding finger meant little. Clearly, no man who dressed so smartly could live alone. There was a slavey somewhere. At any rate, he couldn't greet a camel-haired consultant in a duffle coat. After all, courtesy wasn't a code. It was awareness of the needs of the other. You did not cause embarrassment.

Mr Bevan softened the salt-and-vinegar crisp in his mouth for a long time before scrunching it. That was out of consideration for the fellow in the next seat, because the munching would be too audible otherwise. Actually, you could be a saint in all sorts of situations. Indeed, if you were striving for sanctity, you shouldn't be deterred by social form. Therefore he would in fact salute the surgeon, but on the way out. He would do it visibly. He would do it vocally. It was his human right.

Later, though, as the radiant congregation descended the blinding, balustraded staircase that had been built for the *Titanic* and never installed, he saw no sign of the head that he had shaped so often but could not see inside.

★

Cut to the Barber of Seville and enter Mr Horngrad.

'Watch now,' Mr Bevan said in a breathy whisper to the surgeon's ear. 'You'll see for yourself. On a warm day like this one, he'll wear a short-sleeved shirt. The tattoo is on his left arm. Or is it his right? The mirror reverses everything.'

'Quite so,' said Mr Roper.

'You'll be sad to learn,' said Mr Horngrad, his voice a cadenced counter-tenor's as he sat with a three-coloured ice-pop in his fist, 'that Stan Laurel has passed on. But I can't remember if he was the fat one or the thin one, so I don't know who to grieve for.'

'The skinny side-kick. Let me take your jacket,' said Mr Bevan. 'Did you happen to hear on the radio about the Crucifixion?'

'I heard about it before radio was invented,' Mr Horngrad said. 'I have been hearing about it all my life. I gather I am somehow to blame.'

'That's the point,' said Mr Bevan. 'You're not. Pope Paul has just apologized on all our behalves, Roman Catholic and Reformed Catholic. So there.'

Right enough, the man was tattooed. It was the sallow hallmark of his mettle, the badge of tragedy. But why didn't they go for a skin graft? Skin grafts were two a penny these days. Hadn't that manic stevedore burned his sweetheart's image off his elbow with an oxyacetylene torch, and lived to strangle her later with the same arm? As a matter of fact, many a guinea pig from the war years wore his own behind on his beaming face. But even in a godless world, the surgeon reflected, we idolize our afflictions.

'And who is to be the new scapegoat?' asked Mr Horngrad. 'Did the Pope indicate that?'

'The Italians, I think,' said Mr Bevan.

'The Italians,' said the waiting customer, 'are a most fucked-up set of foreigners. Not like your folk in the Sinai, Mr Horngrad, blowing the bejasus out of the Arabs. Six days, no bother; and on the seventh, I suppose, they hit downtown Tel Aviv.'

'No politics or religion in this club,' said the barber.

'The Arabs,' said Mr Horngrad, 'are all faggots. They can't face a fight.'

'Faggots?' Mr Bevan said. 'You mean they're for burning?'

'I mean faggots,' Mr Horngrad said. 'Bumboys. Men for pleasure, women for breeding. That's an Arab proverb.'

'I know a man who was that way,' said Mr Bevan. 'I know a man who was a faggot; and he had a DSO. He had a Distinguished Service Medal.'

'He was a fiery faggot, so,' said the man with the camp tattoo.

With a flick of his foot, Mr Roper spun round in his seat and addressed them. His accent mentored and tormented them.

'Faggots saved the West at the battle of Thermopylae,' he said. 'Three hundred Spartan faggots stood between us and ten thousand well-adjusted Asiatics.'

'*Touché*,' said the barber.

'There you go again,' said Mr Horngrad. 'First you charge me with murder; then you charge me with bigotry. I can't win. I'm always being accused of something.'

'Be honest now,' said the waiting customer. 'Do you think that Cassius Clay has a soul?'

'I don't think anyone has a soul,' Mr Horngrad said. 'We've been down this road before. But I respect Cassius Clay and I would break bread with him. He's a magnificent creature. He's Michelangelo's *David*, for God's sake. He inspires me.'

'Do you know who inspires me?' said Mr Bevan. 'Sir Francis Chichester inspires me.'

'*D'accord*,' said the surgeon.

'You don't have to go to Cape Horn to feel crestfallen,' Mr Bevan said. 'There are times down here when I don't feel I have the strength to go on any longer. After all, the Barber of Seville is not the be-all and the end-all of the world that God created. It's not on any Cook's Tour. But then I think of this old man out there in the middle of the ocean, washing his Y-fronts over the side and steering by starlight. And what does he eat? The hold of the *Gypsy Moth* is full of Irish potatoes. So you see.'

'See what?' said Mr Horngrad.

'His dignity,' the barber said. 'His daring. His derring-do, if you want.' And his facial colour rose a tad, and sank again.

'Being broken down, I suppose, and still standing up. That's what I mean.'

He swivelled the surgeon round and resumed his clipping. Actually, Mr Roper hardly needed a cut at all. Why had he bothered to come? You took an awful chance on those steep stairs.

'Who inspires you, Mr Roper?' he said then. But he said it in a jocular fashion that took the familiarity out of it, so that the doctor thought about it in a genial way with his eyes closed. The cold sore at the corner of his mouth had dried and disappeared since the last time. Then he laughed out loud.

'You do, Mr Bevan,' he said. 'You keep the show on the road.'

'Did you see it yet?' said the barber, and his elated scissors circled a little mud-stain of psoriasis that was probably all due to anxiety. '*You Only Live Twice*.'

'Spare me the details.'

'You'd love it. I swear to God.'

'I'm an aficionado,' said Mr Roper. 'I'm not an addict. Desist.'

And Mr Bevan let it go at that. He tucked the label of the surgeon's shirt down inside the collar carefully. It was one of those drip-dry affairs that people with Pyrex dishes bought. More to the point, it was the first time he had ever seen his personal hospital consultant wearing anything off-the-peg.

*

On the other hand, it wasn't always a charmed relationship. There were times when you could sense something between a rift and a rupture in the sedimentary deposits of their banter. It might even be defined, given the venue of their meetings, as a hairline fracture.

'What do you make of this man Christian Barnard?' said Mr Bevan one Tuesday afternoon at about ten past five. He had actually closed for the day when Mr Roper clattered down the stairs in a de Valera cape.

'A chancer,' the surgeon said. 'A charlatan. He jumped the gun to be centre-stage at a photo-opportunity. The English team were just about to make the first incision. I suppose you think he's Dr Schweitzer. Well, he isn't; and neither was Dr Schweitzer, either. He was a complete cunt.'

And that was upsetting from a professional person who had won a Gold Medal in some ology or other in the Royal College of Surgeons, and who was never supposed to take a sabbatical from suavity and seriousness. In fact, if you were to post a letter to Mr Roper, FRCSI, Bedside Manor, Dublin, it would be sure to reach him. It was very wrong of him to utter cornerboy English.

'Enid Blyton has gone to her rest,' said the barber one Thursday morning when the chair was still warm from the buttocks of Mr Horngrad. 'I heard on the BBC that she authored – that was the word – nine hundred books. Can you imagine that?'

'Everything about that woman is unimaginable,' Mr Roper retorted. There was no other word for it. 'She was a silly little snob who was married, I gather, to a surgeon. That, at least, argues a degree of discernment wholly alien to her written inanities.'

Mr Bevan had only asked in order to prise domestic detail from the most recalcitrant customer he had ever invested affection in. But it was no use. After how many years, four, five, six, the man was still an enigma. Yet he had begun to write down snatches of Mr Roper's small talk because there were words in it which he had never witnessed outside crossword puzzles.

'Discernment, indeed,' he said, batting it beautifully. 'How discerning was Jackie Kennedy the other day? I could have wept. I could have. But I was at work.'

'You should have,' the surgeon said. 'People are supposed to cry at a wedding.'

'Oil money is all he has going for him. You may call him Aristotle or Plato or whatever you like, but it's all about petro-dollars.'

'Onassis? He won't have long to look at her,' said Mr Roper. '*Myasthenia gravis*.'

'It would make you think all right,' said the barber, who was very pleased that he had got into petro-dollars. It was still in quotes in both broadsheets.

'He has his eyelids bandaged back already,' the surgeon said. 'Otherwise he has to hold them up with his thumbs. He's feasting his eyes while he can, greasy little adhesion that he is. All the oil in the world won't help him now.'

This was not right. It was not righteous. There was a point at which you passed from mischief into malice, and they had passed it. So Mr Bevan searched among his witticisms for some passage into leniency.

'He sounds like the baddie in the new Bond film.'

'Have you seen it?'

'I'm saving it for the weekend.'

'Hamlet without the Prince. The new Bond ponces around in a kilt, but he's no lookalike. You don't believe he's a killer; you don't believe he's a ladykiller. Ergo: no go. It's all set in a rotating restaurant that's cemented to a summit miles above Wengen in the Swiss Alps. I've been there. Five pounds for a cup of coffee and a Cinemascope view of Toblerone mountains. Then you can ski all the way down the cordoned learner's piste at fifteen miles an hour to the nursery slopes where the cable cars start from, and pretend you're on Her Majesty's secret service while you're at it. But there is this vicious old dyke in the film who looks the image and likeness of my anaesthetist. It was worth it for that.'

Then he smiled, relaxed, relented. His fist became a hand again. A shaft of sunlight minted its way through the glass door of the premises, down the peculiar staircase, and lay at their feet on the lino like an oblong ingot. And Mr Bevan's being rose up like a Magnificat, for this was what he loved: when he could groom the cherished head until it gleamed like the bobbing skull of a seal, all tweaked and squeaking, from the domical forehead through the perfect parting, as straight as any Roman road, to the anticlockwise origins of hair near the old, abandoned fontanel.

'You could leave it a little longer at the sides,' Mr Roper said. 'Maybe the back too.'

'You're not going to grow sideburns, are you?' said the barber. 'I think they're very common.'

'I won't wear sideburns,' said Mr Roper. 'But my students have ponytails. You have to move with the times.'

He bowed his head to the barber's clippers.

'Do what you will,' he said.

Mr Bevan thought of what a canon had said to him years before. Not an Irish canon, of course, but a Canadian, and possibly even a French-Canadian one at that, so you had to take his words with a pinch of salt, as coming from the hillbilly hinterlands and not from the bench of Bishops. Yet he had told the barber that the beloved disciple of Jesus in the Gospel of Saint John would have been the Lord's closest friend, his confidant and sleeping companion in the perishing small hours of the Galilean winter, and that they would have deloused each other, God and the man, under the shrieking olive trees in the atrocity of the midday heat outside Jerusalem. The fingers of the beloved disciple would be roaming the Master's hair, splitting the head lice deftly between his nails, listening for the brittle report of the puncture before casting the broken fuselage to the ground, and inhaling all the while the sour sephardic pungency of the body of Christ.

★

The surgeon hadn't been to the Boat Show at the Royal Dublin Society since the time, three years before, that he had finally sold his folk-boat, remaining on at the yacht club only as a dining member who dropped by for an occasional game of billiards and a browse through current issues of *Punch* and the *Spectator.* Whatever drew him now, it was certainly not the motor launch from *Dr. No* or the Spectre-manned torpedoes that a few redundant London models were piloting in a prefabricated glass aquarium until half past four each evening as hooligans ogled their adipose tissue.

'A pound? It was twelve and six the last time.'

'It was twelve and six when my granny was a girl, sir.'

Kayaks to catamarans. He walked among them, their land-locked, stationary yearnings. Worse, there was a saline smell from the breakers less than a mile away at Sandymount to torment them. Tides sipped at the sea wall twice a day as their pennants stiffened under the halogen lights.

'That one's got hairs under her arms. Lookit!'

When he found himself there by accident, at the shallow end of the sci-fi waterhole where swim-suited centrefolds were entertaining a heterosexual press of boys at puberty, Mr Roper saw his man immediately. It was the barber in civilian life, Bevan at large in the lit, incongruous domain of everywhere that was not his basement practice. A hooded coat with wooden pegs for buttons made him monkish and stunted. His moccasins too were spattered a darker shade in places as if he had sprinkled himself at a urinal. Under the canopy of his discoloured ceiling he seemed always endearing in his eccentricity. But this was not it.

'Not that one, you spastic. The bird with the gun.'

The consultant veered discreetly to the right and slipped among the hulls of ocean-going cruisers with their slanted names at bow and stern. *Birthright. Salamander. Gemini.* Their impervious emulsions fashioned his flitting outline as he waded through buggies and paper windmills to the door marked Exit.

⋆

'And where did you disappear to in the last fortnight?' said Mr Roper, settling into the chair without a say-so, and arranging the spaghetti strings of the apron around his own neck as Mr Bevan swept the detritus of a dozen clients into a balsa-wood fruit-box stamped Fyffes. He was always afraid that the sight of so much human hair strewn about might disconcert Mr Horngrad.

'I had to go for a check-up,' Mr Bevan said, but he had taken a long time to commit such a small sentence.

'Three times I came by,' said the other, 'and the sign still said Open. In the end, I went off to the Shelbourne. There was a man there with a white streak in his beard like dried Milk of Magnesia, and all he could talk about was parking meters.'

'That's the way,' said the barber.

'Page two, top of, left to right,' said the waiting customer, coughing. 'Israeli archaeologists have dug up the skeleton of a crucified man.'

'Don't blame it on me,' Mr Horngrad said in a striped and long-sleeved shirt with matching tiger's eye cufflinks. 'Everything ends up on my desk.'

'Are you all right?' the surgeon said.

'I'm all right,' said Mr Bevan. 'I just got a bit of a fright.'

'That's a Jewish plot if ever I heard one,' said the waiting customer. 'That stinks.'

'The whole of Europe is a Jewish plot,' said Mr Horngrad. 'A Jewish cemetery from Brittany to Belorussia.'

'Come into me and I'll have a good look at you,' said the surgeon. 'Come in Tuesday. Will you do that?'

'I feel fine. I look fine. I am fine,' Mr Bevan said.

'That's what worries me,' said Mr Roper. 'Everyone blooms in the mortuary chapel.'

'Skeleton of a crucified man. Very fucking convenient,' said the waiting customer. 'That really takes the biscuit.'

'Did I dig him up?' Mr Horngrad said. 'Am I suddenly an Israeli grave-robber? When I came in five minutes ago, I could have sworn I was a white-collar worker from the South Circular Road.'

Mr Bevan snipped a long hair from the consultant's eyebrow with a cuticle scissors. He must get a silver tweezers at some stage. Eyebrows could be more ageing, actually, than nasal hair, though the worst of all was what grew out of your ears. That was the body calling Time now please, gentlemen.

'What did you think of the new one?' he said. 'Now that Connery is on the job again.'

'*Diamonds are Forever*? I liked the song. I loved the silhouettes at the start.'

'And Plenty O'Toole. Was that her name?'

'It was. Not nearly as good as Pussy Galore, mind.'

'Not at all. Pussy Galore was in a different league all together.'

Mr Bevan set aside whatever he was doing and looked at the surgeon in the mirror. He could hear the distant bronchitis of the two customers arguing.

'The two fellows,' he said. 'Mr Kid and Mr Whoever-it-was. I can't remember now.'

'The fairies?'

'Whatever. Fairies. Queers,' said Mr Bevan. 'Ponces. Nancyboys. Homos. Homosexual is a bit long. Gay is a bit short. Maybe something in the middle like: people. Do you know what I mean?'

'I do.' You could tell by his voice that the surgeon was astonished.

'Because I was loving the film until they turned up in it. Then there were catcalls whenever the camp one opened his mouth. Cornerboys in the balcony. I just thought.'

'You thought justly.'

'I don't know what I'm trying to say,' said Mr Bevan.

'Never let that stop you saying it,' Mr Roper said. 'It never stopped me.'

Mr Bevan picked up the clippers. But what he wanted was the stainless steel comb.

'Do you know,' he said, 'I'll be charging you in decimals after Christmas.'

'You will,' said the surgeon. 'If the Lord preserves us.'

'Take it from me,' said Mr Horngrad, butting in, the bloody fellow. 'If there is a Lord, the only thing He preserves is silence.'

★

'. . . will warrant further comma more vigorous comma attention.'

Friday at six o'clock as the pre-recorded Angelus played from the campanile of the nearby parish church, Mr Roper set aside the Dictaphone and rubbed his eyes because he had seen Burt Lancaster do it so often in American films. Like it or not, he would have to reconcile himself to the new technology of pocket-sized recorders. He would miss the deference and reverence of the convent schoolgirls he had kept supplied in Coke and Cadbury's while they touch-typed complex case histories, but since the nuns had stopped teaching Latin, no one could be trusted to spell correctly the metaphysical intimacies of the body. Besides, the cassettes were cheaper, though he would have listened more alertly to his English master in his early years if he had known that the mysteries of punctuation would so terrorize him in his later ones. Only the colon made complete sense to him. The semicolon belonged to particle physics; and the simple dash had already garbled many a medical court report.

He twirled in his swivel chair among his certificates. Outside the window there was a moon. On the moon there was a man. Two men. He had forgotten their names and their likenesses before the bulletin announcing their arrival there had ended. They would splash-land in the ocean just like 007, close to the Stone Age tribesmen of New Guinea, in a day or in two days. They had left clean shaven and would return bearded. That was as much as could be said about any male experience in or out of this world. Growth on the cheeks was truly astronomical.

Bevan, he thought. He's a lovable fellow.

*

Mr Roper, the barber thought. Where would I be without him?

Those bells from the church were only beautiful. Better recorded music than live noise had always been his position. Best of all he had loved being swept off his feet at the consecration when the adolescent bell-ringers in the Jacobean belfry proclaimed the Risen Lord in their early morning Sunday service of Holy Communion. And to think that their Roman Catholic neighbours still regarded them as Protestants.

It was time to go home. He would do a fry, white pudding as well, and listen to the astronauts. They were at prayer in the firmament, and doing some measurements too. It was nice to hear them read from the Authorized Version, though it was a pity about the American accents. Genesis did not seem the same when it was read in Texan by a youngster. They should have brought Alec Guinness with them in the lunar module.

I must look at my underpants, he thought. I must see if I leaked through the first pair into the second. Thank goodness it is blood and not the other. Thank goodness it is not excrement.

He twirled in the barber's chair, and the surrendered hair on the lino rotated with him, Horngrad's and Mr Roper's, the dun, the chestnut and the auburn, carrot and caramel, russet and sand; copper, jet, dove-grey, slate grey, and the thousand shades of ash. All the walking wounded between the canal and the river had found their way to him. And for what?

He faced his reflection.

*

In spite of the fact that his life had been saved at the public expense three years before by a quick-witted surgical intervention, the pump attendant did not favour his benefactor above other motorists, and Mr Roper was therefore obliged to queue for his petrol along with at least a hundred other cars. Yesterday's customers had become today's clients, and the proletarian was blithe.

'Don't give out to me,' he said to the surgeon. 'Give out to the Jews. If they let the Arabs win once in a while, there wouldn't be an embargo. Besides, if I move you up to the front, there'll be a pogrom.'

So it was almost three o'clock when Mr Roper parked in a consultant's spot outside the Catholic hospital with its sanguinary carving of a saint or an archangel, perhaps, decapitating a Chinese dragon with a drowsy sense of reciprocal pleasure. If it were the third hour on Good Friday, the chaplain would be in procession at this point with a life-size cross that spent the remainder of the church calendar outside the brick incinerator at the mortuary chapel; and sick men would be struggling from their beds, with their goitres and their gall bladders and their golf-ball growths in their scrotums, to honour the Passion of Christ by kneeling on the bare planks of the ward. Thirty years before, when he was a senior house officer with his churchwarden pipe and cravat, he had found it moving, Mediterranean without the ultra-violet. Now it saddened him that even the most important human pain – loss, leave-taking, all the lethal forms of finitude – cried out for the anaesthesia of pantomime.

The stairs as they were, one hundred and two marbled steps from the lobby to the nurses' station on the second floor, a Via Dolorosa for the pensioned charladies with their black, bandaged legs; and the elevator too unaltered, the crash of its old accordion doors meshing and buckling as the trolleys crackled. And then the age-old, old-age odours of the male surgical ward: Lucozade, secretions of the armpit, Woodbine, warm, carpetless wood, disinfect-ant fluid, the perfume and periods of the trainee nurses. It is harder to quit a place than a person. He realized that too.

'*Voilà*,' he said, and drew the curtain with unconscious clinical expertise behind him.

The swollen, simplified face of the barber turned to him. It beamed with embarrassment.

'Mr Roper,' it said. 'There is no doubt.'

'Dr Bevan, I presume,' the surgeon said.

'The same, in spite of appearances. Shaken but not stirred. I am sorry for not standing. And I apologize for my five o'clock shadow. I hadn't got around to shaving.'

'Absolutely,' said the surgeon. 'Absolutely.'

There was nowhere to sit, of course, and he did not want to camp on the bed. At least if you went private, you could keep your dignity. There would be an economy armchair under the fake Constable on the social side of the bed, with your own private business in the pinewood closet on the other. Civility of that sort mattered more in this world than all the awful feel-me-heal-me histrionics of the distaff side. But what could you expect? Unmarried women were running all the committees.

'I'm afraid I can't ask you to sit on a chair,' said the barber. 'And the little table's a bit nervous. But please . . . the bed.'

Mr Roper took his overcoat off slowly in order to think through the whole decision-making process. He had never anticipated this circumstance.

'Actually, Mr Bevan,' he said, 'I've never seen you not standing. In all our conversations over the years, I've been in the chair. You might say that I have been the chairman. This is a complete reversal.'

'It is that,' said the sick man.

Mr Roper lay his folded overcoat on the bed as a compromise.

'I saw Mr Horngrad the other day,' he said. 'He looked badly in need of a cut and a shave.'

'I think there's a time in the year when Jews don't shave,' said Mr Bevan. 'Or is that the Sikhs? You've had a bit of a trim yourself, I suspect.'

'Never.'

'I'm a wise old bird. Somebody else has been at your hair.'

'The Shelbourne,' said Mr Roper. 'I pretended to be Finnish because I got that bloody bore again. Parking meters, remember? And he kept saying: I could swear I've met you somewhere before. So I said: "*Nodicke, nodicke, dicke*." And do you know what he said then? He said: "You poor fuckin' poof, wait until you get back to your car and see the summons."'

'That's the Shelbourne for you,' said Mr Bevan.

Mr Roper was examining the chart at the bottom of the bed. He hadn't for a moment intended to, but his hand could not withstand its own instinctive mapping.

'I know the man you're under,' he said. 'Good pair of mittens, too. Mind you, he borrowed a signed copy of a book by Oliver St John Gogarty from me the time of the Suez affair, and he never brought it back. There's no statute of limitations on my resentment, you see. He borrowed a girlfriend as well during the war, but I don't mind that. She hated shaking hands with a man in case he'd been to the toilet and the last thing he'd touched was his penis. "They don't wash afterwards," she'd say. "That's the long and the short of it."'

'I'll tell him,' Mr Bevan said. 'About the book.'

Mr Roper sat down on his own coat on the bed. Why was he rabbiting on? There was no way around it.

'How are you, old man?' he said. He remembered the theatre faintly.

'Ah. You know yourself.'

'I do?' Of course that was then. It had probably been modernized since.

'You read the chart.'

'That's only there to impress patients. Did you not feel the fear of God when I was looking at it?'

'Well, I didn't feel I was going to take up my bed and walk.'

'Proves my point. The surgeon has to mind his mystique.'

There was a child squealing with excitement outside the linen drapes around the bed, out there in the spacious world of the male surgical ward with its blue sash windows open to the cumulus nimbus. Mr Roper hoped it didn't belong to the man in his mid-thirties with the tracheotomy tube. Even if it did, the mother might be young enough to marry again. So much depended, though, on her features and her figure. Truly life was a bitch.

'I thought it was haemorrhoids for a long time,' said the barber. 'I had haemorrhoids for years. They'd come and they'd go, like.'

'I understand,' said the surgeon. 'They're a pain in the arse.'

'It was only spotting for ages,' Mr Bevan said. 'I thought, if it was anything serious, then I'd be in pain. But I wasn't in pain. I was as happy as Larry.'

'I know,' the surgeon said. They would have done the operation in fifty minutes; the biopsy within twenty-four hours.

'I was happy in my work,' said the barber. 'I was happy in The Barber of Seville.'

'We were all the same.' The statistics were as bad as the lung but not as bad as the liver.

'Then the spots were more like stains; and the stains were wetter.'

Mr Roper looked over his reading glasses in Mr Bevan's eyes. He had been doing this for almost three decades. In fact, he did it very well. There were times when he had been as moved by himself as by his patient patients. But not now.

'You'll be fine,' he said. 'When you're better, we'll go and see *Live and Let Die* together at the Capitol.'

'I'd like that.'

'I'd like that too.'

'It's a date so,' said Mr Bevan.

'Absolutely it is,' said Mr Roper. 'Now I have to admit that I've seen it already, but I'd love to go again. There's a terrific crocodile sequence and a state of the art chase, with this sadistic black ball-breaker, a right-hand man who doesn't in fact have a right-hand at all, only a prosthetic pincers. Roger Moore, the new face, isn't too bad. Admittedly, he wouldn't be my type; never was, even on TV. He just can't play patrician; he can't play privilege. Of course you wouldn't want him to try to be Connery. Connery is *sui generis*. Connery is God. If not God, the Son of God. The most you can ask, I suppose, is that he won't be as lam entable as Lazenby, though even Lazenby has been pilloried disproportionately. Generally, the whole style of the series has gone completely camp and caricatural. It's *The Saint* to the power of *n*.'

'It would make you think all right,' said Mr Bevan from far away. His eyes were playing slow table-soccer with their motes on the arctic whiteness of the ward ceiling.

'It would,' said the surgeon. 'It would indeed.'

The man in the next bed down, or perhaps in the second next one because they were all so close together, like in the dormitory of an orphanage, was imitating Peter Sellers imitating Clouseau and Dr Strangelove and the Indian fellow who chanted the *Doctor, I'm in Trouble* duet with Sophia Loren sometime back in the early sixties when her breasts were one of the glories of Western civilization alongside Brunelleschi's dome and Einstein's theory of curved space. But was he singing to amuse his callers or was he whistling in the dark, shaking a leather tambourine in the breathing labyrinth?

'Do you know this part of the city at all?' said Mr Bevan.

'I know it well,' the surgeon said. 'I was educated down the road.'

'By the Brothers?'

'By the Fathers. The Jesuits. In Belvedere.'

Mr Bevan's face lit up.

'Sure we got food parcels from Belvedere every Christmas in Summerhill,' he said. 'That's why my grandfather called it Wintervalley. Plum pudding, Madeira cake. We got presents as well up to Confirmation and then nothing. You were on your own after that.'

His left eye scored a penalty. Several of the key players had drifted into the stands.

'My father used to cycle through the Monto every day for years,' said the surgeon, talking to the curtain material in front of him. 'He was supposed to go two sides of a triangle from Sandymount to school, but he cut straight through. One time he peeped into a girl's ground-floor room, and it was wallpapered with holy pictures. It was more of an oratory than a bordello. I don't know how anybody managed an erection in a place like that.'

'My da used to fetch messages for the girls,' said the barber. 'That was after his Confirmation. They bought him a pair of shoes one time that shone like the Poolbeg lighthouse. Then this particular prostitute got sick and she was dying, and he had to carry her downstairs on his back, at thirteen years of age, out into the street where the Catholic priest from the Pro-Cathedral was waiting to give her Extreme Unction. But it was the sleet and rain of the outdoors and the night air that killed her with double pneumonia on top of the tuberculosis. He had his top hat and his cloak on. My side was as bad, of course.'

'Your side?'

'Protestant,' said Mr Bevan.

'Church of Ireland?'

'Church of Ireland. The Church in Ireland is the Church of Ireland. That was my da.'

'Me too,' said Mr Roper.

'Go way,' said Mr Bevan. 'I often wondered.'

'Long story. Mixed marriage. Four services on a Sunday.'

'Eucharist, Morning Prayer, Mass, and Evening Prayer.'

'Something like that,' Mr Roper said.

'Roper could be either,' the barber said. 'That's what had me wondering. I knew a Roper in the Third Order of Saint Francis; and I knew a Roper afterwards who was a Freemason. It's handy, like. You'd need to know the Christian name to be sure.'

'Gregory,' said Mr Roper. 'My mother called me Gregory the Great when she was pleased with my homework. She named me after a Pope, you know. She had certain expectations. More to do with prestige, I imagine, than with prayerfulness. Women know what's what.'

'Gregory could be High Church too,' Mr Bevan said. 'Gregory could easily be bells and smells.'

'Bevan is both,' Mr Roper said. 'Catholic and Protestant. And Jewish, for that matter. Am I right?'

'Not with Christopher de Valera in front of it,' Mr Bevan said.

'I suppose not,' said the surgeon.

Then they said nothing for a while as they thought about things. Things in general and things in particular. Visiting time must have been coming to an end because the shadows of people were passing the screen, and two of them were carrying children, and one of the children called out: 'Byebyebyebyebyebye'; but an adult voice from the far corner of the male surgical answered: 'Shhhhhhhhhh. Don't wake the dead.' And Mr Bevan was deciding that loyalty was a quiet form of love, an undemonstrative cornerstone, and that not enough had been said about it, really, by those who studied the behaviour of the heart in its covert operations; and Mr Roper was remembering how the affection of equals had been taught to his class by brief allusion in a course on forensic medicine which was optional for females.

'You'll have to go,' said a student nurse, inserting her head between the folds of the curtain and making an impromptu guillotine around her spotty swan neck. 'It's half past.'

'This is Mr Roper,' said the barber. 'He's a surgeon.'

'Is this a consultation?' she said. Now that he looked, she had a sebaceous cyst among all those hairclips. He used to love squeezing them.

'It's only a visit,' said the surgeon. 'It's not a visitation. I haven't worked here since the Second World War.'

'You must have been a very young student,' she said.

'This ward would have been jam-packed in February,' he said. 'Pulmonary cases, mainly.'

'It still is,' she said. 'And the private hospital is full of skiing injuries until Easter.'

Then she was gone, leaving the faintest watermark of something astringent in the atmosphere.

'Hydrogen peroxide,' Mr Roper said. 'She's bleached the hairs on her lip.' He could get up and leave now. There would be no shame in that. He had done enough.

'Could I ask you something?' said Mr Bevan. 'But stop me now if I'm intruding.'

'Ask away.'

Silence had resumed in the ward outside. Real illness was always speechless. When they were garrulous, they could go home.

'Were you married at all?'

'I was married. I am married. I have a wife and four sons. Hamburg, London, Stepaside. The youngest has terrible cerebral palsy and shouldn't have survived. He looks like the wreckage of a head-on collision. But that's the tragedy of modern medicine. It saves too many lives. I save too many lives. It's wrong.'

'And you wife? What does she think?'

'For the last seventeen years, my wife has decanted all her pity and all her anger into remains in a wheelchair. It leaves very little for anyone else.'

Mr Bevan ran his recessed hand through the frail strings of his hair and across his stubble.

'Still and all,' he said, 'there's something nice about a home with, maybe, pipe-cleaners on the mantelpiece and slips or a pair of stockings on the clotheshorse. It seems to outlast everything. The Roman Empire, the British Empire, even the Holy Roman Empire although I know that it was neither holy nor Roman nor an empire.'

Whitest of feet in flip-flops with a plastic daisy padded past the hem of the curtain.

'Have you a scissors handy?' Mr Roper said.

'A scissors?'

'And a razor.'

'I have a scissors,' said the barber, 'and I have a battery shaver. But you look very spruce to me.'

'It's not me I'm talking about,' the surgeon said. 'I'm talking about the barber from the Barber of Seville.'

'You must be joking. Is it me?'

Mr Roper yanked at the door of the metal bedside table and found inside it two paperback novels by Ian Fleming, a bacon scissors of sorts, assorted batteries, one shaver wound in its own helical flex, jelly babies, the Book of Common Prayer, and a dull service medal from the desert campaign.

'Did you know,' he said as he sat on the tuck of the regulation bed-sheet near to his patient, 'that once upon a time, and a very good time it was too, barbers and surgeons belonged to the same brotherhood.'

'Did they?'

'They did. The barber's pole, you know, was the surgeon's sign. White for bandages and red for blood.' And he ran the shaver lightly over the chin and the jaw; then, with more weight and agility, into the groove of the throat and over the Adam's apple across to the long lobe of the listening ear.

'They were neither surgeons nor barbers bur surgeon-barbers. Surgeon-barber Bevan and surgeon-barber Roper.'

'Imagine.' Yet he yawned as he said it.

'Nothing imaginary about it,' said Mr Roper, and the blades of the shaver sipped at the hairs on the upper lip until Mr Bevan drew it down over his top teeth to bare them. 'They were feared the length and breadth of Europe. It was the surgeon-barbers who carried out autopsies on the cadavers of criminals. It was the surgeon-barbers who performed the anatomical demonstrations at the universities while mere medical doctors commentated behind their pomanders. And it was the surgeon-barbers who amputated the arms and legs of wounded soldiers in the aftermath of carnage.'

'Dear me,' said Mr Bevan. 'You make us sound like Burke and Hare.' But there was a tear, as slow and solid as mercury, snailing along the chafed overhang of his cheek.

'Never,' the surgeon said. There had been friendship between them, and that was something. Muted and minor, perhaps, but what about it? Closeness was too costly. One's near and dear were pathological partners full of resentment and sentimentality. This, in the dignity of its distance, had been pure; or, at any rate, purish.

When the barber drowsed and dozed and fell asleep, his denture whistling modestly in the half-open orifice of his voice, the surgeon sheared soundlessly at the damp, disordered twists of hair, picking the coils from the pillow as he worked, tidying the sides and the little, delinquent spikes, thinning the springy fringe. It was strange to be so intent without boots and gloves and a fragrant scrub nurse and the solar ferocity of the overhead lights like the panels of a satellite in space. Yet he hummed as usual.

As he left, the nurse smiled at him from a trolley of bottles. Many men would mount her.

'Thanks,' he said. 'You're great.'

'No bother. Do you want to talk to the consultant's houseman?'

'No,' he said. 'I'll get back to him. You could say I was in. Roper.'

'Maybe I oughtn't to tell you,' said the nurse. 'I got into trouble once over telling. But they didn't operate. There was nothing they could do. It was too late.'

'They opened him up?' said the surgeon.

'They opened him up, took one look, and closed him again. That was it. He was back in the bed before the Gay Byrne show was over. Gas character. Are you good friends?'

Mr Roper thought about that. Because it would be reported back. It would be relayed forward. It would have its own precarious itinerary among the strict witnesses.

'We were very close,' he said to her. 'We came within a hair's breadth of each other.'

Blánaid McKinney

These Important Messages

The thing is the colours. No, not just the colours but the sheer number of colours. I had seen such flashes on television but back there, they were always moving, from flash to blip to harmless swoosh. Never still. And never stinging my eyeballs with the solidity of these billboards, right here, right now. They are just there. Immobile, huge and just there. They are bigger than my whole dormitory wing and they are truly lovely.

I've never planted myself in front of the likes of that for fifteen minutes at a time, rooted, static, like a moron in front of the brilliant bulk of those billboards before. It is almost like a shrine. It is a damned shrine. I am so happy, just looking at the enormity of the text's crispy, olive lines and the gleam of the girl's five-foot eyes and the fizz and dainty dementia of the message. It's an advert for a beer. Fifty yards high.

I've tried beer twice. Once when I was sixteen and, again, when I was seventeen. It didn't take.

I stand in front of that damn thing, outside Victoria Station, for an age. Then she pulls up in her rag-top MGB and grabs me by the ear and hauls me on to the passenger seat, laughing and clamping her teeth on my collar, and kissing my neck. The scent of her skin is enough to send my shoulder muscles into spasm. I hug her so tightly, she gasps in near-pain.

I am in my street clothes, thanks be to God. Even so, I find it hard to relax immediately. I just want to hang on to her, bury my head beneath her collarbone and block out the daylight. So we cling to each other like that for a minute, until the taxi drivers start up a racket behind us. I'm forty-four and she makes me feel as if I'm an awful lot younger than that.

'Jesus, Matt, let go!' she laughs.

'Sorry. Let's go.'

I rest my hand on top of hers as she shifts gears and we pull away. I can't even drive but it gives me the sense that I know what I'm doing. The roads swim by, and the neon, and we are at her apartment before I know it. We barge up the stairs in a mad tangle of kisses and hand luggage and elbows and pure, svelte desperation. We fall into her bed and stay there for three hours, without even closing the front door, which creaks and thumps in the soft breeze like a mutant metronome, the whole time.

I love her so much. It's like being skinned alive, painlessly, in ice water.

When I am with her, the gentle dynamic of her body leaves me, afterwards, in a shameless shambles and I barely, nor care to, know who I am any more. The skirmish of my previous life, that despicable choir of responsibility and duty and obedience – *everything* – just disappears and I am left with her body, her smell and the absolute certainty that I have made the right decision.

That evening, we go out on the town.

'So, Matt, what do you want to do first?'

'Jesus, Laura, sweetheart, it's your town. I don't know. Could we just walk for a bit?'

So we walk. All over. I had only ever been to London once before. I didn't recognize a damn thing. It would have made my head hurt if it hadn't been for her. We go down to Chinatown and halfway up Gerrard Street, she puts her hands over my eyes.

'Point,' she says.

'Point?'

'Yeah. You want to eat? Just point in any direction and that's where we'll eat.'

'You mean they're all the bloody same?'

'No, I mean they're all equally brilliant. Now point.'

So I flail off, blind, pointing to the south-west, I think, and that's where we have the best food I have ever tasted in my entire life. We never had food like that at home. Well, of course we did, in the form of takeaways. But it was nothing like this. There is a damn orgy going on in my mouth. King Prawns in Garlic and Wine Sauce. Lemon Chicken. Singapore Noodles. She notices the expression on my face and the expression on hers is almost one of pity. I feel like such a hick, but when she begins to laugh, and to lean over the table, and to trail a dreaming palm along the bridge of my nose, all I can think about is how happy I am at that moment, with the most mischievously exquisite food in my gob and the most miraculous woman in the world by my side.

'Come on. We'll walk some more and I'll show you what I do for a living.'

'Laura, I know what you do for a living. And I see it every time I walk down the street.'

'Yeah, but you've never seen it in living colour.'

So we walk some more, through Piccadilly, and we stand for a while looking at the neon signs, high above our heads. Her company, of which she is assistant managing director, was responsible for two thirds of the blinking, winking stuff, up there, that leaks into my peripheral vision even when I'm staring at the pavement. And a lot of the posters, around and about, too. The tourists dawdle by and the hawkers hawk and the sheer, blinding brightness of it makes me want to hug her and cover my own eyes, myself, at the same time.

The mythology of buying.

She is so clever and so kind.

I can hardly believe my luck.

We walk on and she talks but I can hardly hear. It is as if all those adverts have rendered me half-deaf as well as near-blind. I love the feel of her hand on my arm but my own skin feels a little alien under the glare. It's my own fault. I live a very quiet life.

She has a theory about advertising and she tells me as we walk. Walk and traipse through and around Soho, and as we stroll she explains to me the limelight, feral philosophy that has made her both rich and happy. I begin to count the fly-posters, because a fair proportion of them are just fantastic. And an awful lot of them are hers.

Outside the Coach and Horses, a guy is hunkered down on the pavement, pointing a camera at the rooftops. And then I realize it's not a camera, it's a telescope. And it's not pointed at the roofs, it's pointed at the stars. Crowds are crashing, but quietly, past him and this idiot is trying to see the stars. In the middle of the busiest, most spot-lit part of a damn city. He can't possibly see any stars, but still he sits there, terse and tense, ignoring the noise and gazing at the arctic heavens. He is a ramshackle-looking individual, but the telescope is state of the art, top of the range and the most expensive-looking piece of kit I have ever seen.

The telescope. Me and my kind, we weren't ready for that one. Up to that point the earth was the centre of the universe, and humanity was the centre of God's attention. And then along came the telescope and Galileo and Copernicus and we weren't special any more. We were just desolate dust floating, fragments of bits and bobs that didn't mean a damn thing on a galactic ball of nonsense that didn't mean very much either. God just wasn't that interested. Four hundred years later, I don't think we've ever gotten over the shock.

'Matt, are you okay? Jesus, you're shaking.'

'I'm fine, I'm just a little cold.'

'So what do you think of my masterpieces?' She's only half-serious.

'It's all beautiful. You must be making a bloody fortune!'

'I am, but it's all been a little pointless recently. Because you weren't here. Have you any idea how much I've missed you? Why didn't you come over earlier?'

'There was something I had to take care of. It's nothing. I'm here now, and I'm staying.'

'Promise. Promise me, you bastard. Promise me you'll stay with me this time.'

'I swear.'

The last time I swore that kind of oath, an oath of undying love and devotion, was thirteen years ago, lying on the flat of my belly at Maynooth, with the candles dribbling nearby, above my head, and their shimmying, muscular light bleeding into the sides of my vision. My brothers and my betters were with me, praying with me and for me, in a sorrowful, rumbling, male mantra, and in the course of those ten hours of darkness, terror and the best kind of alchemical and muddy joy, I swore to be faithful to God, to forswear all other notions of love and, in my own head, to be the best priest that I could be. And for a long time I was. I was the best priest the school ever saw and the best pastor that neighbourhood ever knew. I told the headmaster I was going on a long weekend to see my father in Donegal.

That was two weeks ago.

They have no idea where I am.

'Well, okay then,' she says, and I know that she is the last person to whom I will ever deliver an oath. Of any kind.

She steps over the man with the telescope, accidentally swiping the contraption out of his hands with the swirl of her coat, and throws her arms around me. I kiss her so hard, right there in the middle of that percussive street that I don't even realize, until much later, that the man neither protested nor complained. He just picked up the pieces, thankfully unbroken, screwed them back together again, and carried on gazing upwards. At that moment, I want to crouch down alongside him and try to see what he thought he was seeing. A world simpler than the one we now inhabited, perhaps. A world where we all knew our place, and where our place was the place to be, where we were all bosses, under God, and where the stars were just there for decoration, for our amusement, a black and celestial curtain of contentment and verification. But the world has moved on. Or back, depending on how you look at it.

I know that I am on trial here. I'm staying. But I can't make it easy on myself.

That would just go against the grain.

If I'm honest, it's all up to her.

Because that's the kind of man I am.

That's the kind of good priest I am. Or was. We'll see.

'How is Belfast these days?' she asks, as we lie down on the grass outside the National Gallery.

There are only a few people wandering about. It's pitch dark and some moron is bathing, naked, in one of the fountains in Trafalgar Square.

I love public spaces. I just wish that they were all *bigger*.

Trafalgar Square is fine, but let's face it – as city squares go, you couldn't swing a cat in it.

St Peter's – now *that's* a city square.

'It's perfect. Almost peaceful. Not where I work, obviously but – yeah, it's great.'

'And the kids? You and the Fathers have got a replacement teacher organized?'

The laser spot on Nelson's Column beams and my guts churn, and I say 'Yes, pretty much.'

'Good. I wouldn't want you leaving anything unfinished.'

'Me neither.'

'Matt. I love you more than anything. Don't shiver away from me like that.'

'I'm not, Laura. Honestly. It's just that, well, this is a big move for me.'

'I know. Sorry.'

The moron is now being arrested, but gently so, by a kindly duo in blue. They've given him a pair of shorts and he seems sadder for it. He actually sags down between the cops and it doesn't seem to have anything to do with alcohol.

She curls her arm around my hip and slides her palm, hard, down along my crotch and says *sorry* again, and I roll over on top of her, and bury my mouth in hers and we start dry humping, right there on the grass, in public, even though it is night-time. Through cotton and denim, hard as hell until, forty seconds later, we both catch a panting grip and haul ourselves up.

'Laura, we're going to get arrested.' I'm gasping the words out.

'Yes. Yeah. Yes, Matt. Let's go home.'

So we catch the No. 53 bus and, on the empty top deck with her straddling me, and with her lovely blue cotton dress wrapped around her ribcage, and my palms on either side of her face, we fuck each other, trembling, in utter silence the whole way home.

And behind us, I'm sure, the skinny seminar of the square, the near-virtuous, luminary ruffle of that gallant public space just carried on and on without us.

*

The strange thing is that Laura and I have known each other since we were children. We both went to school in Enniskillen. She went to Mount Lourdes Convent, I went to St Michael's. We spent seven years at the back of the bus, talking shit and carrying on, like all the other kids. And then we both went to university in Belfast. That's when we began to drift apart. She took Media Studies. I took Scholastic Philosophy – I only started that course because the History course was so awful, and because the tutors, all of them priests, had the kind of glacial calm about them that I've only ever seen since in policemen. Usually during riots. I knew that there was something about her that I'd never had the courage to go after, but I also knew that, in my tutors' intelligence, there was a snazzy and whispering thing that I just *knew* was going to come and get me. Sooner or later. And it did. I enrolled in the seminary after graduation and, well, that was me. They magicked one breed of insubordinate courage out of me but, unwitting, seeped in another. The bravery of being willing to disappear, to become as nothing. To check the yelping checklist of what it is to be an autonomous human being, and to throw it all away, for and before God, and to simply sit there and wait. To wait for Him to tell me what to do. And He did. There were no cranky disintegrative doldrums in my faith. I leaped right in and I was happier back then than I have ever been in my life. And I was a damn good priest. I worked my arse off. I was the best. I still am the best.

What I have here is a gallant bargain, and sanctuary too. I know that you cannot call in a marker with God. But I'm calling it in anyway. All I'm asking for is a little noisy and dreadless ablution. Every time I close my eyes I am praying to Him. Just to be left alone, just for a little while. To sort out what I'm going to do with the rest of my life.

And the notion that the rest of my life might actually belong to me, is the most terrifying, loneliest thought I've had all day.

I don't want autonomy. I want to belong to someone.

I want to be owned, thrown, roped and branded.

And right now on the blessed top deck Laura, coming, screams quietly and bites me hard on the neck.

It hurts, badly.

I hope it leaves a scar.

*

I'm a good teacher. I can teach anything. Back in Belfast, at St Bernard's, which is practically out in the countryside, I taught anything that was needed from day to day. Geography teacher one day, Maths or Latin teacher the next, counsellor pretty much all the time. But my favourite was Religious Instruction. Honestly. I just loved it. A couple of the Fathers couldn't wait to get away from that stuff, since we'd all been buried in it up to our ears in our mid-twenties. But I couldn't wait to get back to the theology. Talking to a bunch of restless boys about a restful deity, the ultimate Mathematician under whose executive gaze all our lives made sense, and in whose realm there existed nothing so cruel as a random event. Where the divine equation was just that, where every death had not simply meaning but meaning that could be explained, in deft and comforting detail. Even the good things could be explained in terms of a loving Father, and didn't have anything to do with individual merit or luck or effort. What a relief that was, then.

But at least our own sins belonged to us.

At least He gave us that gift.

And we were happy to take possession and pretend, in the sheerest and most pesky way, that we had control over our own destiny.

Our sins were the best, glossiest thing He ever gave us.

And the boys, for the most part, assumed that I was talking shit and, sensibly, sniggered their way through most of my classes. Sin was not a concept they wanted in their lives. They wanted my retro, rubbish benediction during the day, so that they could go out and get both hammered and laid during the night and the word 'evil' just made them piss their pants.

My words were a mere, sweet, dumb cat-call to prayer and they didn't want to pray.

They knew it.

I knew it.

But I loved that class.

And I despaired for them.

'Matt, I have to go to work.'

'Christ, Laura, it's the middle of the night . . .'

'It's six in the morning, you moron . . .'

'You go to work at this time, sweetheart? Jesus Christ . . .'

And off she goes. She dresses better than any woman I've ever seen. She is wearing a suit of azure something-or-other, and her aroma wafts around the bedroom long after she's gone. I lie in bed for a while, then go for a potter about her flat. I've never been here before. It really is gorgeous. God alone knows what the rent is. Almost every inch of wallspace is covered in old posters. Classic adverts from the forties and fifties, mostly, beautifully framed. They seem so dated now. Innocent, almost. Her television is like nothing I've ever seen. Mine at home is twelve-inch, black-and-white, and I haven't turned it on more than twice a year. This one is in a different league. It's almost two metres wide, more than a metre long, three inches deep and hanging on the wall like a painting. Jesus, the thing is actually framed in wood, exactly like a painting. Cherrywood, I think. I turn it on and I can practically make out every pore on Michael Buerk's face. It actually gives me a jolt. The aftermath of some bomb or other, or something, is going on behind him and the plumes of smoke have a near-tidal, lazy beauty that is quite mesmerizing. I can't tear my eyes away from it. I find the remote and spend the next three hours upside down on one of her deep armchairs, clicking and clicking. This television is just amazing. There must be well over a hundred channels and the definition is so good it almost gives me a headache. I think about turning it off and I don't, so I lie there for another hour, grazing through a world on its head. I try it right side up for a bit but it's not really an improvement. I flip through at least seventy channels and settle on the Shopping Channel. The jewellery looks so real, my arm actually reaches out, almost of its own volition, as if to grab it. What a telly. It makes me want to laugh out loud but it gives me a small pain in my chest too. It's as if all the tiny bits of feral energy brought to a standstill in my brain have migrated south. Maybe I should get myself satellite and stop being such a snob. But I don't feel like a snob.

I just feel lost. No, that's not it. I feel as if she's racing away from me and I'm too damn useless to be able to catch up. I love her dearly but sometimes I'm terrified that she's just too fast for me. I'm the luckiest man in the world and it makes no sense. Adored and redundant at the same time. Sooner or later she's going to start to feel short-changed. I'm sure of it.

I think, again, about turning it off and, again, I don't. I haven't even showered. I graze some more. History Channel. Nice. Discovery – nice also, and back through the louder stations, and it slowly dawns on me that it's not the majestically stupid programmes that are annoying me. I *like* glimpses of cop shows from my youth. I like the adrenal and sheer love that goes into the assemblage of gobby, feeble and occasionally smashing music videos. Christ, even the near-imperial desperation, the *repetition* of all those news channels have me smiling to myself. No, I like all of this stuff.

In her armchair, I've watched more television in four hours than in the last ten years put together, and I decide that I love all these programmes.

All of them.

It's the stuff in between that I cannot stand.

It's the slime in the middle that's driving me mad.

I finally turn the set off and the silence is so striking that it makes my head wobble.

While I'm showering, I wonder how my boys are getting on. I'm sure the headmaster has drafted in a good supply teacher. I'm sure they're okay. They're good kids. Smart and bolshy enough to know that only 30 per cent of anything we priests say is worth a damn. But even so, I still worry about them. Sometimes I think the album title says it all. Modern life really is rubbish, and those kids are drowning in it, no matter how hard I and my fellow Fathers try. I have been sturdy enough, and cowardly too, to ignore 70 per cent of the earth's nonsense and I had hoped that some of that shrewd and droning arrogance - there's no other word for it – had rubbed off on the boys. Just to give them protection, some permafrost, a little soul-teflon to separate them from the mountain of bullshit that is the world. Nowadays and thereabouts.

And because I am such a sensitive soul, the headmaster, three years ago (after ten years of studiously avoiding the entire subject), asked me to take a couple of seminars about what we have always euphemistically referred to as the 'Troubles'.

I nearly choked on my coffee and dribbled a substantial mouthful of it on to my shirt.

I don't give a flying fuck about the Troubles.

I'm sorry, but there you have it. I grew up with this shit and I just don't give a fuck.

My boys are going to have an infinitely worse world of trouble facing them when they leave. They are going to have to *live* in the fucking thing, and death is *not* the worst of it. They are going to spend every ounce of energy trying not to disappear first, and most of them aren't going to make it.

I know that for a fact.

Anthony didn't make it. He was eleven and as keen as mustard. He wanted to be a priest. I was his hero, God love him. But he had the stern good sense to want proof. One day, after class, he hung back and asked me a question. The question was – how could I prove to him that God really exists? I wasn't being cruel when I laughed right in his face, I just thought it was funny. Hadn't he been paying attention? How the hell was I supposed to answer that? And then his expression began to annoy me. It was a combination of solemn common sense and babyish expectation. I told him that there were some things he was just going to have to take on faith, or some such cliché, and saying it made me feel a hundred years old. Anthony gave me a look that I have never forgotten. He knew that I believed every word. And that he wasn't going to get what, for him, was a satisfactory answer. I went from being his hero to a sad, passive lump in two seconds. The look was one of purest pity. He might as well have stabbed me.

I got over it. He was eleven for God's sake. I had fifty other kids to teach.

The kid was unstable to begin with, and he had a strange home life. Everybody sort of knew that but, when he died three years later, he proved to all of us that even though he was clever and studious and almost pious, he really was just a baby.

Three parts bleach to one part *orange cordial*, for the love of Christ . . .

*

That was four months ago. I phoned Laura immediately after the funeral. We'd always kept in touch, on and off, and I just needed to hear her voice. She invited me over for the weekend. And that's when it started. I was amazed at myself. I wasn't unhappy in any special sense. And when we fell into each other's arms at the airport and she tucked the white band from my collar into her pocket, I didn't give it a second thought. It was as natural as breathing.

Better, even.

And now here I am, again.

I know these three days are a trial run. Laura and me. But I am hopeful.

Laura and me. Me and Laura. Jesus, I love the way that sounds.

I spend the rest of Saturday pottering around this gorgeous flat. She gets back from work at about eight and we spend the night cooking and making love and talking.

'Are you thinking of getting a job here? Matt, it would be wonderful if you did.'

'Yes, definitely. But what am I good for? I'm not sure that

ex-priests are good for very much. I can teach, but references might be a problem, given the—'

'Fuck's sake, Matt, would you climb down off the Cross? We could use the wood . . .'

'Jesus, you don't take any prisoners, do you?'

'I don't need prisoners. I've got you.'

'Yes. I know.' And she has. She has me, absolutely.

'Besides, you're the smartest man I know. You could blag your way into any damn job you want. You could probably do *my* job, if you wanted. Most people are so *stupid*. They just need a little oiling and they'll buy *anything*.'

'*Populus vult decepti*.'

'Matt, don't do that. I hate it when you do that Latin shit.'

'Sorry.'

A moment's silence. Then she sighs.

'Okay, I give. What's it mean?'

'People want to be deceived.'

'Damn right – Jesus, I could *use* that . . . Stay with me, baby. Please.'

Stay with me, she says. And then she drifts off to sleep, with the germ of another mini-campaign building in her lovely head. I watch her sleep. She looks like the most innocent thing. In her sleep, she wraps herself around me, thrice over, in a dry, slow slither, and I have to tie myself in corresponding and dreamy knots to make sure she doesn't wake up or fall out. Her body never ceases to amaze me. I feel like some two-bit engineer, like a lowlife, clay and clanking golem just lying next to her. She is so neat in every way. With her, the panic and sheer shindig of sex remakes me. I wasn't a virgin, but I might as well have been. I stay awake all night and just let her continue her sleepy-bossy, slow-motion strobe through the sheets.

I don't sleep much these days anyway. I don't know when that started.

Laura kicks awake at noon and we go out. Today is Sunday. Our first proper full day together.

She's taking me sightseeing, all over. I'm excited. A full day together.

In her world. I'm all dressed up in my best togs.

We cross the road outside her flat and the first thing we see is a fox. Trotting across the white line, as bold as brass and followed by a taxi. I've never seen a fox before, even when I lived in the countryside. He's a big fellow and utterly oblivious. I'm the only one giving him a second glance. He lopes to his left, behind a tree, and comes out with a careless baby squirrel in his jaws. Its tail is only like knotted string, it's that young. He doesn't even break stride and disappears around the back. I'm laughing already, inside.

'Vermin . . .' Laura says, under her breath.

We head into the West End. I'm ogling the window of Comic Showcase on Charing Cross Road like a greedy child (I've always loved comics, but had to sell my collection years ago), when a man walks by. It's Brendan Fraser. I knew he was in town, doing *Cat on a Hot Tin Roof* but Jesus, God, you don't expect to see Hollywood stars just wandering around the streets, surely. I'm about to grab him by the hem of his jacket and ask for, well, I don't know, an autograph probably, when Laura rams her nails into my armpit and hisses 'Don't be such a fucking peasant, Matt!' and I am suddenly ashamed of myself. But then she laughs and apologizes and I feel better.

From there we get the tube to Hyde Park, to see the preachers at Speaker's Corner. This was Laura's idea. I wonder if she's trying to make a point, or something. Is she being sarcastic? I doubt it. It's not in her nature to be sarcastic. I actually think she's afraid. Afraid I might remember my day job, and run away from her in a hurtful flurry of righteousness and religiosity. Scared that I might remember how much I loved my former life. I think that it's her idea of a test. She is a brave woman, at the very least. But these guys don't bother me. I love them, in fact. They're brilliant. Every nut-job one of them. Brilliant and utterly, utterly stupid. And most of them seem to be convinced that the world is in big trouble. It's depressing, listening to their ragged rants about this, that or the other. But it's kind of funny, too. One elderly gent, in particular, is letting us all know just how many things need fixing, and doing it in a dull, arctic baritone that is sending most of his listeners to sleep.

'Social reform,' he intones, 'prison reform, technological reform, law reform, housing reform, transport reform, education reform—'

'Chloroform?' I shout from the back.

Everybody laughs, Laura giggles into my chest and I am inordinately chuffed with myself. The gentleman stops. He blinks and looks directly at me. He steps down, buttons his coat and walks away. He seems hurt, and for a moment I feel a little guilty. But not for long.

We walk on, and the sheer pessimism of most of the speakers entrances me. They haven't a clue. They actually seem to believe that the world is a bad place.

Well, that's just plain wrong. The world is a paradise and that's all there is to it, really. Some minor kinks to be worked out, tops.

We walk on up towards Westminster. We stop on the

bridge and look at the House of Commons for a bit. It's astonishing, that building.

'Bastards,' snaps Laura, flatly.

'Why, bastards?'

'What do you mean, why? They're politicians, aren't they?'

As if that explains everything.

'Don't you think their hearts might be in the right place?'

'No. I think they're all in it for what they can get out of it. Isn't everyone?'

'Are you?'

'Of course. It's what makes life interesting,' she says, 'and I'm good at it, too.'

'I don't believe that.'

'See?'

I can't think of an answer so I lean over and gaze down at the river. Laura tells me that it's recovering, that all sorts of fish and wild birds are coming back, that there was time when, if you went into the Thames, you were automatically carted off to hospital to have your stomach pumped. It still looks pretty dodgy to me. We walk on, northwards.

I'm a country boy by heart, and the noise is getting to me a little. At first I assume that it's the weight of traffic, and it is partly that. But it's something else, too. Something I can't quite get a fix on. And the closer we get to the heart of town, the more I realize that the sensation has less to do with my ears than with my brain.

We're back in Leicester Square. I'm not the most adventurous tourist in the world . . . I hope I'm not boring her. A guy called Momo is playing flamenco guitar and, on the other side, a troupe of Zulu dancers are doing their stuff.

Both are brilliant, and having money thrown at them left, right and centre. But they don't even look at their coin-filled cases. They're lost in their own benevolent, self-made skank, where cash is at the bottom of the heap. The guitar player has his eyes closed the whole time. Anybody could run off with all his takings and he wouldn't know. That's a shameful thought to be thinking.

Just then, the Swiss Centre clockwork spiel starts up, all mechanical cowherds and milkmaids and rustic bells. And goats. At least, they look like goats.

Laura thinks it's a kitsch classic. She's thinking of basing an advert on it. She doesn't have a product yet, or a client even, but that doesn't matter. It's the idea that counts. She gets an idea every time she turns around. She's humming the guitar guy's *Light My Fire*, and she has an idea for that too. A car advert would suit. Not a people mover. Something along the lines of a small, nippy convertible. Something women would like.

And she just loves that mechanical clockwork contraption.

I think it's the stupidest thing I've ever seen, and I'm afraid to say so.

The weird sensation in my head is getting stronger.

And then I realize what it is.

It's the colours again and, again, the number of them.

It's the advertisements.

Everywhere I look, I see a commercial. Moving, waving, shining or static and huge.

Everywhere.

The place is packed with people and I can't make out a single face. Every forehead is bathed in the reflected glow of neon, every limb is just part of the foreground, or the background, of a poster. Every apprehensive, svelte and startling individual is an extra, not even a walk-on, in some huge, silent circus they don't even know they're in.

The advertisements are everywhere.

On every lamp-post, doorway, bus, taxi, window, wall, banner and tree.

On every T-shirt, dress, rucksack, hairstyle, cap, shopping bag and running shoe.

On every brick, plastered and swamped.

Now I'm *really* looking. And the more I look, the more it dawns on me that the flood of logo-effluent, crowding out our eyes, is all there is.

And that every public space possible, isn't.

There are no people. Not really. What is fizzing its rotten and jaunty way behind my eyeballs right now, is not a softly ruffling collection of bored humanity, but a cracked and positively orchestral explosion of disconnected information.

An overload of mental ecology gone badly wrong.

It never occurred to me before that all these adverts would feel so wrong. That their presence, in abundance, would actually, almost physically, hurt.

It's making me a bit mad, quite frankly.

But beside me, Laura is turning in slow circles, arms akimbo, eyes closed, breathing in what is, to her, the most astonishing air. This square is her world, and she is the best in her world.

She is smiling.

It is a patrician smile of benign acquisition.

She is in heaven.

I have the worst headache I've ever had in my life.

I stand back and watch her, her slow, swooping turns signalling ownership. She doesn't even know I'm here any more.

Everybody else in the commercials business is just a lousy, scoffing slattern, but she is queen. Monarch of the seamless, ten-second story, and everybody comes to the queen. Her contentment is a small and seismic thing, and a world away from me.

None of the passers-by gives her a second glance. Just another headcase, albeit a very well-dressed one. They have no idea that she owns them. Brain and soul, every damn one.

I feel very strange right now.

I take her by the elbow. Her eyes snap open, she laughs a laugh of pure joy, and we walk on. My arm is around her waist and her body feels weird. Cute and angular instead of just soft. I don't want to talk. I just concentrate on walking. We just keep heading what I think is north.

We head up Regent's Street. She has a carnival gait, now.

I grip her waist and feel as if my head is about to explode. What the hell is wrong with me?

We go for an Indian meal this time. It's two in the morning and the city is still blaring outside. I don't know where we are any more. North, somewhere, I suppose. I eat a little, although I am not hungry. I just don't want to go out there again. I feel trapped. Laura has disappeared to the ladies twice in thirty minutes, and she won't stop talking about her work. She's flinging ideas for adverts around like confetti. About how she could use this, with a sort of neo-Fascist-with-humour theme, or use that, with a kind-of religious-iconography-with-dwarfs theme. About how I could help her with the priest stuff. I'm not stupid and, frankly, I don't give a flying fuck about cocaine either.

She is probably smarter, funnier and lovelier, stoned, than most people are sober and straight. I love her. But I'm beginning to hate her universe. She gets more chatty and scatty by the minute. Now she's throwing a few small insults across the table and I don't think she's joking. She's pissed off with me. With me acting like a lumpen tourist, like a useless and uninvolved heap. Fair enough. I've given up trying to have a proper conversation tonight. I am exhausted. I'm afraid that I may have made a slight mistake.

While Laura is blathering, but cleverly, it dawns on me like a slow itch in my brain that I haven't prayed in a week. I used to pray to God a dozen times a day. I used to pray even when I didn't know I was doing it. When I shaved, or ate or just opened my eyes in the morning. I have my hands clasped in front of me on the table, in what must look like supplication, when Laura comes back, bouncing, from the loo for the third time. I'm not praying. I'm just resting my eyes. But she looks at me as if I am the filthiest goon on the planet.

'Are you fucking *praying*?'

Her voice is like a razor. It's not a question. It's an accusation.

I'm tired, and I don't like her tone, so I look her square in the eye.

'Yes. I'm praying. Leave me alone.'

And to my amazement, she does. She quietly picks up her coat and her bag and she walks out. But before she does, classy girl that she is, she leaves a £50 note on the table. She knows I'm skint. And she knows a decent insult when she sees one. I guess I got up on my hind legs and begged for that one . . . The waiter, bless him, carefully examines his shoes.

'Make your own way home, arsehole.' This, also, is said quietly.

'Laura, please . . .'

And then she's gone, out the door with elegance and the minimum of fuss.

I lower my head on to the table and, this time, I really do pray. But I'm half-drunk, so I'm not sure if it counts. The first beer I've had in over two decades and it still didn't take.

It's four in the morning, and I'm walking home alone. Well, I'm calling it home. If she lets me in. Back southwards. I wouldn't know what bus to get. The city is a little quieter now, but the signs of the wake-up are creeping on. The place is shivering itself to life. It's still dark, sort of. I walk on and splash some water on my face from a public fountain. I feel fresher. I find a sandwich shop and treat myself to a huge salt beef and mustard bagel and a tall latte. There is nothing on God's earth better than bread. I stare at the wall opposite and think about bread. *Company*, from the Latin *cum panis*, meaning 'with bread', or 'to break bread'. Of course, His bread at that supper would have been a flat, grit-ridden, unleavened affair.

This bagel is probably the best thing I've ever had. Chinese notwithstanding.

I think I'll leave Laura alone for a couple of hours, until she isn't annoyed with me any more. I'll just hang around town for a while. It'll be okay. This place isn't so bad. I'm just tired. I wander down the Strand, find our exact patch of grubby grass outside the National Gallery and lie down and nap, curled up like a drowned kitten.

I'm woken by the beginnings of the traffic an hour later, and I'm amazed that I haven't been arrested for vagrancy. Or whatever it's called.

I feel good. My head feels clear. I decide to go for another long walk, this time by myself. Perhaps it's not her universe, or the world, or the city. Perhaps it's just me.

But it isn't. Sunrise is still an hour away and it doesn't make a damn bit of difference. The street lights go on and off at precisely the right time, to assuage any jolt to the eyes that the jump from artificial to natural and back again might cause. There is no such thing as true, terminal darkness. Even at this time of the morning, as I'm walking up Shaftesbury Avenue and wiping gunk from my chin, the racket inside my head starts up again, the empty spaces shrink, and I walk and I look and I look and I grow madder with every step.

I love the traffic, I've decided now. I love the crowds and this man-made noise, and the buildings, both gorgeous and hideous. I love every inch of this place. Every sloppy concrete anomaly, every forlorn and stupid statue, every dour delta of alleys and lanes. Every inch.

Every inch, that is, that isn't plastered with adverts.

I walk up the avenue and down the avenue, and up again. On my third pass, the homeless guy lying in the doorway of the Apollo Theatre doesn't even bother to ask me for money. He just looks at me as if I'm an utter nutter. As if I'm the one who needs help. I have to stop myself from talking to myself.

All these adverts are driving me crazy.

I'm not kidding. The whole thing is annoying me to the point where I would rather be blind and fall under a bus than have to endure looking at this stuff any more.

I walk down Wardour Street with my eyes closed and manage to get three hundred yards before I fall over a bollard. This is ridiculous. She loves this stuff and I love her. But there is something else, something more going on here. And the knowledge leaks into my brain like a corrosive acid. Now I know what it is. I'm actually angry. I'm fucking *furious*. Everywhere I look, every time I open my fucking eyes, I see a fucking advert whether I want to or not. Well, I'm sorry, but that's just not fair. I can't live my life with my eyes closed, can I?

I keep walking and I realize that I can identify every shop, chain and brand logo along the street, but I can't remember more than three leaf shapes. Oak, Cherry Blossom, Chestnut. And that's it. I grew up in the countryside, for Chrissakes. I should know this shit.

And with each step, I grow more disoriented and more depressed. It's as if my mind has been polluted by the worst kind of toxin. *Every fucking place I turn my eyes.*

And I don't even watch television. Okay, now I'm actually becoming quite frightened. One of the things that scares me is that these adverts are all the same. Doesn't matter what the product is – they're all the fucking same. Preying on the same things. Envy, pride, lust, shame, you name it. We have nowhere left to run. Neither dim exemption nor simple space to stroll. Not even inside our own heads. We've been colonized. Roped, thrown, done and dusted. And all of it in the one place we thought was sacred.

And the more hardened, the more inured we become, the louder, busier and more crowded those sterile fuckers have to get, just to keep our attention.

Morons. All of us. On both sides.

I read somewhere, once, that there is more information in one issue of *The Sunday Times* than the average person living during the Renaissance would have absorbed in an entire lifetime.

I'm in Leicester Square, again, wandering like a cretinous wraith. I've had three strong coffees in a row. I feel okay. Dawn has arrived. It's really pretty. The starlings are going quietly berserk, up and beyond, and a couple of guys from the Council are standing around with cameras and fancy compass-type things and yellow jackets. They must be surveyors. They stand and stare at each other, equipment and cameras pointing, from opposite ends of the square. They stand like statues. In this early, muddy-misty light, they look heroic. There's no other word for it. And behind them trails a stream of party-goers, staggering out from what must have been a themed all-nighter. One young guy is dressed like Starsky, big cardigan and all, and his friend is wearing a beige leather jacket and the worst blond wig in the world.

They look really happy.

The light is coming along properly now.

The gates to the Square's garden are open, so I wander in and park myself on one of the benches. My mind is utterly empty.

And then I look up and see him.

A big, muscular guy in overalls and a mask, is standing in front of the fountain. There are pickaxes, saws, screwdrivers, huge knives and cleavers strewn on the ground, all around him.

He is holding a chainsaw.

And beside him is a three-metre high block of ice.

He's a sculptor.

I remember how to breathe again, just in time, and the big guy gets to work.

He rips on the chainsaw, hoists it up to shoulder height and swipes the corners off the top of the block. The ice chunks fall to the ground with a slushy, groaning clunk. He moves around the block and uses the roaring tip to dip in and around, up and down, delicately, to excavate a diagonal series of slivering crevices. The muscles of his arms and shoulders bunch, and the sweat on his skin freezes, sheen, in the cold air. He dances, a lumbering dance, around the diminishing block, as he darts the chainsaw this way and that, poking and sluicing.

It's impossible to tell what it's going to be. Flurries of ice chips fly through the air and the noise is deafening. He is oblivious to everything around him. He's like a stout and crafty bouncer, touched by some demented Muse. He is mesmerizing.

I get comfortable. A few other people, not tourists, gather round, and we sit and watch him.

He turns off the chainsaw, stands back and folds his arms, gazing at the ice.

We gaze at him, and we still haven't an idea what is going to appear from within.

He stares at it for ten minutes and he doesn't move a muscle. It's as if we are waiting for some exotic animal to emerge from its lair. He moves forward and picks up a hammer and a chisel. We all lean forward. Nobody has the nerve to speak to him. We can hear the sounds of the city outside this space rumble up and take possession of the day. But here, I and my spooked half-dozen are deaf to it. We want only to watch and wait to see what the big man is going to do next, in his project of playful and brilliant violence. This is great. I love it.

He approaches the block, which has now taken on a vaguely humanoid shape but with weird points and high projections, and begins to tap gently. The chisel is long and slender and he holds it between thumb and forefinger, like a pencil. His breath steams out and bounces off the ice like a solid thing and as he chips and taps, the thinning shape changes in tiny, incremental ways, twisting into smackly visible common sense. Two hours later, it becomes a shape vaguely familiar and of frozen relish.

I stare at it and the hairs stand up on the back of my neck. Twenty minutes after that, he is almost finished, and now we can see what it is.

His whole body is trembling from the effort and his overalls, despite the cold, are drenched with sweat. No one applauds. It all happened much too slowly for that.

Instead, we all sink into a reverential hush, afraid to make a sound.

It's an angel. It's an angel. Its body is a stern and rigid reed, and the small, Asiatic face and hands are white and tidy things. But the wings. The wings are *massive*. They are less than an inch thick and two metres high, pointing towards the heavens in a glorious arc of curved, translucent bones and individually carved, icy feathers.

The sun is well up now and its beams begin to steam towards us, through the immoderate, body-shaped ice-window of this angel. We all turn around and look at each other. Every one of us is covered in an intolerable, ludicrous and luminous pebble dash of colours and antic, blinding stripes. We look gorgeous. We look inhuman. We look divine.

We sit there for a bit, stunned by the angel and by ourselves.

A baby starts to cry on his mother's lap, on the next bench.

The big man takes one last look, nods to himself, collects his stuff into a sturdy holdall and walks off, stooping and a little unsteady on his feet.

The baby stops crying and settles down to a comfortable snuffling.

The other people make soft, appreciative noises and they drift away.

I sit staring at the angel.

I have looked at images like this for all of my adult life and I never really paid attention.

And now I can't move for looking at it.

I park there for another hour, and I am thinking very, very hard. About my life.

I'm staring at this desolate, now-melting, deity and it dawns on me that I'm going to have to come to some kind of damn decision. Some kind of choice.

I'm in love but I don't know if it's enough any more. I'm very tired.

I'm tired of trying to squash myself into Laura's world.

And I'm tired of her glee. Of her energy. Of the joyful way she will loot and ransack *anything*, all in the cause of the brief. The brief, the concept, the client, the contract.

Just before she caught me, head down, in the restaurant, she had been talking about how beautiful Jesus was. He looks like a cross between Jamiroquai and David Beckham, she said.

I could use that, she said. If it can be done, then it should be done.

And she is convinced that it is the noblest, most creative thing a body can do.

Maybe in this world, and in this time, she is absolutely right. I love her but, now and here, there is a notion calling to me. Something I thought I had forgotten.

This was not a slight mistake.

It was a colossal mistake.

I am a priest.

I don't belong here. And I don't mean the city. I love the city.

I mean *here* in this situation. This place of dreary waste versus sacred thrift.

This rancid stasis, utterly bereft of the machinery of forgiveness.

If I don't slide in, with a nice, doofus grin, I'll be thrown out, by both Laura and the world.

This world does not seek things out to salvage them; it seeks them out to destroy them, and it does so without the most valuable component in the universe – doubt.

I lied to that troubled child, four months ago. I lied through my teeth and I did it with a smile on my face. Not a day has gone by in my adult life when I haven't been convinced, for ten minutes at a time, that I am engaged in some awful, intangible folly.

But I live with it.

At least I have the balls to do that.

My world has a thin skin and is a dusty amalgam of solid faith and the worst kind of percussive treachery. Every single day. And every single day, I am deceived.

Deceived by a God who promised to love us, then shows us that He might not.

But I live with it. Because I love Him.

And because it is more difficult to keep on loving after you have been deceived.

I like hard work. That's what has kept me sane, sensible and a good priest.

Dux vitae ratio. There you go.

I've made my decision.

God cannot be denied and that's all there is to it.

A few feathers fall off the melting angel's left wing and crash in a tiny tinkle on the cobbles. It still looks amazing. A beauteous and chill admonishment, aimed right at my guts.

I get up quickly and leave the park. My own shadow runs ahead, shivering.

I don't want to be around to see it disintegrate.

I hurry away, and the slow, frozen cacophony of ice clumps, bigger now, falling to the ground rings in my ears.

I read somewhere, once, that fifty-five of the world's largest economies aren't countries.

They're corporations. Laura would love that statistic.

And I read somewhere else, once, that by the time they hit thirty, the average person will have seen over a million adverts. Laura would love that one even more.

*

'You're leaving me for *GOD*?!'

She says this as if the Creator is a poor second string.

'No. But I have to go home. I just have to.'

She is crying and pacing around the flat like a mad thing. Oh Christ, I hate this.

'Matt, this is *stupid*. You promised you were going to stay. I love you, for God's sake.'

For God's sake.

She is red-eyed and heartbroken, and I feel as if I am miles away from her.

Her computer is on in the background. It seems to be tuned into some web radio station or other. She keeps crying and swiping me, helplessly, across the shoulders with bunches of paper. That would be her latest project. It looks very impressive. Very colourful.

I can feel tears welling myself, but I fight it. I put my arms around her and she goes limp.

She sags, and her whole body is heaving with annoyance and sorrow.

'I'm sorry, Laura. I love you. But I just can't breathe any more.'

'Then get out, you *bastard*!' She pushes me away.

That's the first honest thing I've heard in a week.

Even in her state, she's too kindly to use the proper word.

Coward.

That's the truth of it.

The worst coward in the world.

I finish packing. She sits by the window, crying. She doesn't look at me.

As I leave, I realize that the computer is tuned into a New York police radio frequency.

A static-laden, crackling voice is shouting about a Caucasian male, mid-twenties, assault and robbery suspect, heading towards—

I close the door.

★

Back home, I go to the headmaster's office, expecting to be crucified.

He is a very clever man in his sixties. His name is Barney. He's been a priest for forty years.

The man oozes authority.

He just looks at me with an expression I can't quite make out.

And then he tells me that he hopes I'm over that bad bout of 'flu.

I think about telling him the truth, then I realize that he already knows.

He probably knows everything about me and my little sojourn.

Don't ask, don't tell. Whatever.

I take up my classes pretty much where I left off.

No one says anything and everyone is very kind.

My life goes on as normal.

I never saw Laura again.

Months later, Father Barney reminds me that it is a year since young Anthony passed away, and would I like to conduct the memorial service? It would be nice for the family. It is on the tip of my tongue to say that suicide, theologically speaking, is the worst sin possible. It is the ultimate evil, the worst possible insult, sneer and treachery against life itself. It just isn't forgivable, and besides—

Then I see the look in his eyes, seeing mine. And hear the firmness of his tone.

'Anthony had an accident, Matt, okay? Everybody knows that.'

Then he sighs, and shrugs, but his eyes have me pinned to the wall.

His voice is like ice.

'These people need something, Matt. So stop being so high and mighty, okay? And so damned cruel, too. It may offend your purist sensibilities, but I'm afraid I'm really going to have to sell you on this one. It does the soul no harm to be bought and sold, occasionally. To love God is our side of the deal. Even if it's a bad draw.

Bargaining is part of living.

It teaches us that we are not above the world.
It teaches us good manners.
Now. Matt. I'll ask you again.
Would you care to conduct the service?'
It is not a question.
'I'd be delighted,' I say.
And it is not actually a lie.

ÉILÍS NÍ DHUIBHNE

It is a Miracle

It is the feast of the harvest moon, the last weekend before the schools reopen. Everyone is celebrating, with wine and aquavit and crayfish, with paper hats and Chinese lanterns. But what good is any of that if you have no friends?

'We should have thrown a party,' Sara says to Thomas, her partner. Thomas smiles benignly and says cheerfully, 'We are having a party. Our own little party.' He wears a badge on his T-shirt engraved with a picture of a smiling moose and the words, 'It's going to be OK!' That is the motto of the insurance company he had a policy with, or it had been one of its mottoes during an advertising campaign several years ago. Thomas got several copies of the badge and wears it constantly. 'Two's company!' he says, patting Sara on the cheeks. He has hung two garish Chinese lanterns on the verandah, and has put a Mozart CD on in the living room. He seems to have forgotten the paper hats.

'Yes,' Sara says wanly. Sometimes she finds Thomas's proverbs and maxims comforting, wise and profound. At other times, their predictability is what strikes her, and then she finds them unbelievably annoying. Thomas is not unaware of the range of reaction but he loves his clichés far too much to drop even a single one. On the contrary, he adds to his collection, savouring particularly trite specimens.

He squeezes Sara's hand and chuckles heartlessly.

'I'm going for a swim,' she says abruptly, releasing his hand.

Thomas is taken aback. 'What, now?' he says. He is just about to cook the crayfish. It is almost nine o'clock.

'Just a quick dip. My last evening!' Sara grins, pleased that she has succeeded in dinting his complacency, and slips down the path to the lake before he can stop her. Not that he would dream of doing so. He looks after her for a few seconds, bemused and hurt. Then he shrugs and finishes setting the table.

The midges bite. They are mustered in clouds over the reeds, ready to stab as soon as she approaches the water's edge. But Sara removes her old towel robe, hangs it on its hook at the edge of the dock and lets them do their damnedest. She is liberally sprayed with insect repellent, so only the most relentless succeed in puncturing her. Still, they circle, as always at this time, causing her to itch, until she slides from the wooden steps into the cold soft water and swims away from the shore.

She swims out into the lake, with lazy overarm strokes, keeping her head above water so she can see the apricot colours of the sun setting on the western shore behind the rim of darkening trees. Lamps are lit already in some of the cottages, and on several docks the orange light of summer torches flickers. She can hear music floating like a beam of light from one of the cottages, hidden in its shelter of reeds and trees. All around the lake, the parties are starting.

The water laps against her skin as she moves languidly through it. A small fish jumps, plopping close to her with its quiet quick flip, a sudden comforting sound. When the sun vanishes behind the black spiky rim of the forest and the northern star is a white spot in the dark blue sky, she turns and swims back to the shore, faster than she had swum out.

The torch is lit on the verandah when she returns, and she can see candles flickering on the table there. The live flames keep the mosquitoes at bay.

'We can eat as soon as you are ready,' Thomas says, as she passes into the house, wrapped in her robe. He is happy again and has as usual decided to forget and forgive. It's going to be OK. 'I'll be just a few minutes,' Sara smiles and pats his head. Swimming always lifts her spirits and she knows Thomas likes having his hair ruffled.

She flip flops into the bedroom, and pulls on loose cotton trousers and a muslin shirt with long sleeves. Her wet black hair she pulls out of its band and brushes quickly, then ties back up again, in a mean knot on top of her head. In the small mirror, she looks tired and old, although her body feels rejuvenated after the swim. How she feels is not necessarily how she looks any more.

They sit on the wooden verandah, overlooking the untidy garden and the long narrow stretch of wild flowers and grass and reeds that leads down to the lake. Ten o'clock and it is quite dark, just the flicker of lights on the docks is visible. The sound of music is louder now, and occasional bars of laughter come floating over the lake. They sound to Sara like silvery canoes of joy, bobbing around out there on the lake.

The bulging red eyes of the crayfish stare at her over the edge of their white dish. The eyes look accusing and sad. She eats them purposefully. Small Turkish crayfish, frozen until an hour ago, they consist mainly of shell; you have to bulk out the fish with bread and salad, and wash it down with a lot of white wine. The music, a Mozart clarinet concerto, plays soothingly in the background, and jets of other kinds of music join it from along the shore and across the lake. The mosquitoes buzz but do not descend on the table, the lights flicker in the blackness of the night, the Chinese lanterns grin, red and blue and yellow, from above. The full moon is gleaming like a yellow lantern in the dark blue sky and its reflection floats in the black water of the lake.

Sara eats and drinks, and thinks that although the food is good and the setting lovely, although she likes sitting here with Thomas, at first she feels she would just as soon read, she would rather watch television, than sit here on this verandah, trying to have a party. And she knows Thomas feels exactly the same. But it is the harvest festival so they are obliged to celebrate it, just like everyone else. As the wine bottle empties, however, they feel better and talk more; by the time they have drunk two bottles they feel they really have had a party, as good a party as anyone could wish. They tumble happily into their separate beds.

Thomas is a writer; every Christmas, almost without fail, a new work appears on the market, and sells 5000 copies, then does not sell again except in tiny numbers for the rest of its existence. In addition to his royalties, he usually receives a grant from the Writers' Union which supplements his income, and as a result he is reasonably well-off. How he could find topics for so many novels is a mystery to Sara, since he seems to have difficulty coming up with topics for conversation, at least with her. They have been together for ten years and have grown so alike that people sometimes ask if they are brother and sister.

Sara works in a library. She has been working in the same library for fifteen years, ever since she arrived in this country. Initially the work was greatly challenging; in order to get her job, she had to take a course at the university, for two years, which she had managed to do while working in a supermarket, stacking shelves. The transition from supermarket to library was gratifying, was wonderful; she spends her time talking to customers about books or about other things – many of them are old people who want to tell her about their grown-up children and their illnesses, to hint at the condition of their bodily functions and discuss their plans for the important calendar festivals. In her library, there are sofas and easy chairs for the readers, and a pot of coffee always ready, so some old folks spend a good part of the day with her, drinking coffee and chatting. Her function is as much social worker or psychologist as librarian. But there is even more to it than that. As well as providing counselling services for the readers, tidying shelves and checking books in and out she organizes lectures, exhibitions, readings by popular writers. It was in this way that she met Thomas, who had been invited to read from his latest novel at Christmas one year. Attracted by Sara's foreign accent, he had chatted to her about his own life. He had just come back from the summer cottage on the lake, where he had been the only resident in November. The lake was covered with ice, the gardens snowed up, and the house heated with a log fire.

It had all sounded very romantic to Sara. She imagined being there by the big fire, with the flames making shadows on the wall. In her picture she was reading and listening to classical music; there were candles, mulled wine, it was Christmas. Thomas was not actually in this picture but then she hardly knew him at the time.

A week after the reading (it was the day before Christmas Eve) he rang her up and they celebrated Christmas Eve together; Sara could not return to her family for Christmas, since they never celebrated it, and she had no real plans of her own. Thomas didn't either. He had been divorced a year earlier, that was why. His parents were dead and he did not feel like inflicting his company on his sister although she had invited him to her home in the suburbs. He treated Sara to meatballs and herring and cold beer in his flat, a large flat full of books and smelling rather dusty. Although it had a window overlooking the river, decorated with fairy lights now for Christmas so that the view was magical, the flat itself was completely undecorated. There was no Christmas tree, not even a Christmas card. And it was dark and dull, cluttered, untidy. No fire. Still, Sara liked Thomas well enough and she liked the view from his flat. Snow-covered fir trees, strings of starry lights glittered on the pack ice in the river. She thought of the summer cottage, and the relationship prospered. Now they live in a house on the outskirts of the town, perched on a rock among pine trees, with a big lake far beneath: the country is full of lakes, it seems to Sara. Everywhere you look, there is one, glittering like an eye among the dark trees.

She still works in the library, spending much of her time there, while Thomas sits in his own library at home, typing up his novels.

★

Sara feels her heart sink when she drives out of the cottage garden and honks goodbye to Thomas, who stands by the flagpole, cheerfully waving her farewell with big exaggerated childish waves, and a big childish handkerchief. Now that she is leaving him she feels a big gush of love for him, and the cottage, ramshackle, looking like an old magpie nest in its untidy cluster of trees, seems incredibly appealing. Sadly she makes her way along the narrow dirt track that connects the lakeside to the main road, glancing at the neat wooden houses, pretty as toys with their carved porches and bright pennants, the gardens still filled with petunias and nasturtiums and summer roses. They are lovely, but she has not cared about that during the past month, cycling along the roads in her shorts and T-shirt, grumbling in her head about the futility of the whole place. Everyone dashes down here on Midsummer's Day but what did they do then, apart from walk or cycle or swim? Occasional staid parties, wine and shellfish, or coffee and cake in the afternoon. They measure out their lives in swims and cycles; one summer succeeds another, they come to the cottage, they return to the city, they come to the cottage. Then they get too old to come to the cottage, and then they die.

So what's wrong with that, she is thinking now, as she leaves it. Now it all seems peaceful, civilized, charming, and she is in no hurry to return to the bustle of the city. It is summer, but autumn will descend quickly after tomorrow, and then winter will close in on them, and it will be dark and cold all the time until the ice melts again in April. Lucky Thomas, whose work allows him to prolong the summer, to stay in the country, walking in the woods, swimming in the lake. At night he will be lighting his candles and listening to the lap of lakewater and the buzz of the mosquitoes for another month. Lucky Thomas. If he loved her wouldn't he sacrifice that and come home with her now?

She reaches home in mid afternoon, and she is in the living room, with its green silk chairs and pale silk walls, opening the windows, letting the fresh air in, when Lisa, her friend at work, calls and asks if she can come round. It is an unusual request – normally she meets Lisa at work or work-related occasions, they don't visit each other's houses; in fact surprise visits, or unarranged visits, by anyone, are a very rare occurrence – but Sara says yes with some alarm, and waits for Lisa with a sense of apprehension.

Lisa has two children, now in late teens or early twenties. They are students and whenever Sara has met them have seemed sulky and taciturn. But Lisa adores them, and has spent most of her life, it seems to Sara, rushing home to look after them, although that is not how she would put it herself. 'I've got to hit the supermarket,' she says. Or 'There's a heap of washing to be done.' Or, more often than not, she is rushing home so she can hop into her car and leave it straightaway, to give one of the children a lift somewhere. She is an unpaid chauffeur, and she doesn't mind if Sara tells her that; ironically, although she claims to be feministic and assertive and liberated, Lisa is pleased to be an unpaid chauffeur, an unpaid washerwoman, an unpaid cook, and an unpaid charlady too, as well as a badly paid librarian. 'I'm so tired!' she says, but good-humouredly. 'How long can this go on? I thought I'd be free to do hobbies when they got to be fifteen.' But it is very clear, at least to Sara, that Lisa has no wish whatsoever to do hobbies. She enjoys all this rushing around, the juggling, the hard work. She even enjoys grumbling about her husband, or ex-husband – he left, was thrown out, years ago. They divorced but they never quite separated. 'He's gone, out, never darkens my bed!' Lisa said, with emphasis, waving her hands about to underline her words. She is short, roundly built, with fair hair tied on top of her head and a round, childish face. Her eyes are round too. He never darkened her bed but he darkened her door almost every day, and ate dinner with his ex-family five days out of seven. Such arrangements were not common but strange arrangements were getting more usual, it seemed to Sara. Separating but not quite separating, having a sort of *ménage à trois*, or *à quatre*, with nobody screaming 'Betrayal!' had replaced the all or nothing mentality which had prevailed here as elsewhere not so long ago. Lisa did not have another friend, and as far as Sara knew neither did her ex, but they could have had.

Lisa arrives, looking calm and relaxed. She sweeps into the cool dim hall.

'Welcome back!' she says. 'Was it good?'

'Very good,' Sara says. The sun is still shining so they go out and sit at the rear of the house, on a terrace, a loggia hung with vines, overlooking the suburban valley with its small central lake. Sara's house is built on quite a steep hill, dotted with houses and trees. The gardens are patches of hillside, so steep and rough that the lots are not separated by fences, although everyone knows exactly where their boundary is.

They drink a glass of sparkling wine, which seems appropriate on such a sunny, glowing afternoon, and given that Lisa is dressed in a very summery, indeed rather girlish outfit – a pale cotton skirt, flowery and long, a pale T-shirt with pink lace around the neckline. Also a wide straw hat with a floppy brim, and a delicate white daisy in the yellow band. She has lost weight and got a tan since Sara last saw her. Her whole appearance suggests that she has good news and the hat suggests what the good news involves: love.

'I have got married,' Lisa says.

Sara's face does not drop but her response is slower than it should be, as she pauses to absorb the surprise. This is more than she anticipated.

'Congratulations!' she says, laughing, and kisses Lisa on the cheek, catching a whiff of perfume. 'That's wonderful!' She sits down again and takes a drink. 'Who is . . . the lucky man?'

It has occurred to her that it could be Lisa's ex-husband. Remarrying the old spouse is an event which now occurs with some regularity, and Sara knows three or four people who have done it. But would that call for such a physical transformation, for a hat with a flower in it? Probably not.

'He's someone I met on holiday,' says Lisa. 'You know Kirsten and I went to Turkey?' Kirsten is the younger daughter, she is nineteen or twenty, a student of commerce. 'To this resort on the Black Sea. Well, she made friends with some young folk at the hotel and I was left alone most of the time, going to the bazaar on my own, sitting on the beach in solitary splendour. Well I even had to eat alone. You know how it can be for single ladies!' She laughs gleefully, no longer one of them.

'Oh yes,' Sara sees a green baize door, and boiled sausage in a nest of sauerkraut. 'I know all right.'

Lisa pauses for a split second, sensing a story, but she races on with her own.

'I was sitting outside a restaurant, eating lunch, quite happy, it doesn't bother me to be alone. I like it. Sun and wine, what do I care? A man came and asked if he could join me. Cheeky devil, I thought, but for some reason, I guess sun and wine induced, I said yes. Anyway one thing led to another and now I am married. To somebody who picked me up at a restaurant in Turkey. It's unbelievable.'

The only unbelievable thing is that Lisa married him, that he married Lisa. Suddenly Sara remembers a woman she knew when she lived in London, who suffered from nervous problems. In and out of hospital. She worked with Sara, in the school she had taught in back there, and was one of the single ladies who seemed to be so numerous in those days, although now she realizes they seemed more numerous than they were, because they were the only women who worked in schools and offices and libraries, the married ones were all at home, glad to be there and smug about it too, as she recalled, marriage still being a victory then for a girl or a woman, a passport to economic security at least if you belonged to the middle classes, and an escape from schools and offices. This woman, her name was Bridget, began to joke about having married the school gardener, an old man, aged about seventy, called Paddy. She described the wedding and the guests, what she wore – an off-the-shoulder cream silk dress, calf length, and a cream hat with a silver veil and a mauve flower – and what they ate – turkey and ham and peas and roast potatoes. The honeymoon was in Tenerife and they had bought a terraced house in Wimbledon. The story went on for days or weeks, became more elaborate, more embarrassing for everyone else in the staff room. Eventually Bridget was back in the hospital again, getting whatever treatment it was she got there. She drank, that was part of her problem.

So did Lisa. Lisa was possibly hallucinating.

'He is called Tamcumsin,' she says. 'He is divorced and is a lawyer.'

'So where did you get married?'

'We got married in the city registry office here in this city,' says Lisa. 'It's as valid as hard bread.'

'Has he moved in with you?' Sara is more and more concerned.

'No,' says Lisa. 'But I will move there, to where he lives, in Istanbul.'

What about your job and your precious children, not to mention your country, your friends, your home? And that now-you-see-him-now-you-don't husband of yours.

'It's ME-time,' says Lisa. She closes her eyes and smiles at the sky, where the sun is beginning to sink down into the dark dark trees. She opens them again. 'I've already handed in my notice at the library, so there's no need to worry about that! The children will stay in the house here for the moment, I don't need to sell it. They're well able to look after themselves.'

So Tamcumsin is not a con-man, after your house and meagre salary? And access to the most civilized country in Europe.

'He's rich,' says Lisa. 'He's got a big apartment in Istanbul, and a summer apartment on the Black Sea. His former wife has their house which is a palace.'

'Have you seen his apartment?' Sara doesn't have to ask about the palace.

'I've seen the summer place,' says Lisa. 'Of course. Don't be so suspicious, Sara, he's bona fide!' She giggles and gives Sara a kiss. 'I'm a big girl, I can look after myself. And I want you to come and visit me in Istanbul as soon as I settle in. You might like to come before Christmas? Do a little shopping?'

'That would be lovely,' says Sara with as much enthusiasm as she can muster.

'I am so happy,' says Lisa, and she laughs aloud, a laugh of pleasure and triumph and bliss. Sara does not ask what Tamcumsin looks like, or what he is like in bed, but she can guess.

In the spring of this year, I went alone to a strange restaurant. This was in a city to the south, in the middle of Europe, in another country, where I was attending a conference on digitization of library records, the sort of conference I attend three or four times a year. The topics are sometimes dry but the venues are always pleasant, and I have seen most of the great cities of Europe by virtue of accepting invitations to attend, sometimes also giving a talk on catalogues in the internet age, or information networks in the twenty-first century. When the conference was over, I usually stayed on wherever I was for a day or two to look around. I was lingering in this way for two days on this occasion, keeping to my small room in an old hotel in the centre of the city. It was described as charming in the brochure, which seemed to mean that there was old furniture in the bedrooms – one baroque chair, dusky pink, in mine – and faded prints of the city in the eighteenth century on the walls. Also it had literary associations and a large portrait in the tiny lobby of a famous writer who stayed there at the beginning of the twentieth century: Kafka.

Some of the other conference members had stayed on, too, and were visiting a Nazi concentration camp about an hour's journey from the city. But although I have never seen a concentration camp, I decided to forgo the experience. I am not attracted to concentration camps and this wasn't a very well-known one anyway, I had never even heard of it, in fact. So instead I had spent the morning in the great museums and galleries of the city. These had been built by the royal family centuries ago, to store the collections which they had taken from other countries, sometimes looting, sometimes buying (but at rather cheap prices). They were still doing it. I had seen a feather headdress, Mexican, which Cortez was said to have been presented with by a great Mexican king. The brochure said this information was wrong, was just a myth, and that such a headdress could not have been worn in the time Cortez met the king. This is the sort of information museum staff love to give their visitors, telling them the truth, letting them know that the popular story, what they knew, was wrong and the staff know better. I had never heard of the headdress anyway, and did not know the popular story. Why bother preaching at me, telling me it was false? The museum people appeared to believe that stories about the headdress were common knowledge, that people were busily spinning yarns about fifteenth-century Mexican feathers!

There is something surprising in the museum: a reconstructed house from Greenland. It is part of the Inuit collection, a little wooden house, not an igloo, a wooden house made, probably, from a pre-fab in a packet and built by a Greenlander in 1950. It is a Scandinavian design, a bit like the summer houses along our lake although much much smaller, more like a garden shed. One room, a gallery, a picket fence around the garden, a little Danish flag flying. Inside holy pictures, a few sticks of furniture, a range. The owner had sold it to the museum in 1980 and moved to another house, better one hoped. And now his old house is here, at the end of one of the huge marble halls of this sumptuous museum, surrounded by ornate pillars and carved friezes, and, on exhibition, other bits and scraps of Greenland life: a kayak, snowshoes, some old and lovely sleds. A group of schoolchildren were sitting in front of the sled getting a lecture on it from a guide, or their teacher.

I have visited Greenland, with Thomas, who wrote an historical novel once about the Norse settlement there, which had died out in the Middle Ages, nobody really knows why. I do not remember houses like this one, everyone seemed to live in a high concrete block of flats designed on some Soviet Union template perched on the edge of an icebound fjord. But perhaps there had been a village with little houses, certainly a little shop. Thomas was excited there, and I was infected by his excitement. I had borrowed it, lapped it up from him, I had read all about the old settlement and the new settlement too. I had read everything I could lay my hands on. I could have written a novel myself, at the end of the visit. But I did not. I have always known I could write a novel if I put my mind to it; watching Thomas, I can see how easy it is. But I don't want to. Why should I? There are more than enough of them in the world. So I went back to the library, and ordered a few books about the Inuit, and soon lost interest in them. It was revived by the sight of this funny little house in the middle of the great marble museum, but not for long, not for long.

My mind was on more important things. Lunch. I decided to eat in a restaurant specializing in local cuisine, since all through the conference we had eaten Italian food, French food, Greek food, but nothing belonging to this country. Perhaps there was a reason for that? Maybe the native cuisine was too stodgy, uninteresting? What the city is famous for is its cakes, rather than its dinners. But there was an old-fashioned restaurant near the hotel where, the receptionist told me, authentic food was served, so I went there. When I stepped inside I wondered if I had made a mistake. A thick baize curtain separated the entrance from the restaurant, and when I pushed through this curtain I found myself in a dark, cluttered place, which looked smoky although in fact nobody was smoking. The tables were covered with heavy green cloths, the walls were panelled with dark wood, there were no windows. It looked more like a pub than a restaurant, but the tables were crammed with people eating and waiters were running around carrying plates and trays. I decided to leave and go back to the safe little Italian place at the hotel but before I could escape a waiter came and said he would find me a table. He seated me on a small sofa near the desk and I felt obliged to stay, to wait. Five minutes passed. Eventually someone came and guided me to a table. But it was not empty. Would I mind sharing? It was a strange request, but I agreed, and sat at a tiny table opposite a man who was finishing some sort of stew, not picturesquely presented, and drinking wine. I buried my head in the menu and ordered what looked like the most typical local dish, as far as I could make out, since the menu was hand-written and the hand was not very legible. I also ordered a glass of wine.

The man opposite smiled at me. This is where I made my first mistake. I nodded, returned the smile.

He looked like a local, an authentic type. He was dressed in a white shirt with a black waistcoat, made of boiled wool, the most typical cloth of this country. Of course I could just see him from the waist up, alas I did not catch sight of his trousers. His hair was black or dark grey, his skin a pale bronze. He was very handsome, with the sort of flawless good looks which were not, I decided at first, all that attractive. He reminded me of a woodcutter in a fairy tale. He could have been Red Riding Hood's father. This region is rich in fairy tales, and seeing him I could understand where some of the characters had come from.

But he turned out to be foreign, like me. Probably a local would never wear an outfit like that, an outfit which hinted at woodcutters. He was Italian. As soon as I heard this I wished I had not nodded, because of course I am not a racist but I know what Italian men are like when they come across a single lady, I've been to Italy more than once. Too late. He was already telling me the story of his life, or making it up. He had come for the weekend, he often visits this city, he loves it. He was asking me about my own position, and I decided to make up a little story of my own. I said I was at a conference of writers, that I was a writer of detective novels. I was about to say I was giving a reading later on but decided in the nick of time not to, in case he said he would come. So I said I had a meeting again in half an hour, I had just slipped away for a bite to eat. I could tell he did not believe a word I said anyway; probably I am not a very good liar.

My glass of wine came, and he looked at it meaningfully; if you drink wine they assume you are up for anything, it gives some sort of message. Respectable Italian women don't drink wine when dining alone, and not very often otherwise, but sometimes I think I'd be abstemious too if I lived in a place which was overflowing with the stuff. Living in a country where you have to buy it at a government office that doesn't open at weekends affects your attitude and then of course on top of all that I'm Irish originally, or at least my mother was. So hump him, I was thinking, watching his eyes linger knowingly over my beaded rim . . . Then my food arrived. A huge sausage, boiled so that it looked fleshy, obscene in fact, draped grotesquely over a heap of pickled cabbage. It was not clear if he found the sausage repulsive or suggestive. All the food here looked disturbing though, to put it mildly; it was country cooking, no attempt was made to prettify the dishes, to make them look like flowers or paintings. In fact most of the food looked like something you might give to a not-very-fussy cat.

I told him I was married, thinking it important to get this message across as quickly as possible. I am not in fact married, since Thomas does not approve of marriage any more, but I might as well be. The man was married too, he had a daughter aged twenty who was a student, and he himself was a doctor in a city in northern Italy. He went on and on, entertaining me in his broken English, as I dug into my enormous sausage, which tasted much better than it looked. The cabbage too was excellent. I hadn't had any real vegetables for days, just scraps of tomatoes and peppers, the odd lettuce leaf, decorating the edges of plates. I really appreciated this big heap of sauerkraut, a cabbage patch on a plate. My body was crying out for iron and of course I was constipated, I always am when I go abroad anywhere. The woodcutter ordered more wine, enough for both of us which was really going much too far. I refused, I looked annoyed, but he would not take no for an answer; the waiter colluded with him, ignoring my protestations with a knowing smile, filling my glass against my wishes. Of course I drank it, I seldom refuse, I'm practically an alcoholic anyway. I was beginning to feel reckless, what does it matter, we are in a restaurant, surrounded by about fifty people stuffing themselves with schnitzel and strudel. The waiter smiled whenever he passed our table, he was smug and pleased with himself, as if he had set this up, two lonely people in his restaurant, now hitting it off. Perhaps he was some sort of broker, a matchmaker, on the side?

Mr Riding Hood was separated from his wife. This is the usual story and maybe it is usually true. But presumably if you are chatting up a woman you do not tell her you are happily married? I found it difficult to understand exactly what he was saying, because his English deteriorated as the meal continued, which is always the way with people who have a mere smattering. They sound okay for about five minutes and then it's downhill. He knew no German and I did not even attempt to speak Italian. Since I had been trying to speak German for the past few days whatever smattering of Italian I had picked up on holidays seemed to have vanished completely. When I tried, in response to a question, to tell him what my books were about, I could see he did not follow more than a few sentences, which was just as well because I found myself forgetting the plots (of course I just summarized a plot of one of Thomas's novels, they've never been translated to anything and never will be, the woodcutter could never have read them). I gave up talking and soon I gave up listening. Why should I exert myself? I was imprisoned by this woodcutter, I did not ask him to start telling his story.

I drank more wine, and began to feel more relaxed. But even as I felt the wine taking effect I felt a slight panic rising. The waiter came and took away my plate and I ordered coffee. His wife has thrown him out. It sounded as if this happened a few days ago, perhaps yesterday. But it could have been years ago. He only used one tense, the present. 'I try to love her but I love life!' he was saying. Actually what he said was 'Wine, life, I love. Women!' He mentioned

Homer saying he was reading the *Odyssey* at the moment, that everything is there. I assumed he was telling me this just to impress me, because he thought someone who was a writer would appreciate an *Odyssey* reader. Actually I couldn't remember much about the *Odyssey*. I read it once but somehow it didn't make a great impression. Adventures. Encounters with monsters. Dragon teeth, are they in the *Odyssey*? Pride and passion of a kind. Love? Circe, he was thinking of, probably. Penelope at home weaving, waiting. The subtext was that he had been unfaithful to his wife who was not weaving and waiting but who had thrown him out, and now he was in this city on a holiday trying to get over it by flirting with strangers.

'Oh dear!' I said, making a decision to believe the story and to be concerned for the sake of his marriage. But I was still sceptical. Would someone who has been thrown out of home in Italy immediately come to spend a weekend, alone, in a foreign city? I started to comfort him. 'Can you telephone?'

'I phone. I write letters. I write my daughter a long letter saying I am sorry, I love her . . .'

Then he revealed Exhibit A. The letter. It was long, pages and pages. So it was true. True that he had been writing a long letter anyway, and it was clearly not an official letter but something personal. I glanced at the pages covered in blue handwriting, but I could not see the opening line, to check if it started in the correct way. Whatever it might be. I would have recognized it if I'd seen it.

'It's going to be OK,' I said. 'Your daughter is twenty already; she knows you love her.'

He looked puzzled then, and stared into my eyes, stared more than before, he was very skilled at eye contact. It's not clear if he understood or not but he felt some goodwill, he felt something new in the air (replacing the scepticism which had filled it before).

'My daughter I love,' he said, and I had to suppress an urge to correct his word order. Wouldn't it be just as easy to say 'I love my daughter'?

'And she loves you,' I said gently. It was probably true. They usually love their fathers, daughters, and he looked like a very loveable one. In fact I began to wish he was my father. Imagine! That would make me Red Riding Hood, but I wouldn't have minded that. My father was more like the wolf. He's dead though, I don't have to worry about him any more.

'You think?' He looked vulnerable now and I could see how really beautiful he was. He could have anyone. I imagined his wife, a slim blonde Italian with one of those smooth beige cashmere sweaters, fine brown boots, lots of gold jewellery. I have seen such women, Paolas, Claudias, Leonoras, on the streets of Rome and Florence. Princesses. Why would such a beautiful man try to flirt with a woman who looks like me? I was never a beauty. And now I'm fat-ish. At best I must look substantial, with my expensive suit, my diamond earrings and necklace, my leather bag (picked up in Florence, ironically enough). I probably look mature. Let's face it, I always did! And that attracts some men, they want to get to know someone who doesn't remind them of their daughter. In fact he is a few years older than me; he's told me his age, just like he has told me everything else, and it seems to be the true one. He looked younger, which is why I believed him to be telling the truth. So maybe he was telling the truth about everything.

Then something extraordinary happened. The man in

the Red Riding waistcoat started to cry. Tears rolled down his lovely bronze cheeks.

I felt shocked. I felt startled. I felt confused.

'It will be okay!' I was turning into Thomas. This can happen to me. 'Don't worry! A cry will do you all the good in the world.' I ruffled his hair but he went right on crying.

'I . . . I . . .'

He couldn't speak any more.

'It will be okay,' I reiterated. Pity I didn't have one of the badges for him. 'Telephone your daughter. She will understand. You will see her on Monday anyway.'

He began to pat his eyes with a table napkin.

'Well,' he said, crying more gently. 'I am sorry. I do not know . . .'

'It's all right,' I go on and on. 'Have a good cry. Why shouldn't you cry? It'll do you a power of good.' That's something my mother used to say, back home in Terenure. Goodness, I hadn't said it in about thirty years, if ever.

He smiled then, and dried his eyes. He poured more wine – he had ordered a second carafe, the sneaky devil. I didn't even bother to protest.

'It is a miracle,' he said, quite composed now, his old self.

I just drank the wine. I was shaken.

'In all this city, I meet you.'

'Well,' I don't know what to say.

'How many people in this city? A million.' I haven't a clue, but now that he mentions it it looks like a million-city, what is called a million-city in the country I live in, which is a great country for measuring things, populations, statistics, temperatures. Never a 'hot day' there. It's thirty degrees. It's fifty-three kilometres. She weighs seventy kilos.

'A million, and I sit here and you come here and you are

the one person I can talk to. It is a miracle!' He throws up his hands, emphasizing the wonder of it all. I smile in spite of myself. I have been called many things, but never a miracle. It was quite nice. Quite nice.

His English had picked up again, he was quite coherent and easy to understand, and he had stopped crying. He got down to business, in fact I had finished my coffee. He told me that he was staying in the city until tomorrow.

I tried to catch the waiter's eye, quite an achievement because he was determined to ignore me, to leave me to my fate. The restaurant was nearly empty by now. I asked for the bill.

The woodcutter invited me to meet him later in a wine bar, the most fashionable, the best wine bar in the city. Nothing if not hyperbolic.

'I will be at the conference,' I said. 'I can't. I'm busy.'

He did not bother understanding, pushed cards into my hand, his phone number, his hotel, the name of the wine bar. Then he insisted on paying for my lunch. I argued, then gave in, thanked him. 'Six o'clock,' he said. 'Just a nice glass of champagne. That is what we drink here for an aperitif.' 'I won't be there!' I laughed. But he was laughing too. Either he didn't hear me, didn't believe me, or didn't care. Any of these possibilities existed.

I said goodbye and got out of the restaurant before he could follow me. The last thing I wanted was for him to see where I was staying, in the hotel just across the street. As soon as the green baize curtain closed behind me I ran and didn't stop until I was in the lobby of the hotel, under the portrait of Kafka. Even there the receptionist smiled in a knowing way and I felt mistrustful of him and the entire staff of the hotel.

And after that, in that city, everyone seemed to look at me in an odd way. It happened when I was sitting in one of its innumerable coffee houses, drinking a tiny cup of coffee and eating rich cake and cream. Women, sitting at tiny tables also having coffee and cake, would look at me and then glance at one another, smiling, as if sharing a joke or a secret. It happened when I was walking around the cathedral square, a tourist among many others, that natives, wearing the little hunting hats with feathers which they liked so much, looked over me, questioningly. Was I too dark, was it something about my clothes? They knew something about me that I did not know.

So it seemed. I was glad to get away, after another day, to get home, or back to the place I now call home.

In this city, her home, there is a famous and vast amusement park, prettily laid out on the slopes of a hill. Sara has been there many times; people go to listen to music, to eat in the many restaurants, to walk around, not just to ride on the amusements. Now Lisa wants to go there, to celebrate her marriage; she wants to have some fun in the sense in which her own city understands it. She wants to go immediately, because soon, in a few days, she will be leaving for Turkey and her new husband and she seems to suspect that she may not be back again for a long time. She wants to go tonight.

The Coffee Cup. The Flume. Grandfather's Motor Car. The Ghost Hotel. The Hangover. The Roller Coaster.

They stroll through the fair. It's dark but warm, the coloured lights twinkle and the tinkling sound of fairground music sparkles in the dark air. There are not many people at the funfair though; it is the last Sunday of the holidays, schools open tomorrow, lots of workplaces open their doors for the first time after the summer holidays. This is a night when people are preparing for the winter, going to bed early, even though it feels like the height of summer.

They go on the Coffee Cup, which is a gentle merry-go-round, in which you sit in a big cup. Each cup holds about ten people and is usually patronized by toddlers but occasionally old women, or middle-aged women, use it too.

When they get out Lisa says: 'Let's go on the roller coaster!'

The roller coaster is huge. It consists of almost a mile of track, swooping and soaring in imitation of steep mountains, looping high above the fairground. From its cars even now you can hear people screaming, with delight or terror or a mixture of both. You see little faces far away, mouths open and eyes closed, and the cars into which their owners are strapped racing up and down the steep tracks, looping the loop so that their occupants are upside down for seconds at a time.

Who could enjoy all that? Sara has never even gone on the easy roller coaster, a gentler version that is hidden among trees and bushes, that pretends to be a rather adventurous version of a country railway.

'Let's go on it,' says Lisa. She means the roller coaster, the real one.

'What?' Sara is disbelieving.

But Lisa persuades her.

How does this happen?

Sara knows she has never in her life wanted to go on the roller coaster. She has visited this amusement park often, occasionally with Thomas, with other people, visitors from Ireland. She has visited it with her nephews from Dublin, the older one – he was thirteen then – went on with some other boy from here, and came off shaking and white, saying, 'It was cool!' Sara hadn't even been able to bring herself to watch him on the thing.

She has actively not wanted to go on the roller coaster. And still she allows herself to be persuaded. She finds herself in the queue, quite a long queue since this is the most spectacular, scary and popular ride. She is handing over money to the girl in the ticket office, a rather brusque and impatient person who, when she hesitates to step into the car, tells her crossly to hurry up. She finds herself fastening her harness, smiling uncertainly at Lisa as Lisa says, 'It is my first time. I always knew I should do this.'

Slowly the car climbs up the first track, a few yards at a time, as the other customers embark. By then they are close to the top of the first track, and, although they have inched their way slowly up, Sara is already feeling frightened, and reluctant to look down at the ground, about a thousand feet beneath. She flies half a dozen times a year, she has climbed mountains higher than this roller coaster at its highest point, she is perfectly safe, strapped into a little car on a machine which has been tested and double-tested by safety inspectors, in the safest country in the world. She tells herself all this, and other things: you have to do it; it will do you good; you have to take the risk. But she still feels as terrified as she has ever felt. More terrified. Once she was attacked by an Alsatian, who pulled her around by the coat-tails for a minute or perhaps an hour, she did not know how long, before biting her neatly on the calf of the leg and running away. That experience was terrifying – she had thought of nuns torn by dogs in Nazi concentration camps. As the dog snarled and pulled her coat she believed he might bite her face, any part of her body. But she was able to work then too, like a Christian confronted with a lion, she was able to try to get away, and was in fact working on a strategy for escape when he bit her and abandoned her. This felt much worse. That the roller coaster went around a hundred times a day did not comfort her. She was strapped into it, it terrified her, and she could not get out.

A whistle sounded, curdling her blood, and then the pace quickened. It was still slow when she reached the crest of this hill, the first hill, but they hurtled down the other side at a speed that made her want to crumple up and die, then sped up the next higher slope. She watched the crest looming with dread, grimaced at Lisa who was smiling broadly. (Was she pretending? Did she really like this?) Then they went hurtling down the other side.

We went down. My stomach did not lurch, it was not that . . . not yet. I closed my eyes, screwing them up tightly. I said, 'Oh God, Oh God!', although I do not believe in God, I do not pray, my family converted to Protestantism as soon as they arrived in Ireland and I am an atheist myself. I said, 'This is ridiculous, soon it will be over and you'll have done it.' I said, 'It's a good experience, you care about nothing now while you're up here, all you want in the world is for the thing to stop, if you get off you will never worry about anything again.' Is that why people do it then, I wondered? Are they doing it to put other problems in perspective, are they doing it . . . Words failed me, questions failed me, a lot of people, not that I could look at them, seemed to be screaming at the tops of their voices and I thought, you should scream. Maybe that's part of the fun, if it could be fun, which I sincerely doubt, but how else to explain the existence of this? Fun to test yourself, to experience danger that is not real danger, contained risk, no risk at all, no risk at all, to have permission to, encouragement to, scream. I tried to scream but I could not, I can never scream, I could not scream even when the dog was biting me . . .

We are looping the loop. We are upside down, my hair is hanging down for a second, we are defying gravity (or is it that we are strapped in?). I scream. Lisa screams. Everyone screams and I hear the huge scream all over the park.

Then we are back on the ordinary slope again, and now it seems easier than before, that happens too. We are hurtling around and all I have to do is close my eyes when we reach the crest of one of the ghastly hills and lurch sickeningly over. How many times do we go round? Why didn't I count when I was standing there in the queue?

I look at Lisa and she laughs but the machine is so noisy, there is loud music playing. Abba, *Dancing Queen*, a song I loved once but never again. I can't talk to her there is no point. We are going round for the second time, in a second we will hit the loop, we are there . . .

The machine stops. It stops suddenly and the timbre of scream changes from one of exultation, pretend terror, to a real scream of fright. Every car is frozen right where it is, on the crest of the hill, on the slope, or on the loop. Sara and Lisa are upside down. The harnesses are secure and they do not fall (to their deaths – that is what it would be). But they hang suspended from the top of the loop track, the cars are fixed to it by some sort of magnetic force. Not quite upside down – their car has passed the zenith of the loop, in fact no car seems to be there. They are on the side of the loop but not far enough to be sitting upright.

They are upside down but they can talk.

'What's happening?' Lisa asks.

'It's . . . stopped. It's broken,' says Sara. It is not nice being upside down but it is marginally better than being in motion on a roller coaster. 'I'm sure they'll fix it soon.'

Abba have stopped singing.

Minutes pass and they begin to get headaches, their heads are red.

A voice on a loudspeaker tells them that due to a fault in the machine the roller coaster has stalled. They are trying to fix the fault as quickly as possible. They should not panic, they are in no danger. Apologies, apologies . . .

'We're upside down. How can we not panic?'

'We're not quite upside down.'

'I am more upside down than I ever was before. I don't like it. I feel sick.'

Time passes slowly. More announcements come. They can't fix the fault, the air-rescue service has been called, help will be at hand shortly, be patient.

'It's a wonder they don't send an angel around with free drinks,' says Lisa. Her hair is floating downwards in the wind, she looks different upside down, younger than her upright self.

'Do I look different this way?' Sara asks. She is getting light-headed in more ways than one. 'You look ten years younger.'

'Great! I'll try to do this more often. Maybe if I walked on my hands it would improve matters.'

Sara finds that although she feels sick and dizzy, she does not feel frightened at all.

⋆

On his way back to Italy, the woodcutter was going to visit a Nazi concentration camp, the camp of Mauthausen, near Linz.

'Why are you visiting Mauthausen?' I asked. It was where my colleagues had gone. I had wanted to ask them the same question but hadn't dared to. It had irritated me, I don't know why, that they were all so agog to go to the concentration camp. Hitler lived in this city for years, as a young man, and although it is a city whose greatest associations are with music and art, with psychology and scholarship, with architecture and every aspect of civilization, a city at the heart of European civilization, it is this aberration, this mistake, this tragedy we might as well forget, which obsessed all the librarians, so it seemed to me. They went to the Jewish Museum, they took day trips to the concentration camp, they distrusted the citizens of the city in a visceral way. 'They look like woodland animals, in those little hats,' one woman, from Birmingham, had said, with a sneer. 'Their fur coats, their little noses.' You would think the English had a history free from guilt.

'It is good to get close to the concentration camp,' he says, something like that. 'It is good to feel it in the heart. You read about it but you do not feel it unless you go to the place.'

'Yes, I suppose it would be,' I said, although I believe this sort of thing is voyeuristic, vulgar, on a par with visits to those torture chambers which have sprung up in any town with any pretension to a medieval origin all over Europe. People like to visit them too, to contemplate not the sins of politicians and clerics but the pain of the victims. Misery likes bedfellows; tasting true horror on a vast scale, in the safe confines of a museum, puts minor personal pain into perspective. Relativity. Healthy people make such comparisons, without knowing it, weighing a divorce against execution in the gas chambers, arthritis against the Iron Maiden. That's why he is going, now, the weekend after his wife has turfed him out, or the week or the month. But of course I didn't express my view to him. I couldn't have anyway, in words that he would understand.

'Also I am Jew,' he says. 'My family was hidden in a Carmelite convent during the war and some of them survived. But some of them went to Mauthausen.'

'And they did not survive?' I was beginning to feel sick.

He shook his head philosophically.

'It was a Level Three camp. Nobody survived.'

'Oh dear!' I said, because what can you say? I mean what? Couldn't we talk about divorce, Schubert, chocolate cake, the Hapsburgs, my novels or anyone's novels?

When she met Thomas at the library, he had read from a thriller, an excerpt in which a woman is strangled and then tied in a sitting-up position on an ordinary kitchen chair. When the detective arrives on the scene he sees this woman and thinks she is still alive, sitting in her kitchen. Sara could not quite envisage it: wouldn't she look unusual? Dead, for two days at this time? Would anyone believe that such a person was really alive, sitting on their chair, rigid, tied. How did he tie her up so she looked so natural? Wouldn't her head droop or did he tie that in some way too and if so how? These details were ignored in the novel and Thomas had made the scene convincing enough.

Thomas read his grisly scene in a low key, ironic tone, and then read other even more graphic horror scenes. The old ladies listened with polite attention, smiling and clapping their hands delicately and appreciatively when he was finished. When the reading was over they queued up to get books signed and to congratulate Thomas and thank him for coming to their library. He was kind and polite, he chatted to them all and thanked them. Thank you! No, No, thank you!

All she knew about him, when he phoned, was that he had written some nasty and to be honest not terribly popular books, mostly about murdered women.

The amusement park management brought everyone from the roller coaster to the hospital for a check-up, then sent them home in taxis. It is after midnight by the time Sara gets home, and she sees the message light flashing on the telephone. Thomas has no doubt been phoning, wondering what has happened to her. She phones the cottage but there is no reply so she leaves a message herself.

She writes an e-mail to the woodcutter, whose name is Ernesto.

> Dear Ernesto
>
> You may remember me? I am the woman who had lunch with you in Vienna last March. You told me about your divorce. I have been thinking about you and wondering how you are.

She crossed out 'and wondering how you are' which she guessed might confuse him and replaced it with a full stop and 'How are you?' Then she finished.

Thank you for everything. The lunch, the wine, the conversation . . . It was a miracle.

I am sorry I did not meet you at the wine bar. But please write. Tell me about yourself. Tell me about Mauthausen.

My family was Jewish too, until a generation ago. I forgot to mention that when I talked to you.

Best wishes
Sara Feldmann

But she puts this e-mail in her draft folder, as she has been advised to do with all e-mails. Leave them for a day, re-read them, before launching them into the ether. Then she writes another e-mail, to Thomas, telling him about her misadventure on the roller coaster, about Lisa's imminent marriage, and about the journey back from the summer cottage. The house has not been burgled, the grass is not too long, the asters and goldstorm have blossomed at the edge of the loggia. This e-mail she sends straightaway. The rules about keeping them for a day do not apply when you are writing to your partner or your loved one. You can tell them anything.

SEAN O'REILLY

Playboy

Gaunt and sweating, Ishka Moynihan appeared on Grafton Street around lunchtime and leaned his sandwich board against a streetlight next to the flower sellers, mother and daughter, who waved to him enthusiastically from their deck chairs. Ishka performed a regal bow in response, lost his balance and staggered forwards into the path of two men who pushed him out of the way without breaking their step. Stumbling on towards a stack of big yellow buckets, he seized one with both hands and pulled it down over his head. Then he fell to his knees and threw back his neck towards the sun in prayer.

He was watched by people in line at the cash machine, some who found him amusing and others who thought he was a fool and should suffer for it. There were those also of the passers-by, who without knowing why, felt compelled to stop at the sight of him, their hearts struggling to remember some blessing, some lament . . . but the crowd soon forced them to move on. Out of nowhere, a red-haired youngster approached at speed and drummed violently on the bucket with his palms but Ishka stayed in position. A grinning tourist shouldered a video camera and zoomed in. It took Ann-Marie, the daughter, to sneak towards him and pull the bucket off his head. Ishka blessed himself solemnly and got back on his feet.

Poetry for sale, he cried out at the summer throng. The great classics. Bishop Patrick, O'Rathaille, Denis Devlin, Synge, James Clarence Mangan, Jonathan Swift. Poems to the brightness and the darkness. To the water and the land. The metal and glass of Dublin. The sun is out and the boiling in your blood and the heat between your legs is called poetry. There's madness in the air. No need to be alone today. A poem for company, or for your girlfriend or boyfriend, your mother or sister, your dead uncle. A poem for a complete stranger. A spell of beauty on the world today. Yes, a poem for everybody today in Dublin, the Irish and the Spanish, the Italians and the Americans, the refugees and asylum seekers, the guards and the gun runners. Everybody is listening. They can't help it on a day like today. Will you come a-boating, my gay old hag, will you come a-boating, my tight old hag, will you come a-boating, down the Liffey floating? I'll make a pair of oars from your two long shins.

A happier one, a funnier one, Ann-Marie called to him.

Ishka raised his hands above his head as if he was about to begin a dance: In Siberia's wastes, no tears are shed, for they freeze within the brain, nought is felt but the dullest pain, pain acute, yet dead.

Sun-burned Ann-Marie shook her head and sighed above her bucket of giant daisies. He always did the opposite of what you wanted, she reminded herself and gazed sullenly at the mingling crowds on Grafton Street, like two rivers meeting, trapped between the hot steep banks of glass, hiding from the sea. At the passing of two young women, the usual sour jowly blondes in business suits, she watched Ishka step out in their wake, dodging, skipping, wriggling until he was behind them in the crowd.

Love poems, poems of seduction, sweat and passion. Horny and randy and wet as the hosed-down steps of a club on O'Connell Street on a warm summer's morning. Come on girls, let me paint your eyes and pierce your ears with the fruit of some sweet agonies.

Ann-Marie watched closely as one of the women turned around with a face transformed by pleasure, her mouth open to drink. There was happiness, Ann-Marie had time to think before the woman got a good look at her seducer, Ishka, leering back at her with his mocking, bloodshot eyes. The woman abruptly shut her mouth, and her face wilted in an instant, the colour, all her self-possession, confidence, hope was replaced by fear, or something else, pain, anger. Ann-Marie tried to laugh but the spectacle saddened her. Ishka did this again and again, trying to humiliate people, or himself, with his starved cheeks and stained lips, the grey all over his hair, the filthy comical clothes. He was skipping from foot to foot and singing: We have thousands of women who'd keep you busy, with breasts like balloons or small as a bud, buxom of body and hot in the blood, virgins or whores – whatever's your taste – at least don't let them go to waste.

The woman screamed. Ishka vanished like a ghost and a moment later was back beside his sandwich board, calling out the names written there, Mahon, Joyce, Heaney, Pádraig Pearse, Ní Chuilleanáin. Before long, a group of tourists stopped in front of him, two American couples, big people in shorts and sandals who listened breathlessly as Ishka reeled off poem after poem like he was never going to stop. Laughing this time, Ann-Marie watched the Americans hand over their money gratefully, it looked like a twenty euro note, and hurry off.

Almost immediately, an old woman stepped up beside the sandwich board. She was wearing lipstick and blusher on her tiny tree-bark face, her scorched tweed coat was held together by a pin and she was walking around the city in house-slippers. Ann-Marie couldn't understand her feeling of irritation towards the old woman, and scolded herself guiltily. She was sure the woman would smell of disinfectant and have a well-spoken voice that was hard to hear. But Ishka was leaning away from her as she spoke and his eyes avoided looking at her.

Who was that? Ann-Marie hurried over to ask.

My death, Ishka groaned. He was squatting behind the sandwich board. I forgot about her again. She was here last week. My own death.

Ann-Marie had started back towards the flower stall.

What? Where are you going?

You know I hate it when you talk like that, she said. It's not funny. I can't think. Every week there's something. Do you know how to have a normal conversation?

She gave me some poems to look at, written by her first love. He's dead now. She said he used to be big buddies with all the big names. But they all forgot about him when he died young of a heart attack. So she wanted to know if they were any good now, these love lyrics, or if she should forget about them.

You look scared, she told him. You lost them didn't you?

Ishka nodded and covered his face. Ann-Marie stared down at the huddled, washed-out shape of him and felt afraid; he was trembling and helpless and this frightened her. Like the night she had met him by chance in a pub when she was out with her own friends. Ishka came over to join them, he was already drunk if not more, and soon he had all of them laughing, a gang of them, by doing different voices. She was delighted that he didn't care who her friends were or what they did or where they came from. The problem was he didn't know when to stop. The lads began to get restless and the girls shot looks at her, and it was as if Ishka was aware of this, and he started getting dirtier, creepy, his eyes swelling like a mad fish. Then one of the lads punched him. One punch and no one said a word. Ishka fell on the floor and curled up like a baby. Ann-Marie had to beg him to get back on his feet. She took him to the toilet and he tried to put his hand up her skirt.

Doreen threw me out last night, she heard him say, looking up at her.

Hardly the first time. She's your mother.

She was waiting for me when I came in. It's been coming for weeks. I could sense it. Unconsciously. That's why I was staying out so much. You're thirty years old now, when are you going to settle down, there's an ad in the paper for a baker's apprentice or she's had another dream and I was wearing a uniform but she can't remember what kind so she's been to the library to do some research and while she was in the library she – it doesn't stop.

Where'd you sleep? Ann-Marie said to cut it short.

That's the problem, I don't remember. I went out and must have got hammered. I woke up this morning under a tree in the Phoenix Park with the deer all standing around me in the mist. I thought I was dead. They wouldn't go away.

She'll let you back, you know she will, Ann-Marie said. The poems are another problem. You can't let an old woman like that down.

They were the only copies. I looked at some of them. In pencil on old paper. They were awful. They were probably her own you know. It's probably some fantasy of hers.

The point is it doesn't matter. You have to get them back to her. They'll be in some pub won't they? Look for them now. Now, not at night.

I must have left them somewhere.

You probably ate them.

Ishka looked up at her alarmed.

I was only kidding, she had to tell him, and he grinned, a nervous, ugly grin.

When her mother shouted for her, Ishka watched Ann-Marie walk back to the stall, a thin arse in boys' loose jeans, haunchless, the disappointed swing of a drab ponytail. Suddenly he was delving with his face in the smooth teen crevice between her buttocks. His tongue ached as it jabbed at her unpierced arsehole. She was bent over the flower-filled buckets, her face smothered in the gaudy petals. The cheap elasticity of her soaked thong was tormenting, infinite and – the image vanished, leaving him choking.

It was the sun. He had to get out of the sun, it was driving him mad with lust. Look at that woman passing now with the cramped rounded breasts and cross-eyed nipples or her with the fresh brown ankles. Or see the way that one holds her head, the gentle grace, the coy serenity and underneath she is fighting the urge to grab hold of that young lad with the long arms and waft up her skirt and sit on him there in the street. Ishka saw a man stop and step out of his jeans as another man knelt in front of him. The sun gave the eyes back their power to dream. The flesh came alive and seized control over the concrete. Pores opened and swallowed up the dust. He ran out into the street and pulled a woman to the ground and the crowd was cheering, stripping, clawing, sucking. He could fuck indiscriminately, man or woman; he could fuck a shop doorway, wedged between the sliding glass. They all dreamed of it in their beds at night, then set the alarm clock. You could get so hard, the sun inside your head, you could understand why they needed the cops. Look at her, the yearning expression in her eyes that says she doesn't know whether she's asleep or awake, she's out walking, she feels the breath of every man brushing by her, the sun on her bare shoulders, she is faint with it, just touch me, somebody please put their hands on me before I . . .

He ducked down behind the sandwich board again with some idea of cleaning it, anything to get some control over himself. Or he could run into some pub and pull the sunshower out of him in a cubicle, it wouldn't take much. He picked off a bit of something stuck over the TT of Beckett. The paint was chipped in Kinsella. He would have to do it again soon, a new glamorized make-over in the coy style of new Dublin, stained glass maybe. Buy himself a suit and hat and do it Sinatra-style, clean, sauve, a smirk at the past. On his thumb he noticed a red smear and he tried to rub it off on his trouser leg. Then he noticed there was red grime in under his fingernails. He held out his hands. It was blood. In between the fingers and matted on the hair on the back of his hand. He searched for a wound, a cut, some explanation. He stood up straight, fast enough to make him dizzy, patting his body in search of a sign of pain.

Ann-Marie saw him lurching into the crowd, hitting himself like a man on fire. She thought it was another joke. People stopped to watch or got out of his way while others seemed to want to hit him. Goat the Busker put down his guitar and looked over. She saw a frowning security guard speak into the radio on his chest pocket. Ishka ricocheted around amidst the shoppers, slapping himself, pointing at the sun and calling for water, poor Christy needs a-drowning, a-sopping, a-splashing . . .

Ishka was lying on the sofa in a velvet green dressing gown, a glass of cold vodka resting on his chin. There was jazz playing; Coltrane drumming up the sore Spanish light, the trumpet of the sun, a fiesta in a one-welled thick-lipped pueblo.

Wake up, Caroline warned him.

His clothes were drying on hangers in front of the open window. It was as if he had stripped and jumped before the clothes had time to hit the floor, and he was now out there falling, free-falling, arms and legs stretched wide like a kite, his cock hard and pinpointing the spot far below. He looked at the trousers, faded brown corduroy bald at the knees, and wondered what they said about him. And the vivid green bars on the shirt he had stolen from a busty Spanish girl earlier that summer which always seemed to sag across his narrow chest.

Caroline wore a long grey linen dress and sandals. It made her look maternal, a woman who, saddened by the lies of the marriage bed, had decided to devote herself to her children. To somebody who didn't know her, she would give the impression of a woman who saw behind the unstoppable charade of people around her but had not lost her compassion for them. Honest, gentle, touched with weariness, a good listener, loyal.

Did you hear me? You crossed the bloody line, she shouted at him.

It might have been one of those perfect moments, an idle stoned summer afternoon when the mind breathes out and the sunbeams are spiked with sudden revelations and coincidences. He was in the mood to talk, about being alive, about other people, about joy and destruction, about his first swim in the sea after a storm on the Aran Islands, anything at all, to talk until he reached that point where you had to sing, and everybody began to sing, they had been singing all along, even the furniture, the streets were loud with song . . . if it wasn't for Caroline and her spitefulness, her bleak monotonous anger.

She was sitting in the big chair across the room, as ugly as he had ever seen her. Her complexion was like raw meat. Every gulp of vodka showed off her double chin. She was a woman at the end of her thirties, a Belfast woman who he had met almost a year before, yes, it was nearly a year, he would have to remember their anniversary. She would pretend not to give a damn if he mentioned it, she would mock him for being sentimental. But to forget would mean trouble. Maybe not on the day itself, no, a few weeks later, on one of their drinking sessions her face would darken and her mouth would froth over with rage and she would tell him the fucken truth, the fucken truth about the wee shite stain that you are, the wee fucken conniver, the liar and the scranner, but you're not pulling one over on me creep, with your sick fucked up head, get fucken out of my house . . .

He had met her in a nightclub, a bare underground waiting room where middle-aged women drank expensive wine at candle-lit tables and moved their car keys around like they were involved in an inscrutable game of wits. Some nights Ishka sometimes found himself hammering on the cell block door, after the usual clubs had closed, alone, drunk, with a baroque craving to see the sleaze coagulating in the eyes of some divorced mother of three with her own business and a big house out along the bay.

He had already investigated the tables, the car key double bluffs, pawn takes queen from behind, and flirted with himself on the empty square of dance floor, when he went up to the bar hoping he had enough change in his pocket for one more glass of red wine. A big woman was sitting on one of the stools swearing in a northern accent at a Spanish girl behind the bar. The woman wasn't attractive in any way but she was drunk and her sarcasm was sharp and self-deprecating. Ishka moved straight in on her, hanging over the bar next to her as though he was drunker than he was, and gradually nodding along to what she was saying until she ordered him a glass of wine without looking at him. They were last to leave. She took him home in a taxi for more to drink. The next morning he woke up on the sofa, his trousers at his ankles and discovered that he had sprained his wrist from hours of slapping her.

In the middle of Grafton Street, Caroline continued to fine-tune her humiliation. In broad daylight. What if somebody had seen me? Crawling around my feet like some demented animal. And then just in case I wasn't shown up enough some girl throws a bucket of water over you, some shrill wee knacker from Tallaght. It's gone too far. Enough's enough.

Ishka gazed into the water, the tranquil pool of apology, and saw the reflection of a hundred other times when he had stood there, hearing a voice shouting at him from far away in the dark forest.

And bloody listen to me, Caroline went on. I'm not done yet. Then he starts shouting in the street about killing his mother. It's beyond a joke. You run a mile if someone looks crooked at you. You're a born coward. You haven't an ounce of strength in you. Pure gristle, like something you hang out for the birds to peck at in the winter. A string of bacon rind with hairs on it.

Well where did I get the blood then? I must have hit somebody to cause the blood to flow.

Caused the blood to flow? Caroline laughed, then began to cough. Oh, he's been at the poetry again. You don't have the first notion about poetry you know that? You've no feeling, no sympathy. You learned it off by rote to pass the time in the loony bin don't forget. Poetry won't cure you. And it won't feed you either. It would be better to manufacture combs. Who said that eh? Why don't you just stand on Grafton Street and blow on a comb instead if you want to humiliate me? The shame you make me feel sometimes – I could wring your neck. But that's it isn't it? The reason you bloody do it, you seedy wee shite. You enjoy standing there in public debasing it don't you, you're laughing at people, at me, me, that's what you're doing, wiping your arse with it, wanking, wanking, pulling your stinking wire all over Grafton Street. Poetry's just a blow-up doll for you. I see right through you and don't you forget it.

Ishka laughed and clapped his hands in praise; he was accustomed to treating her attacks on him as a joke, as a kind of perverse eloquence. Holding the glass under his chin, he began to clap more loudly. He hadn't seen her in more than a month and he guessed this was the source of her anger. That last night they must have drank about ten bottles of wine, he stripped off and she took out her camera. A line was crossed that night, they couldn't look at each other in the morning.

They never went out together because she hated crowds and she was afraid to be seen with him. Usually, he came round to her apartment. She would have cooked a fine meal and bought in plenty of expensive wine to drink, and they would listen to music or sometimes they would recite poems or passages from books to each other. Ishka knew very little about her and felt he was not allowed to ask. She seemed to have lived in Paris for a long time, to have come back to Ireland and might be working in television. She never mentioned other friends. At the start, Ishka had enjoyed their talks – he felt free to be himself, no matter how outlandish. After the wine, there was vodka. Then she would disappear. Ishka would smoke another joint and follow her into the bedroom. He'd pull the duvet off her and walk around the big white bed, shouting orders at her, roll over bitch, lift your fat leg, open your mouth, suck on those fat milk-sacks of yours, show me it, go on up on your back, I want your knees around your head, pull those pishflaps apart you dirty whore. Where did Lucifer kiss you?

I've just remembered something else, Ishka said. I went down to Walshe's after she threw me out and I was talking to this lad, Jerome, he's from the north as well, and we went back to his with a few cans and a few smokes. I was hoping to be able to crash there but his girlfriend came back and they started to argue. I remember leaving. It was nearly dawn. People had put their rubbish bags out in the street. It was like each bag was an offering and I was an evil spirit and the bags were there to make me pass on. The street was misty. Then, I remember now, I turned a corner and there were seagulls filling the street, roosting in the mist, hundreds of them, spread across the road. There was no way by them and . . .

Will you shut up, Caroline roared at him. She got out of her chair, the bottle of vodka in her hand. Ishka imagined her pouring it over him and then setting him alight, aflame in a velvet green dressing gown.

Your mother throws you out and it's tragic farce. People put out their bins and it's the Bible. Some seagulls on the street and you turn it into Leda and the swans. Shut your mouth for five minutes. Just stop talking. You shouldn't even bloody be here, she said and then sighed heavily, painfully.

Do you want me to go?

She didn't answer. She had asked him to leave before but never sober. Once or twice he had dropped in on her unexpectedly and found her drinking alone. She would start in on him as soon as he sat down; snarling, hissing, gulping down drink, she would pace about and describe in hallucinatory detail the scene of his betrayal, how he lay on the floor of some student bedsit with a flat-chested girl and mocked her name as the candle burned down in the ash-tray, and Ishka would listen in wonder, and almost believe her.

Don't try to apologize; I'm sick of your exaggerations, she said, swaying before him. He wasn't able to look at her; he distracted himself by wondering what he would do for the rest of the day if he left, whose house he could crash in that night. Then, he was walking up a flight of dark stairs; he stopped and looked down behind him into the candle flame and the meek whiskery daubed-over face of the old woman – she blew the candle out.

Did I tell you about the lost poems? I've been cursed. Listen—

Shut up, Caroline screamed back at him. 'I can't take any more. We went too far. It hurts. It fucken hurts me. Can't you bloody see that?

Ishka fell backwards in the sofa as though she had hit him. Out of the corner of his eye, he saw her go down the corridor and into her bedroom. She was giving him time to leave. He had managed to get his legs into his boxers before she came back, and threw a handful of photographs at him. They fell across the floor, pictures of his stiff cock from every angle, close-ups and him wanking for her, the jism spurting into the air.

Take this filth with you.

He thought he knew what to do. He took out his cock and moved towards her, pulling on himself, talking to her the way he usually did, a rough lewd drawl, Come on baby, here's big daddy Leda, look at him spreading his wings, he's got a big mouthful of hot milk for his dirty wee ugly duckling.

He was sliding towards her, through the drift of photographs. If he could just empty himself everything would be all right, his head would clear, Caroline would relax. But she kept her eyes down. He was almost near enough to reach her. He willed her to look at him, softly, then threateningly, Come on, come on you filthy bitch, you know you want it, you can't pretend to me, take my sap, the bark is splitting.

Later that night, he went to a club with some people he had met in a pub, a stoned faction of dread-locked Basque youth who he had emblazoned himself on as an indigenous jazz musician, my weapon is the xylophone man, the soft wooden steps that lead down under the water – Atlantis, that's our name. The bouncers at the door of the club warned him to behave himself and then waved him in free of charge when he performed the Proclamation of Independence in Irish for them. Once inside, the Basques started rolling grass joints and Ishka went off in search of white-haired Constance, who sorted him out with some pills which she kept stored in a heavy emerald locket on a chain round her neck.

He had rushed out of Caroline's with his shoes and socks in his hand, taken flight like a man who has seen into the future. Or into the past. Or everything at once. It wasn't simply that he had never seen her crying before; Caroline in tears made him want to run for his life. Maggots, it may as well have been maggots wriggling out of her eyes. Laughing at his disgust, she followed him to the door and threw a Polaroid after his blackened heels.

He aimed himself back towards the city centre, determined to find the old woman's poems. It was the only thing on his mind as he hurried through the hot streets. The day had been a disaster so far and he wasn't able to piece together an explanation. Bird shadows constantly brought his hands up to protect his face. He saw an old woman up ahead at a bus stop and crossed the street. As he passed a window, he was aware of a man staring out at him. The homeless girl he sometimes spoke to on Baggot Street Bridge was sleeping; her face was bruised from a beating. The breadwinners would be out of work in less than an hour.

In the first likely pub, he met Adrian, a junior lecturer at Trinity. They had a pint together and Ishka told him the story of his day. In the next pub he sat down among two people he used to know at school, two website designers now who had taken the afternoon off, and they bought him a drink and laughed themselves into tears as he told the story again. After that, there was Hector and Phantom Pat who claimed to remember him with a sheaf of papers in a hotel bar a few nights before. On the way there, he was stopped by the glamorous Eve Ó Dálaigh, who took his arm and insisted, because he was the funniest man she had ever met, that Ishka entertain her for an hour before she went off to meet some friends and on to the theatre. Ishka did what was expected of him, knowing she would never invite him along. She laughed so much she had barely touched the wine which she left him to finish with a kiss on the forehead and a shallow perfumed impression in the deep leather sofa which Ishka convinced himself she wanted him to defile. He slid across the sofa and imagined it was her delicate white face beneath him. It was then he noticed that there was no trace of himself on the other side. Involuntarily, he slapped the seat hard with his hand. The people in the café bar rose out of their seats in unison. Ishka stood up in the hush; he wondered whether he should deliver a poem but he was afraid he was going to cry, or worse. His head was turning against him. He needed company, to forget himself. He also needed somewhere to sleep that night. The old woman's poems would have to wait; he was probably exaggerating their importance, over-dramatizing like Caroline always accused him of. He had too much of a sense of humour to be a detective anyway.

With two E blossoming triumphantly in him, his eyes were hot exposed roots, Ishka was dancing like a flower in the summer rain of lights under the DJ's caged dais. When a girl joined him, he was delighted by the generosity in her eyes and the awkwardness in her movements was a new kind of beauty. She was young and thin and he shimmied towards her with his hands above his head, Spanish style he thought. The girl began to mirror him, struggling to fight off her embarrassment. Ishka put his arm around her bared waist; the softness was like her own blood had got into his veins. The girl wriggled free but he tried again and this time she allowed him to keep his hands on her hips, brittle hips, sharp teenage bones under his velvet claws. He leaned down to whisper into her ear. The girl laughed and turned her face away and he thought she said his name. He stopped dancing and took a closer look at her. She stuck out her tongue at him.

Don't look so disappointed, she said, laughing, and held out her hand.

Ann-Marie led him towards the bar.

You've no idea how good it is to see you, he told her.

You're off your face, she said.

I've had the worst day of my life. But now it's beginning to brighten up. You should see yourself. You look so beautiful. Like you know what happiness is.

Stop it, she said but she couldn't help herself smiling. Did that woman get you home? I didn't know what to do. Did you find the poems?

Come on, forget about that now, Ishka hugged her. Come on. We're going to have a great night together. I'm so glad you're here. Do you feel it? We'll have a mad one. Do you feel it?

They danced again. Ishka spoiled it when he dragged a chair on to the dance floor and began to make love to it like a stripper. Ann-Marie walked away but she couldn't leave him out there on his own. Finally, she got him into a corner behind a pillar, out of sight of the bouncer. She held his hand while he talked to her, in overheated clouds of words, about what he wanted to do to her, had always wanted to do, watching her with her scalpel among the flowers and the buckets but she was too young and he had to control himself. As though the words were too hot in his mouth, he began to spell them out, blowing on them, b-r-e-a-s-t-s and n-e-c-e-s-s-a-r-y and i-n-y-o-u-s-o-d-e-e-p. She put her lips against his to cool him down.

When they separated he was still talking, now about the sex he had with other people, men and women, one-night flings and two-day orgies and about what he did when he was alone. She could tell he was on E but maybe some part of him was trying to put her off him. As he went on, and his mouth dried up so that he sucked on his gums, she decided he was testing her, searching for her limits the way some men gape at your underwear. He was pleading with her to tell him what she liked. For a moment, she felt she actually wanted to, that it was only words anyway and it would soothe him but the two friends she had come in with spotted her behind the pillar before she could speak. She knew what they saw; some scrap of a man in rags with dead man's lips feeling her up, poor desperate Ann-Marie, where's her airs tonight?

They sat down. It's for your own good they said. They refused to go away. Furious, Ann-Marie went off to the toilet. She was delayed there by another girl on her way back and when she reached the table she found Ishka kissing the knees of her two friends. They were screeching with laughter as they dared each other to pull up their dresses. Ishka barely recognized her as she got him back on his feet; he pushed her aside and walked off into the depths of the club, peering dangerously into every face as though he was looking for something that had been robbed from him.

Ann-Marie sat down, asking herself why she couldn't go after him, hating her two friends, her mother, her long-dead father, and the entire city for being too weak to follow him.

Ishka howled at the moon and people stopped to clap and shout encouragement. The street was hectic and loud. Jubilant hordes gathered and dispersed at the junction. They spilled out of the darkness with amazed bloated faces. Under a streetlight, Ishka jumped from the bonnet to the roof of a car.

Half a hundred beyond. Ten more there. A power of euphoric faces. Breasts, a schoolmaster'd be hard set to count, and enough in them to sweeten all the come downs of the dot.com men of Dublin. Did I tell you about the time I killed my mother? The cobbles of Stoneybatter were as hot under my feet as my mobile phone after a call from my dark Rosaleen in Gdánsk. Ah, now, they stole her away one morning in the open air and her trimming the spuds on the doorstep with her white hands in the cold murky water, a plague of portly spuds like she thought the neighbours would brighten towards her. Ah, she loved to see them throw her a smile as they rushed out into their cars of colours she couldn't name. But wasn't it my very own mother who did the foul deed and called the authorities, a mean crusty worm of a woman, I caught her giggling out in the yard bush and the gulls gone mad in the sky of mystic Volvo blue, squawking and diving and winking, like they knew just to look at her. Ah now it's sad to tell but the screeching got inside my head and I heard the angels singing and the sun humbling my eyes from any reason and—

He jumped down to the pavement at the sight of two guards coming wearily round the corner. There was more applause. A girl ran up to him, kissed him and then disappeared. The night was young yet, vast and magnanimous. Look at the human beings in their urban carousing, their gaiety in destruction, their mockery of loneliness. Ishka made a plan to walk the streets for the rest of the night, he'd talk to people, it didn't matter who, the people awake on the streets, the homeless, the lost, others like him, the stragglers behind the parade. He had ideas to share. At this stage of the night people understood each other finally. And if he got tired he'd climb over the railings into Merrion Square and recline alongside the painted statue of Oscar Wilde.

He followed three singing women down a street, three married women out on a birthday they told him. Two of them took his arm. They sang a song together and Ishka left them for a group of younger girls, plain girls from the country, students trying hard to have a wild capital city time. They stopped by a kebab shop and Ishka waited outside with the crowd, trying to talk to anyone who looked at him, hoping he might get wind of a party. He stepped up on a car and gave another speech, pretending he was a country priest condemning their insobriety and fickleness. Some threw chips at him but mostly they were laughing. A joint was passed his way.

Ann-Marie saw him in the crowd outside the kebab shop. She called out to him but he didn't hear her. Her two friends stopped and refused to go a step further in that direction. He's a madman, what's wrong with you Ann-Marie? They tried to grab her by the arms but she broke free. As she ran towards the shop, hardly knowing what she was doing, she saw him, showing something in his hand to a girl in a short leather skirt. Other heads leaned in and suddenly the crowd seemed to explode from within. She heard screaming and saw Ishka fall backwards to the ground. One lad pounced on him and then more, kicking him with a savagery that filled the street with screams.

They were still kicking him when she reached the shop, about six of them, they wouldn't stop even when she was punching their backs and grabbing handfuls of their hair. No one would help her. She was pushed against a wall and hit her head. A second later, they went scattering up the street and Ishka was as limp as a flower on the ground. Ann-Marie knelt beside him. The blood bubbled out of a spot above his eyebrow swamping his face, dripping from his earlobe. She thought of the picture shapes the doctors show you and ask what you can see. I can see you, she said and then screamed at the people in the shop to call the guards. The shirt was torn off him; his chest was as hairy as she had imagined but now it wasn't moving. Her eyes scanned the length of him for a safe place to put her hand. Then she noticed he was holding something; lightly as she could, she touched his fingers and the hand fell open. It looked like a crushed chip wrapper. She opened it hurriedly, spread it out on her knee and saw that it was a photograph. Leaning forward with it into the light of the shop window, she made out an erect prick wreathed in a nest of blurred black hair, the eye at the top red and gaping and ready to burst. Stealthily, she put it away into her pocket. She couldn't stop herself smiling. I can see you, she said again. Then she lay down on the street alongside him, her trampled flower.

CLAIRE KEEGAN

Night of the Quicken Trees

In every house in the country long ago the people of the house would wash their feet, the same as they do now, and when you had your feet washed you should always throw out the water, because dirty water should never be kept inside the house during the night. The old people always said that a bad thing might come into the house if the feetwater was kept inside and not thrown out, and they always said, too, that when you were throwing the water out you should say 'Seachain!' for fear that any poor soul or spirit might be in the way. But that is neither here nor there, and I must be getting on with my story . . .

from *Feet Water*, an Irish fairy tale

Shortly after the priest died a woman moved into his house on the Hill of Dunagore. She was a spear of a woman who clearly wasn't used to living on the coast: not five minutes after she'd hung the wash out on the line her clothes were blown halfway up the bog. Margaret Flusk had neither hat nor rubber boots nor a man. Her brown hair was long, flowing in loose strands like seaweed down her back. She wore a big sheepskin coat that fit her to perfection and when she looked out at the mortal world it was with the clear, canny gaze of a woman who has suffered, and survived. When she moved to Dunagore it was past the time when she could bear a child. That power had left her years ago because of the night of the quicken trees.

The priest's house stood on the highest point of the hill beside the mast whose evening shadow fell into her rooms. It was joined to another cottage of equal size and they both looked like two frozen hares across the Cliffs of Moher. It was autumn when she came. The swallows were gone and any blackberry still on its briar was starting to rot. The house smelled of dead insects and urine. Margaret dragged anything she didn't want down to the bottom of the haggard and set fire to it. Being superstitious, she gave his clothes away. If his clothes weren't given away she knew he'd be naked in the next world. She painted all the walls and ceilings with a bucket of white emulsion, disinfected the floors, the doorstep and rubbed the windowpanes until they squeaked under the cloth for, although she did not come from Clare, she knew nothing good ever happens in a dirty house.

When she got the chimney swept she tore across the field towards a farmhouse where smoke was rising. Soon after she was running back, her long legs stretching easily over the wet fields, holding a fire-shovel full of embers. After that, smoke was always rising. She was never gone or slept long enough to let the fire die. In fact she liked getting up while the stars were still in the sky. It gave her satisfaction to see a star falling. If she believed in the forces of nature she was yet determined to avoid bad luck. She'd had her share of bad luck so now she never threw out ashes of a Monday or passed a labourer without blessing his work. She shook salt on the hearth, hung St Bridget's crosses on the walls and kept track of changes in the moon.

When she got the house clean, she drove down the hill and around the coast to Ennistymon. The roads were narrow and steep, their ditches stone. Inside the fields stood bony cattle and small flocks of long-woolled sheep. Down in the village a white-haired man who'd lost his mind stood on the bridge directing traffic.

'Quick! Quick! Winter is round the corner!'

She bought flour and sugar, oatmeal, butter and tea, peas and beans, milk, spuds and salt fish, brought it home, sprinkled holy water around the house and baked a loaf. When it got dark at five o'clock, she went outside and lifted her skirt and squatted in the grass. She wanted to pass water on every blade of grass around her house, she could not say why. Grass was long and sour up there. It was a strange place without so much as a tree, not a withered leaf to be seen in autumn just the shivering bogland and all the gulls wheeling around screeching under restless clouds. The landscape looked metal, all sturdy and everlasting but to Margaret, coming from a place of oak and ash, it was without substance. There would be no shade in summer, no fields of barley turning yellow in the month of August. She decided she would stay in that house as long as she could without harming anybody or letting anybody harm her. If either one of these things happened she would move on. She would get in a boat and cross over to the Aran Islands, go as far west as she could without leaving Ireland. But until then she would do her best to keep people at arm's length for people were nothing but a nuisance.

Not every man can sharpen a scythe or drive a stake. Stack, the 49-year-old bachelor who lived next door, had a bald head and seeds of grey in his eyes. He'd lived and worked the land with his father all his life until his father died. He was thirty-eight when his father passed away and now he was left with all the bogs and an income from the turf. He did not live alone but with Josephine, a sleek brown goat who had the run of the house. By day she stared into the fire and at night she took up more than her share of the bed. Stack milked her twice a day, rubbed Palmolive on her udder and always remembered to bring her fig rolls from the town. He had courted a small farmer's daughter outside Lahinch for twelve years, bought her 624 Sunday dinners but she wouldn't even let him touch the hem of her skirt or push the hair back out of her eyes so he could see her properly. Once she got a bit drunk and he kissed her in the car outside her back door but that was all. In the end she went off and married a man who sold stone and Stack found Josephine through an advertisement in *The Farmer's Journal*.

Stack, like many who have experienced a happy childhood, couldn't bear to part with anything. The spare room was packed to the ceiling with his father's fishing rods, his mother's sewing machine, weed killers, jam jars, a solid fuel cooker. He kept all the clothes he'd ever worn from his matinée coats to the trousers he'd recently grown out of, and kept the door closed because Josephine liked to go in there and eat his mother's slippers. Stack did not like to think he would ever become like the new generation. Young people couldn't catch a fish or skim cream off milk. They went around in cars they couldn't afford with small children who'd never tasted their mother's milk, committing adultery at the drop of a hat. In fact, hats didn't drop fast enough for them.

They drank beer out of the bottle, came back from America and Prague looking for pizzas and couldn't tell a Golden Wonder from a rotten apple. And now a woman was living next door, setting fire to the priest's good furniture, walking the roads with her hair falling loose like she didn't own a comb.

Time passed and little happened in Dunagore. Clouds raced. Wind blew gates open. Cattle and sheep escaped from their small enclosures and were captured. The postman hardly ever stopped except to deliver a bill for the electricity. Once a middle-aged man asked Margaret to sign a petition to get the pot-holes on the road filled. While she signed her name his eyes crawled across her frame.

'Would you be any relation to the priest?' he asked.

'Why, do I look like him?'

He looked up at her nostrils, the gypsy eyes and the waiting mouth. 'You don't look like anybody,' he said.

She slept well, kept baking and walking to the edge of the sea and back. Sometimes she walked all the way to Moher and looked down over the cliffs and frightened herself. Sometimes, when she was down there with the rain wetting her hair and her sheepskin, she thought of the priest. The priest was her first cousin. He used to come to their house every summer to make the hay. He would come with the fine weather, sit on top of the hayrick at her side, dig new potatoes, pull scallions and eat them raw on the ditch. She was only a teenager. Skies were blue back then. They always said they would get the bishop's permission to marry, rear Shorthorns and have two children, a pigeon's clutch. Then he went off to the seminary, became the pride of a family who no longer called him by his name:

'Another drop of gravy, Father?'

'Do you think there's such a place as Limbo, Father?'

'Did my father say where he was going, Father?'

Even though he came back in summer to make the hay he never again sat on the ditches combing the knots out of her hair. Summers passed and the whole family, instead of putting on the record player and dancing when the hay was safe on the loft, knelt and answered his rosary.

Margaret tried not to think of the priest. After her walks she sat with her feet in a basin of soapy water listening to Raidió na Gaeltachta, got into his bed with the hot-water bottle, trapping his lamp-light in the right angle of a library book. Every now and then she came across a passage he'd underlined or a word he'd circled. Sometimes she saw his shadow at the bed-side, felt his cold hand firmly grasping hers and saw again his starched collar, the hayseed trapped in his cuffs. But that was only his ghost. If she wondered, before she slept, what her neighbour was doing in his bed at the far side of the wall, she didn't dwell on it. She tried not to dwell on things. Putting the past into words seemed idle when the past had already happened. The past was treacherous, moving slowly along like deep river water. It would catch up in its own time.

No doubt she was the subject of curiosity. Some said her people were all dead and that the priest was her uncle, that he'd taken pity on her and left her the house. Others swore she was a wealthy woman whose husband had run off with a teenager and that her heart was broken. When it got late down in the pub it was common knowledge that the priest had been in love with her, that she'd had his child and lost it, that he wasn't gone off to the mission at all that time he'd gone off to the mission. On All Souls' night, the middle-aged man who'd given her the embers banged his fists on her door but she stared him down through the glass. And women said she must be going through the change of life:

'The new moon takes a terrible toll on women like her,' one woman down in Lisdoonvarna said.

'Oh it would,' said another. 'The moon'll pull at her like the tide.'

Stack, like every man who has never known a woman, believed he knew something about women. He thought about Margaret Flusk as he drove home from Lisdoonvarna with Josephine sitting up in the passenger seat. She liked being in the front and he sometimes wondered if she couldn't drive. 'Wouldn't it be terrible,' he said, 'if that woman took a liking to me? She'd have nothing to do only break down the wall between the two houses and destroy our peace for ever more.' All she'd need was reason to knock on his door. If she had reason to knock he felt sure he'd let her in. If he let her in once she'd be in again, and then he'd be into her and there the trouble would start. One would need a candle and the other would want the lend of a rake. A woman would be a terrible disadvantage; she'd make him match his clothes and take baths. She'd make him drive her to the seaside every fine day with a picnic basket full of bananas and blackcurrant jam and ask him where he was when he had gone nowhere but into Doolin for a drop of oil.

December came in wet. Margaret had never known such rain. It didn't come down out of the sky but crossways, on the wind. There was salt on the windows and seaweed in the air. People down the town took to drink while the birds went hungry. They played darts for turkeys and hampers, fell out and in again. Town women took dead fir trees and holly into their houses, strung multi-coloured, electric lights under the eaves. Children put pen to paper, sent letters to the North Pole. The postman was run off his feet but Margaret didn't even get a card. The day before Christmas Eve she walked to the cliffs and back. She had written a few lines to her mother without reply. Her mother could be dead and she wouldn't know. The sea was going mad, eating away the land and she wondered how many years it would take before the sea pulled down the walls. By the time she got home she was soaked. The salt rain made her feet cold and hot at the same time. It was getting dark but there wasn't a light in the parish and Margaret knew the electricity was gone. She threw sods on the fire. The turf hadn't really dried; it smouldered unhappily in the grate, burned without turning into flame. She longed for wood, big ash sticks she could split open with an axe. She imagined herself outside on a fine frosty morning splitting sticks with the strength of two men, stacking them against the wall and the smell of resin and the heat that would come off them. But sticks were rare in Dunagore. Her mother, who said little, sang Irish:

Cad a dhéanfamid feasta gan adhmad?
Tá deireadh na gcoillte ar lár.

That night Margaret lit a candle, placed her feet in a basin of soapy water and watched the smouldering turf. She wondered if the priest had gone to Hell. The priest believed in an afterlife; in God and Heaven and Purgatory. All that. He said there wasn't any point believing in Heaven if you didn't believe in the other. 'The Other' is what he called Hell. Margaret wondered if she would join him there but it seemed more likely that she'd be turned into a *pucán* or a dock leaf. She drank two bottles of stout and felt the past rearing up. All those summers of childish commitment, them saying they'd marry and then him going off and the whole family witnessing his ordination. Him coming back to make hay with not so much as a handshake, eating her ribs and parsley sauce and walking alone through the woods. She'd meet him on the stairs, in the cowhouse, on the back lane where the foxgloves turned the ditches pink and he'd pass her with a bare nod same as she was a shadow of what she used to be. One evening a heavy shower fell out of the blue. The house was sullen. The hay was down.

'That's the end of us.' Her father, standing at the parlour window.

''Tis only a shower.' Her mother, always trying to pacify him.

'We may buy it in. I knew we shouldn't have mowed today. Didn't I say we shouldn't have mowed?' Her father willing the raindrops to increase, to prove himself right.

'Tomorrow will be fine, surely.'

'We're finished.'

Margaret went out into the rain without a coat, up to the clearing where the quickens grew. She always felt safer outside, the scent of damp fern and lichen diluted the unhappiness in that house. The quicken boughs shook pleasantly above the silver trunks, their leaves trembling. Out in the lane the priest passed smoking a cigarette, his open-necked shirt wet on the shoulders. The only reason she made her presence known was to ask the simple question of why he never looked her in the eye or asked how she was? Could the man who'd promised her marriage not even ask how she was? And then she caught up on him and he showed her why. They laid down without a word between the berries and the wet grass and she knew while he was planting his seed in her that she would pay for it. Afterwards he got up and paced between the trees and smoked and stared at her and suddenly turned his back, going off without a word.

It was night before Margaret rose. She walked home watching the tops of the shaking trees and, beyond their boughs, the yellow wisp of moon. The experience was like everything else; it wasn't what she thought it would be. Going home she knew where she was by the sound of her feet on the gravel road.

Sometimes she imagined where she would be, what she might be doing if she had not made her presence known. Now she was constantly afraid to take the smallest step in any direction. The greatest lesson the priest had taught her was the lesson of where one step can lead. She came to her senses. The feetwater had grown cold. She dried her feet, cursed a little so she would not cry and fell asleep in the chair.

When she woke the fire was almost out and the candle was burned away to nothing. Outside, no lights flickered in the houses around the coast. Villages were in darkness. The last quarter of what was now a winter moon shone down on her garden. Her neighbour's nanny goat was standing on her hind legs eating all that was within reach. Margaret had neither the energy nor the desire to chase her off. The moon and the clouds looked so still, like painted things. She got up, dried her feet, left the basin on the hearth, and went to the priest's bed and dreamed she was a man.

There was a loft in her dream whose floor sprouted grass. The grass grew higher than houses, their stalks leaning west then east then west again although there was no wind. Margaret lay supine, wearing nothing only a man's trousers and when she put her hand down there, instead of a penis, was a fat lizard which was part of her, his muscular tail swishing back and forth. A woman who looked like herself came in from another century wearing some type of knotted cloth. When she saw the lizard she didn't flinch but took it inside her anyhow and when Margaret woke she felt herself to make sure she wasn't turning into a man. When she saw her hand she got a lovely shock, for she saw blood. She thought all that was over. She got up and went into the bathroom and washed herself. It was almost morning. Grey light framed the trembling curtains. The house was draughty. Outside, a gale was blowing. Margaret was used to the wind flattening the long grass in front of her house but it was strange not hearing its power in the trees. She'd never get used to Dunagore, knowing no seed would take root and grow into a sycamore anywhere near the house. She could smell her own blood. So she was still a child-bearing woman. While she was thinking this she saw the basin of feetwater. She opened the back door and threw it out on the wind. The wind was so loud it shouted like a man.

That same night, at the far side of the wall, Stack couldn't sleep. This often happened. He wondered if other men really slept through the night and woke rested. Some nights he liked being awake when everybody else was asleep. He would sit up eating cream buns, watching television with Josephine. Other nights he craved the company of another human being, someone who would be able to change the channels and boil the kettle. He covered Josephine with his coat. She was already dreaming. She dreamed a lot, and ate things in her dreams. On fine nights Stack put on his hat and coat and walked the bogs. That night the electricity failed, he drank five hot whiskeys and thought about the past. Nothing would ever compare to the past: his mother laughing when she watched him becoming left-handed; his father teaching him to shave; that summer they all got sunburned in the bog and took turns with the calamine lotion and his father singing some song that made his mother blush. But his mother and father were dead. He was thinking about death and how he himself would go when he went, stumbling a little, to Margaret's house. He believed he would die alone and would not be found until Josephine ate the door down and somebody recognized her on the road and brought her back to his corpse. It felt lovely to be certain of something. He stood outside Margaret's back door and listened. There wasn't a stir. It was getting bright. The sun's light without the sun itself was visible beyond the cliffs. Nobody knew he was there. He was in the middle of nowhere and the woman was inside asleep, and safe. He stood for a long time imagining she was his. Then the door opened and Margaret came out, half asleep, with a basin of water and threw it in his face.

He went home. Josephine had gone to bed. Beside her he felt light in the head, was hot in himself then cold. He sweated, stripped, and passed wind. He felt the stone that was always in his throat growing bigger, going down into his stomach. He sat on the toilet for a long time before it passed and when it did it was the size of a stout bottle. He looked in the mirror. A stranger looked back at him. The drink and the night air and the cold water was exactly what he'd needed.

He fell asleep and dreamed of Margaret wearing a bear-skin, riding Josephine across the bogs of Clare. Her legs and arms were muscular. He followed Josephine's tracks until she came to the edge of the sea. The woman slapped Josephine hard with a hot leather strap, urging her on into the sea and the pair took off. The waves were high. Stack stood on the edge of the strand, calling out to Josephine to come back: 'Aw Josie! Come back to me! Josie!' but she got smaller and smaller and in the end he saw Margaret getting down on the coast of Inis Mór and men with red hands surrounding her and leading her, leading Josephine by the bridle, taking her away, bribing her with chocolate.

When he woke he felt like a new man. It was eleven o'clock in the night. He had slept through Christmas Eve. He couldn't believe it. Josephine was standing over him, nipping the soft flesh inside his arms. He opened the door and let her out. Margaret Flusk is wild, he thought. Hadn't he seen her bare white breast under the fur? Sure didn't she piss outside? Hadn't she got up in her sleep knowing he was there and not so much as blinked when he shouted out?

On Christmas morning he took a bath. He hadn't taken a bath since Easter. The electricity was still gone. He boiled water on the gas and nearly scalded himself. He polished his shoes, milked Josephine in front of the fire and put a lump of beef into the oven. He didn't know why he was looking at himself or washing himself except it was Christmas and he felt young enough to swim the Atlantic and drive stakes. If only he hadn't lost his hair. His father, down to the day he was laid in his coffin, had the fullest head of hair. The undertaker had combed it before he laid him out in the parlour and Stack had cried when he got home.

Now he took an eel out of the fridge and put it on the pan to fry. It was a Christmas box from the fish-monger down in Ennistymon who knew Stack had a taste for eel. He was certain it was still good. He looked at the black writhing form frying on the pan. It looked alive and for a moment he wasn't sure it wasn't. He bucked himself up, came to his senses and walked up the path to the priest's house.

Margaret wasn't dressed. She was scratching herself and thinking. She liked to roam around in her nightdress until noon having a think, drinking tea, bringing the fire back to life. She went to the toilet and made sure she was bleeding. It was strange to have eggs again. Wouldn't it be lovely to lay out? she thought, like a hen. She had once followed a hen for twelve days with a hat down over her eyes thinking, because the hen could not see her eyes, that she could not see Margaret but she never found the nest. The hen would lead her astray then disappear through a thicket of ferns. Then, out of the blue, she proudly walked into the yard with a clutch of eleven chickens.

If I could only cut out the man, Margaret thought, I might have a child. A man was a nuisance and a necessity. If she'd a man she'd have to persuade him to take baths and use his knife and fork. She ripped a towel in two and made herself a sanitary towel. Beyond the pane, standing there in his shirtsleeves staring at her, was the bachelor from next door. She wanted to stand there and stare him down as she had stared down the man who'd come on All Souls' but it was Christmas. She opened the door. The bachelor looked clean but smelled like fish.

'Stack's my name.'

'Stack?'

'Some Christmas, and you with no electric to make a bit of dinner.'

'Tis raw.'

'Come in and have your breakfast. I've gas.'

'I'm not hungry.'

'You're not hungry. Well, that's a good one. Don't you know the moon is changing?'

'The moon?' What did he know about the moon?

'Put on your sheepskin, good woman,' he said. 'Hurry. The fry will be in cinders.'

She didn't think. She got the sheepskin and her boots and followed him down the path to her front gate which was opening and closing on its hinges. There were goat droppings all over his front yard. His porch was full of bicycle parts and the cab of a tractor and the kitchen darker than a wood-shed. In the gas light she saw spades and shovels cocked up against the chimney wall and, hanging from the central beam, a well-sharpened scythe. A live snake was being fried in a pool of oil; on the table cuts of brown bread and a tub of fake butter. Margaret, in nothing, only her nightdress and her coat, felt lovelier than the raven. I'm producing eggs, she thought. I'm bleeding. I'm past nothing.

Stack held a bag of defrosted peas up to the candle to read the cooking directions. She could read the directions from where she sat. Maybe he was going blind. And the things he kept: seashells, old calendars, bottle tops, dead batteries, pictures of dead people. There was a picture of Stack when he was about twenty with a head full of hair, three Sacred Heart pictures, barometers, and inside the window, behind the television, a fan to keep the window pane from fogging up. So he likes to see who's walking the roads, she thought. Through an open door, she saw a big unmade bed. She could smell the goat. Maybe the goat slept with him. Just imagine.

'Don't mind the house,' he said. 'I've no woman.'

'No?'

'Well, I had a woman one time and now I'm not sorry I don't have her. She was a fierce expense.'

'Maybe you should find yourself a woman with money.'

'If a woman had money she wouldn't want me.'

'Why, have you a wooden leg?'

He laughed. It was a queer sort of laugh, closer to sadness than amusement. 'No, thank God. And by the looks of you, your legs aren't wooden either.' He was putting the two of them together.

'You must have left school early,' she said.

'Why's that?'

'It gets more complicated after you learn to add.'

'Your tongue is quick.'

When he said the word 'quick' she was back under the quicken trees, in that clearing, alive with enchantment. Neither she nor the priest could help themselves. It was even better because he was a priest. By breaking his vows of celibacy it felt possible that he might somehow make others. She felt him on top of her, panting, rolling over on to his stomach, zipping himself up, ashamed. And the thrill of it: the thrill after a decade of sitting on ricks of hay, eating scallions, him leaving the first primrose on the saddle of her bike. She could see the orange berries of the quicken shaking beyond his head in the rain. There was blood that night too. She felt her face redden and put up her hands to hide herself.

'Josephine is minded better nor any woman in Ireland,' Stack was saying, nodding in the direction of the armchair. There in the dark was the nanny goat staring at her. Her eyes gave Margaret a fright. Stack reached up and took a sprig of holly from behind a picture. Margaret thought he was going to give it to her but he gave it to Josephine, who ate it.

'What part of the country are you from?' he said.

'Wicklow.'

'The goat-suckers,' he said. 'That explains everything.'

'Did you ask me in to insult me?'

'That wouldn't be hard; you're proud. Pull up a chair.'

She didn't want to pull up a chair, didn't want to sit in that awful place eating fried snake with those dead people looking out at her from photographs. Well, what did she expect? What happens when a woman follows a man into his house wearing little more than her nightdress on Christmas morning? But she was smelling burned flesh and toast, watching the teapot steam. She hadn't eaten yesterday. It is the stomach, not the heart, that drives us, she thought. She was grateful the room was dark so she couldn't see the extent of the dirt and could eat in ignorance. Josephine sat under the table with her own buttered toast.

'Most people have dogs,' Margaret said, starting him off on his favourite subject.

'Ah but the goat! The goat is a great advantage. She'll eat anything. She'll go anywhere. She's twice the size of any dog, she's like a radiator going around heating the place and to top it all, I've milk. Do you like goat's milk?'

'No. But they say it's a noble child that's baptized in it.'

'Do they now?' He was looking into the oven at the beef. It had begun to spit and he lowered the flame. 'Are you one of these superstitious women?'

Her mouth was so full she couldn't answer.

Once her mother took her out to eat in the mart. Big dinners were cheap there. A man came in and ordered his plate. He was white in the face. Her mother watched him getting his dinner and going off to a corner with his back to all his neighbours and said, 'Do you see that man there? If you ever see a man like that leave him alone till he's had his fill. A man like that is dangerous.' Margaret now felt like that man. She drank the tea and ate most of the snake. Stack looked at her big nose and her long hair and filled her cup again. He cut more eel and watched her eating. While she ate like a savage he could not help wondering what a child they'd have together would look like.

'And do you miss Wicklow?'

'Every now and then.'

'What is it you miss?'

'I miss the ash,' she said and felt herself redden once again. The quicken tree, the mountain ash, were all the one. Stack bantered on. He talked about young people and turf, the Taoiseach, new year's resolutions and sunburn. When he stopped to draw breath she went home. He's a lonely man, she thought, but he's decent. And that goat! She'd have no time for her at all.

When Margaret got back to her own house, the door was wide open and a litter of black mongrel pups had got in and dirtied all over the floor. She'd no idea where they'd come out of. They'd chewed the corners off her library books, got up on every stick of furniture and left dirty paw marks all over her lovely white bedspread. One black pup trotted over, bit her hand and wagged its tail. She turned him up and saw, on his belly, a penis. She threw him out and thought about Stack. She didn't know why she'd followed a total stranger into his house and eaten all that food when it could be poisoned. She could still see the big bald head and him reaching up for the sprig of holly he wouldn't give her. She felt lucky to be alive. That night she saw children rounding up the pups, whistling, flash-lights shining on dogs' eyes, green eyes racing like demons in all directions. There were dogs in the graveyard the night she went to the priest's burial ground. They watched her without moving while she walked all over his grave. So they were back. She felt a chill, pulled a cardigan over her nightdress, filled the hot-water bottle and got back into the priest's bed.

★

When the pubs opened after Christmas, there was talk. The Flusk woman was seen coming out of Stack's in nothing only a nightdress. He must have sheared her, they said, because there wasn't a sign of the sheepskin. Stack carried her across the muck of his own yard and over her own threshold. Some said it stopped there.

'He must be drinking his Bovril, so,' said the grocer.

'Sure wouldn't he nade a set a steps just to raych her knickers?' said the carpenter.

'Ah, we're all the same height lying down,' said an old man.

'Imagine the two of 'em wudout a stitch,' said the draper's wife. 'They'd frighten wan anudder.'

'Not half as big a fright as she'd get,' said the auctioneer who was doing his best to join in but was in a terrible way with a toothache.

'You mean a small fright,' said the barmaid who was single and getting older and pretending not to care. 'Two hail-stones and a mouse's tail.'

'You should know,' they all said because they knew the barmaid thought that would be a nice cosy little number up there in the cottage with Stack and the lovely view looking down on all the tourists in the summertime and him with plenty of money and nobody to spend it on only herself and Josephine.

Smoke kept rising. Margaret bought two boxes of sanitary towels in the supermarket and set the women talking.

'There could be a babby in Dunagore yet!' they said.

'Wouldn't Stack be over the moon?'

'Sure isn't spring coming?'

Margaret walked between the showers, kept track of her

eggs and the changing moon. Daylight lasted longer but towards evening the red sun always lowered itself into the sea. Dirty suds floated up on the edge of the strand. The heather was thick, took on new growth like hair all over the boglands. Tourists wandered into Doolin looking for Irish music and mussels and directions to holy wells. Men came down from Dublin to test themselves on the golf course at Lahinch, lost balls and found others. A German hitch-hiker knocked on Margaret's door and asked her which way was east. Margaret pointed towards home and the young woman took off as the crow flies over the fields.

On Valentine's Day, she went outside and there, at the front door, was a load of ash sticks. She knew an ash fire would banish the Devil. She got in the car and took off down the road to Ennistymon. She met but could not avoid another car on the narrow road and they both lost their side mirrors, stopped, shrugged and went on again. When she got to the town the mad man on the bridge signalled her to stop: 'Seven cabbages for a pound! Ten bananas twice the price.'

People were buying and selling red roses. Margaret bought an axe and spent the morning splitting the ash and made an almighty fire. Stack had left the sticks during the night. He'd made a phone call while he was drunk and gone up to Limerick and traded three lorry-loads of turf for the load of sticks. Margaret sat at the fire with her feet in the basin, sweating. She drank the sherry she'd bought for a trifle she never made and thought about her son. He would be nine years old, if he was alive. She'd heard the banshee the evening before he died but believed it was nothing only a stray cat. The child was fast asleep in the cot that night. He was such a quiet sleeper, it made her nervous. Sometimes she put her hand over his mouth to make sure he was still breathing. She had placed her hand over his mouth several times that night and the next morning he was cold, the tinge of blue on his lips. She stopped the clock and ran up the wood with the child in her arms and thought about hanging herself. She stayed there all night then went home to face it all.

'Cot death,' the doctor said. 'It happens.'

She would never forgive his words. In any case, she wasn't the type to forgive; forgiving might mean forgetting and she preferred to hold on to her bitterness, and her memory. But she always blamed herself. Shortly after his birth a fisherman from Rosslare heard she had the baby's caul.

'I'll give you me last penny for that caul,' he'd said. 'Me father and the one brother I had on this earth drowned. If you let me buy that caul, I'll be safe at sea.'

'I wouldn't sell it for love or money,' Margaret said.

'Well, money is all I can offer,' he'd said, and went away. She felt sorry but could not bear to part with the caul. And then the child died and she threw the caul on the fire. What upset her most was the little things he would never do. To think that he'd never taken a step or set eyes on his father. She had taken for granted a future of homework on the kitchen table, exercise books marked with gold and silver stars, a mucky hurl, measuring his shoulders for a Communion blazer. And then that future was blotted out, gone like something that falls from sight without sound.

February turned into a March of many weathers. Margaret's superstition deepened. When she stopped in the pub in Doolin for a bowl of soup and saw a cat sitting with her back to the fire she ran out and ordered more coal for she knew the weather would get worse. When the hills looked closer she did the same. The sea looked black when it was about to rain. One morning she woke and saw a crow on top of the wardrobe. She drove to the chapel and lit a candle for the soul of her child. An old woman was kneeling, fast asleep, outside the confession box. Margaret went up to the altar where the father of her child had said Mass. It was the first time she had gone into the chapel. She imagined him standing there giving sermons, placing the Eucharist on the parishioners' tongues while her belly got bigger with his child. She lit a candle at the feet of St Anthony, went up to the front pew and stared at the ambo. She did not intend to pray but when she looked up her knees were sore, the woman was gone, and a group of children were practising their First Confession. She watched each boy, looked for the face of a child she'd never see, filled her sherry bottle from the font in the porch and went across the square.

A caravan was parked beside the vegetable stand. *Meet Madame Nowlan, Teller of the Future*, the sign read. Margaret walked down to the hotel and ordered a fried herring. Outside, the crows seemed anxious. When she finished eating she wanted to have a drink but she did not know how many of the drinks tasted. They had kept whiskey at home for sick calves, and poteen to rub on the greyhounds but nobody ever drank anything except at Christmas when they bought twelve bottles of stout so they would have something if visitors came into the house. People seldom came to their house but when they did they drank the calves' whiskey and her father complained that he'd have to go out and buy more. She walked over to the bar and picked the first bottle. Sambuca, it read. She asked for a large. The barman asked her if she wanted it straight and she said yes, thinking this might be some kind of glass. It looked like water and tasted like liquorice and took away the after-taste of the herring. People came in looking at her. She read their minds. There's the woman who lives on her own. There's that Flusk woman Stack's after. She couldn't stand it. She walked back to the caravan and stepped up into the candlelight. Madame Nowlan had fake blonde hair and a face turned brown by a sun-bed. A pot of tea was left out on the table.

'You want your fortune told, Love?' she asked.

'I don't know.'

'Come on. There's no harm.' Willie Nelson was singing a love song on her radio. 'I'll read your leaves.'

Margaret drank the tea and they talked about the weather. It felt strange to talk to another human being. She hadn't held a conversation since Christmas and found it a terrible effort, trying to make sense of another's words, then her own and all that went on in between. Madame Nowlan pulled out a mirror and put on more pink lipstick.

'Do I look all right?'

The lipstick was a foxglove pink. 'You do.'

Then she picked up Margaret's cup and began to read the leaves.

'I see a dead child by a local man. I see property, a house up on a hill, and terrible shame. There's no need for shame. It wasn't your fault the child died. I see the number seven and a man with an *S* in his name. You already know this man. There's grass in your memory. You're mule stubborn. Don't stay in the place you're in. There's a shadow on the back of your house. You must rear your next child in the Irish tongue. Who is this goat in your life? There's jealousy I can't understand.'

'My neighbour has a goat.'

'It's unhealthy, this goat. Well, you've lost and gained your fertility. That much is clear.'

Margaret felt a terrible ache in her back.

'Your people are hard. They turned their backs on you over this religious man. Have another child,' she said. 'The time is now. The next child will make your life worth living. After him, you'll stop looking down over the cliffs. But give the next sea-man his caul. The last man you refused drowned.'

'Do you see anything about my mother?'

'Your mother? Your mother is gone to a better place.'

Margaret thanked her and gave her whatever she had in her pocket. Driving back, the roads looked steeper, the hedges taller. It took her several minutes before she got the key in the lock and when she did she stripped naked and sat in front of the fire. The pain in her back got worse. She laid down on the floor not realizing, until she tasted salt, that she was crying. She began to wail. Stack heard the wailing. Her grief was floating through the stone walls. A few hours later she was out again, naked but for the big sheepskin and her boots, walking the road to the cliffs. Stack followed her but his legs were not as long as hers, and he did not catch up until she stopped at Moher. She was down on her belly in the wet grass looking down over the precipice. Ages passed. It was getting darker. Stack stared at the back of her neck until she turned and faced him.

'I was in love with the priest,' she said.

'I know.'

'I lost his child. Look.' She opened a button and showed him her caesarean scar.

'That must have been awful.'

'It was. It was terrible.'

'I've never been in love. I've nobody only Josephine.'

'That would break my heart.'

'Your heart's already broken.'

The ocean wasn't angry. Each wave seemed to brake before the cliffs, slowing before the end of its journey and yet the next waves kept on as if they had learned nothing from the ones that went before.

'You must think it strange, me telling you these things.'

'I suppose I do. But I doubt I'll ever understand women. Tell me this: what sort of woman pisses in the grass?'

Margaret laughed. She pushed her head and shoulders further out over the Atlantic and let her laughter fall into the water. She was, unlike Stack, undaunted by the sea. In fact she made the ocean look small and harmless as a pond ducks take to. He watched while her laughter fell like stones, and Stack realized he was more than half afraid of her.

'Come on,' he said. 'It's getting dark.'

They walked home. A few council workers were finishing up for the day, filling pot-holes with gravel and the last of the hot tar.

'God bless the work,' said Margaret.

She was glad to say something ordinary. They had said so much that they were now at a loss for what next to say. From a distance the two houses on the Hill of Dunagore looked like one, with Margaret's smoke whirling around their lighted windows. Stack, not wanting the walk to end, slowed down on the hill but Margaret didn't wait. She walked on, her bare legs mounting the hill and her hair was blowing into her eyes. Her laughter had been more terrifying than her cries. When they reached Dunagore she didn't even bid him good-night but walked into her half of the house and shut the door.

Summer came. The rain eased off, swallows came back, woodbine climbed the ditches and heather bloomed. A stranger knocked on Margaret's door one Tuesday morning, a dark haired man with weight on his shoulders.

'I hear,' he said, 'that you can cure a toothache.'

'Are you in a bad way?'

'I'm demented.' He sat down and covered his face with his hands and started to cry.

Margaret went outside and caught a frog.

'Put her back legs in your mouth without harming her and the pain will go,' she said. 'If you harm her the pain will double.'

He held the frog like an emerald. 'Put her back legs in my mouth?'

'Yes.'

'Well, I'll try anything.'

'How did you find out about me?'

'That Nowlan woman in the caravan told me. She says you're a seventh child, you have the cure.'

He went out with the frog and four days later she got the first letter she ever got in Dunagore.

Dear Miss Flusk,

I don't know myself. No pain since the morning after I saw you and we have the frog beside the rain barrel. Many thanks,

John McPhilips, autioneer

That evening a load of birch was delivered to her door.

'What's all this?' said Margaret.

'I dunno,' said the fellow on the lorry. 'It's from the man with the toothache. That's all I know.'

Then the parish started to come. There were men with boils and women who wanted no more children; women who wanted children, and a child that was born on Christmas Day who saw ghosts and couldn't eat. They had shingles and gout and stones in their throats, bad knees and haunted cowhouses. Margaret placed her hands on these strangers and felt their fears and their fears put her heart crossways. The people left in good faith and their ailments and their apparitions disappeared. She'd wake and find new spuds and rhubarb and pots of jam and bags of apples and sticks outside her back door. Her dreams grew black as the charred doors of Hell. She started to tell God she was sorry, started sleeping late and when she woke neighbouring women would be there frying rashers, boiling eggs. Strange men came and cleaned the moss off her roof, put new hinges on the gate, new putty in the windows which the birds promptly ate. She grew frightened of her own death and passed water all around the house when it grew dark. This gave her great satisfaction. She had once wet herself as a child while making her confession and nothing, except the night of the quicken trees, had ever matched it.

One night, after a rich man asked if she could turn his old friend into a sow, she went in to tell Stack. When they stopped laughing, Stack thought of her slapping Josephine with the leather strap and the strange island men leading her away. The men in his dream outnumbered him. He suddenly knew she'd move away. He couldn't bear the thought of her being gone. He unlaced her boots and rubbed her bare feet. Her feet were bigger than shoeboxes and reminded him of a song.

'You've a fine pair of feet,' he said, 'God bless them.'

She didn't speak. His hands were lukewarm, and strong from the bogs. There were clocks, too many clocks on his walls, and they were all ticking. The strangers were always coming, their palms filled with hatred and compassion and it was all contagious. She thought about the Nowlan woman and what she'd said about the child.

'My eggs are right.'

'Your eggs?'

'Come to bed for an hour.'

When they went into the bedroom Josephine was under the quilt. Margaret laughed. Stack tried to lift her. He unbuttoned himself and then she saw his penis and thought of the lizard in her dream. He hadn't, at first, a notion what to do but nature took over. Josephine did her best to get between them. When Margaret woke, Stack was gone and the goat was staring at her. There was a terrible stink of goat and hair all over the bed. Margaret went back to her own house and ate two tins of red salmon, skin, bones and all. She looked in the mirror. The whites of her eyes were like snow and her skin had turned into the skin of a woman who lives in salt wind.

The next morning she went into Stack's house. He hadn't slept, had walked the bogs half the night with Josephine.

'Do you have a sledge hammer?' she said.

'No,' he said, 'but I've a fair idea what you're thinking.'

'You do?'

'I've been thinking meself.'

'Do you mind?'

'I don't,' he said. 'Isn't it the sensible thing to do. But I should be the one to do it.'

'No,' she said.

She drove to Ennistymon and bought a sledge-hammer. While she drove she wondered what the priest would think. He would look up at her mortal frame, having conceived another illegitimate child, walking around his house. He would still be regretting the day he ever laid a hand on her but it was his own will that made him stretch out his hand. He was ten years older than her and it was him, not her, who had broken his promise to the Lord. She had paid for her side with the death of the child. And that wasn't her fault. Hadn't the gypsy said it wasn't her fault?

When she got to Ennistymon, the mad man on the bridge signalled her to stop.

'There's ostriches on the road! Slow down.'

She was glad there were crazy people in the world. She watched him, wondering if she wasn't mad herself. When she rounded the corner, ostriches were walking down the street. People were standing on the footpaths watching them go past and a young girl not half their height was driving them along with a stick. So being mad was the same as having your wits about you, Margaret thought. Sometimes everybody was right. For most of the time people crazy or sober were stumbling in the dark, reaching with outstretched hands for something they didn't know they wanted. She was pregnant. She knew this the way she knew, after Christmas morning, that it was Stack, not the wind, on her doorstep; it was him who shouted.

Margaret came home, pulled the priest's bed out of the room, took it down the field, and doused it with paraffin. It was slow to burn at first then it blazed and turned into a bed of ash. She went inside and began to knock a hole in the wall between the two houses. Stack stood inside his own house beside the dividing wall and felt afraid. When that wall came down nothing again would ever be the same. He could feel the grief of Margaret Flusk. Her grief was beyond comparison. And her strength; Margaret had the strength of two men. Her legs and arms were the same as in his dream. He heard the plaster loosen, then the stones.

She was there half the day. When she saw light at the other side it reminded her of the time her mother woke her, as a child, on Easter morning so she could see the sun dancing, to witness the resurrection of Christ. She got through the hole in the wall. Stack was singing.

'They say Clare people are musical.'

'They say Wicklow people suck goats' milk from the teat.'

'That's why we're good looking.'

'You're a quare woman.'

'Do you think this child will live?'

'I don't know.'

'Do you know nothing?' she said.

'No.'

'Neither do I.'

'Aren't we blessed.'

Josephine did not like the new arrangement. Stack did not seem to love her any more. He didn't even warm his hands before he milked her and forgot to put Palmolive on her teats. The woman stole her milk, tied her to his bedpost, then told Stack she belonged in the shed.

Stack had never eaten as well. Margaret churned butter, baked bread, made cheese out of Josephine's milk and spent the rest of her days eating chocolate. He couldn't keep the chocolate into her. It was like throwing biscuits to Josephine. He'd go down to the shop and come home with Mars bars and Galaxies and find she'd taken another piece of his mother's furniture down to the haggard and set fire to it. She was always lighting fires, going around with a big belly bumping into things and then running outside to throw up her food. And no matter how much toilet paper he put in the house, she always went outside after dark.

Day and night the whole parish came: every man, woman and child, looking to get rid of ghosts and ringworm. The kettle was always boiling, teapots going and poor Josephine tied up, imprisoned in the shed. Even the priest came, saying he had a bad leg and was there anything his wife could do for him? Even though he well knew they weren't married. Margaret was like a gale going through the house. She could see fingerprints on the furniture, beat him at cards and split a load of sticks while he was thinking about it. She threw out the television, wouldn't let him have holly in the house at Christmas, and watched him when he ate. And at night she kept herself well clear of him, was as bad as the small farmer's daughter who, in fairness, never threw up her dinners.

They say something bad will happen if you don't throw out the feetwater. They say man should not live alone. They say if you see a goat eating dock leaves, it will rain. Every time Josephine ate dock leaves, it rained. But bad luck does not last for ever. Margaret gave birth in the priest's house. There were thirteen women and nine children there that day running around with scissors and boiling water and telling Stack to get out of the way. He sat in his own side of the house with Josephine, listening to the radio. Margaret's screams shook the parish. Stack imagined he heard a slap and the cry of a child for several hours before he heard them and then an old woman's voice which said, 'easy knowing it wasn't her first'. Stack would never understand women. They could smell rain, read doctors' handwriting, hear grass growing.

Margaret christened her son Michael, baptized him with a jugful of Josephine's milk. When a fisherman came over from Inis Mór to buy the caul she would not take a penny for it. She invited him in and treated him like royalty, giving him sherry trifle and custard. Stack went to bed and when he woke Margaret was still in the chair but the fisherman was holding the baby. By that time the two houses were clean as polished wood. The two chimneys that had poured smoke on to the Hill of Dunagore turned into one. Stacks of wood and turf leaned against their gable walls. The opening the woman had torn down was framed in wood and had hinges which were attached to a door which opened, and sometimes closed. Stack looked younger. Somebody saw him in Ennis having a shave, sitting up in the barber's chair with a towel around his shoulders, smiling.

Margaret did her best to give up on superstition. She started to believe nothing she didn't believe could harm her. But however she changed her behaviour, she could do nothing about her nature. In all the years she lived in Dunagore, she never lit her own fire, never failed to pull rushes in February and, hard as she tried, could never throw out ashes on a Monday or go out as far as the clothesline without placing the tongs across the pram. If, on the occasional dark night she thought of the priest, she did not dwell on it. The Lord's work was indeed mysterious. If she hadn't lost the priest's child, she would not have inherited his house. If she hadn't inherited his house, she could not have been washing her feet that night and she might have remembered to throw out the feetwater instead of throwing it like a spell over Stack and eaten his Christmas snake and had his child. As it stood, she had got into that bed beside the goat. And you know what they say about goats: It is said that goats can see the wind. Margaret too could see the wind; could see it shaking those berries like beads of blood beyond the priest's head.

The child was nothing like Stack. For years he waited to see some mark of himself in his own son but none came. It mystified without surprising him. It was as though Margaret had spit the child or laid him. As a mother she was ferocious. Stack saw her bare her teeth at harmless people who stroked the child's hair. And she gave him his own way at every turn, rocking him to sleep until she had him ruined. Stack hardly got a wink of sleep. Margaret didn't seem to need sleep. She'd be up at dawn and up every five minutes to check the child was breathing, then fall back into dreams that made her kick him in her sleep.

Michael never crawled. He got out of his chair one day and walked all the way to the front gate and back. One day Stack went in to milk Josephine and found there wasn't a drop of milk in her teats for the boy had sucked her dry. When the boy got hardy he went around the bogs with Stack, jumping ditches with a pole, drank bog-water and was never sick a day in his life. He'd eat nothing only fish and turnips and sweet things, rode Josephine around the front lawn, bought ducks and pushed them around the narrow roads of Dunagore in his own pram and grew tall as a stake in no time. He could write his name backwards and upside-down. He made up stories, told lies when he was bored and walked around the house in his sleep. Margaret wouldn't let him go to school, said there was nothing the people of that parish could teach him that she couldn't teach better.

Michael was seven before Margaret gave up on the parishioners' ailments and apparitions. She'd had enough of them and knew, if she sent her child to school, that he would suffer. But it was a long time before the people of Clare gave up hope and stopped leaving jam and sticks and herrings for Margaret Flusk and started doing her harm. One morning she got up and found peacock feathers stuffed through the letter box. On another morning all her tyres were punctured.

Stack knew she was going before she went. She let the fire die one night and the following morning Stack walked down to the edge of the strand. He wanted to be there when it happened. He stood at the edge of the strand staring west. Soon a fishing boat full of island men came into Doolin and a currach was lowered into the sea. Then these strangers rowed slowly to shore, their oars cutting neatly into the salt water. When they reached the land they tipped their caps but did not speak. Stack recognized one man as the man who'd taken the caul. When he turned Margaret was there looking him straight in the face then climbing without a word into the currach. The boy cried but Stack knew he would not cry for long. Stack held him in his arms then let him go.

The morning was fine, the sea glassy and calm. Nothing stopped him from getting on board, nothing at all. For a moment the men waited and it seemed that all he had to do to make his future happy was to climb into that wooden boat and be carried away on a tide cut by the strength of other men. But Stack stood in the sand and watched the only woman he had ever loved vanish from sight. It didn't take long. Closer to the shore a pair of oblivious dolphins played. Stack watched them for a long time then climbed back up the hill.

When he got home Josephine had chewed through the rope and was up on the table eating the second half of a rhubarb tart. He was glad of Josephine. He could at least predict her needs. He sat down and looked for a long time at the bare, clean rooms. So Margaret was gone. Hadn't he always known she'd go? Hadn't the dream told him? But he couldn't judge her, not even when she took his son's hand and rowed away with strangers. They were, after all, divided by nothing but a strip of deep salt water which he could easily cross.

Josephine licked the plate clean and stared at Stack. He followed her into their old bedroom, closed the door and shut his eyes. Tomorrow he would go down to Doolin and buy a bag of cement and brick up that wall. He would buy a bottle of whiskey, some fig rolls, and leave the television in to be repaired. He would not be idle. Winter was coming. The turf would keep him busy, and fit. There'd be long winter nights and storms to blot out and remind him of the past. Although he was no longer young his near future was a certainty. But never again would he disregard his dreams and venture up to a woman's house and be placed under the spell of feetwater.

Tom Humphries

Australia Day

Boyle did a little conga through the door, looming behind her with his round shoulders hunched and his full-moon face flushed with seasonal merriment and a couple of early Bushmills. His mitts were fastened to her hips, as if she needed steering.

'Show everyone your coat,' he said.

And she stood there between the tables, wrapped in embarrassment and something which might have been squirrel or might have been sable for all that we knew. The wan Christmas Day sun slanted through the frosted glass high behind her catching little flecks of dust in the air above. I turned away to fiddle with the spirits optics at the back of the bar in case Boyle would see my eyes, alight suddenly like votive candles.

'And none of you political-correctness merchants are to go chucking eggs at my lady,' Boyle said. 'If you could afford the lady you could afford the fur and that's all about it now.'

And he applauded himself loudly and marched right towards me at such a pace that I pushed myself back from the counter as if he and I were the north poles of two magnets.

He was forty-eight then and Boyle's blond hair was a memory that lingered only in the crescent of salty grey hair hung across the back of his head. Shiny skin which in winter was ice-rink white had annexed most of his scalp uncovering as it went a birthmark in the shape of Tasmania. He was tall and broad and carrying a paunch. He dressed and still does, like a man half his age, a mistake which I think gives him a certain raffishness. Me, I am small. All angles and eyes.

Back then it wasn't like he was a regular in here. His pantomime loudness was an unwarranted trespass and on the quiet of a Christmas morning, a catastrophic interruption to the pleasant hour or so of free drinks. I've always handed over the bar to old friends and ailing alcoholics before they ambled away for dinner. There he was though, big and blithe. Furstenburg. And a red wine for herself.

'Sheeds,' he said to me as I tilted his glass beneath the tap, 'this is Maud. But of course you know that already. Anyway Sheeds,' and he paused, 'this is still Maud.'

I said, 'Maud' and bowed my head to her.

She said, 'Peter' and smiled.

'Maud! Peter!' said Boyle suddenly, 'be the hokey but the pair of ye must have been a fine sight doing the promenade on a Sunday morning back in the days when old Sheeds had woo to be flinging. A fine sight. After you Maud! Why thank you Peter!'

No more wondering about that then.

'Well girl,' he said appraising her freshly, 'ya must have been a piece of open commonage back then to have had the like of Sheeds grazing about your pasture. Open commonage. Fenced her off too late Sheeds, didn't I? Came back from Noo Yawk City and fenced her off but just a little too late. You're a big black sheep Sheeds.'

I've learned that he always says it that way, as if he was from Brooklyn Heights and not Judes Cross. Noo. Yawk. City. Again, feeling the need to look preoccupied I tended to a tap but then Boyle leaned over the bar and did the oddest thing. He rubbed my head.

'Sheeds and my Maudy,' he said again, 'you could have been *bean an tí* Maudy! The genial hostess with the mostess!'

'It was all long before you Timmy,' she said, 'long, long, time ago.'

I glanced up and found her staring at me. By reflex I gave her a wink. I wink at customers all day long. Boyle pulled this one out of the air though.

'Darling,' he said, 'Sheeds sends you a big wink. Mind the fence Sheeds. Ah ah now. Mind the fence.'

This is The Boomerang Bar and Select Lounge. My late father named the place for a horse but over the years an antipodean theme has gripped the place. '*G'Day Boomerang. We'll get back to you*,' says the greeting message on the answering machine. The new people who come here for the 'atmosphere' brought an Australian tourist in here one day to record the message on an afternoon of unprecedented shenanigans. For a month afterwards the phone shrilled at least twice an hour with each of them calling up to hear their message. They bought the Aussie, a timid teacher from Perth, pints of Fosters until he was sick on the street outside.

When he tells the story in his staffroom my bar must sound to his colleagues like a vision of hell. The rear saloon has been reclassified as 'Outback' and the same calligrapher's hand has designated the women's toilet as being for 'Sheilas'. The inspiration stopped there and its busier neighbouring facility still retains its three gold on black letters stuck to the door, FIR. They tell me it should say 'Bruces'. I don't care much one way or the other.

There used to be a reading room tranquillity to this bar as men dedicated themselves to alcohol. It was a quiet, solemn, sacred place, a smoky monastery where the devout drinker could sit undisturbed by television or fresh air or wanton chatter. He could sit from morning time till closing time. He could sit for an hour or two after closing time if he moved to the back room and kept his voice down. When it was fashionable and profitable for people around here to drink plenty we had the town's heavyweight drinkers in here, pallid, ruined men who after a gallon or so would pass quietly into the outskirts of inebriation but would keep going in sour, determined, unfussy style. Stout. Whiskey. Water. That's all we needed to offer. There was never a raised voice or an openly expressed demand for prawn cocktail flavoured potato chips. Those men that spoke at all discussed a small range of matters in a solemn, baleful way while those that didn't speak voyaged to and from the room marked FIR lifting just an index finger as they passed. Semaphore. Soft pint to be put on. Will collect same on return voyage.

Then through no fault of mine or theirs we were 'discovered'. The first Nautica sweater burst through the door and swooned before the 'biscuit' coloured walls, the dark hardwoods and the large antique mirror and like the poor Indian spying the *Mayflower* I knew in my heart it was over. He'd be back with Pierre Cardins and Tommy Hilfigers. So it was. The novelty of the place hasn't flagged since. The new types view themselves as co-proprietors and have made free with the décor. They procure trophies which they place above the bar in giddy ceremonies. A boomerang. A kid's koala bear. A road sign warning of the presence of kangaroos. A southern cross flag. A stuffed wallaby. An Australian rugby jersey. A framed and signed picture of Dame Edna Everage. Two of them journeyed to the Olympic Games in Sydney and despite my prayers returned intact bearing a large phallic implement which now hangs suspended on translucent fishing line above my head when I work. My days may be ended by a falling didgeridoo.

Lunchtimes now are for the young office crowd swishing in from the accountants and solicitors and banks whose offices suddenly surrounded us when the town shiftlessly drifted into boom time and found that it needed to stretch its main business street up as far as here. The new housing estates devoured the hinterland and closed in on us from the other side and from behind in a clever pincer movement. We had no chance. About three years ago as reward for decades of steady neglect, for never being smitten by Leatherette or Naugahyde or Formica we suddenly became a landmark of quaintness. My alcoholics frightened by the sound of young hooves, fled. I've come to feel like the last of my species still in captivity.

Not many around here will agree with me, least of all Timmy Boyle, but there's some places that money doesn't suit and if you ask me this town is one of them.

Success has made a travesty of the place. There's flaky paint slapped on the narrow streets like make-up on a decaying trollop and the cars have made the streets narrow like a fat man's arteries and it's gotten so that some of us feel like strangers here.

Gossip and begrudging have come under the writ of prohibition. Judes Cross was put together at a time when gossip was the information superhighway and in those terms we ran a clean operation along these skinny streets. You could have an impure thought on Charles Row at noon and old women would be praying for the redemption of your sooty soul before the Angelus bell stopped ringing above in the square two minutes later. And begrudgery. Nobody ever took two steps up the ladder out of here without being reminded by the gang below that the arse of his trousers was still threadbare.

I couldn't draw you a map of where is where any more. Lots of the good places that I grew up in died when the money came in. Mary Denby's counter no longer has schoolboy elbows leaning on it as hardboiled sweets are fetched from big jars. Hank Moore's bookmaking shop vanished. The Eureka Cinema with its improbably wondrous giant screen and grand balcony is no more. I could keep you here half the afternoon as I recall the names. Last week *The Herald* had startling news straight from the lips of our Timmy Boyle. Judes Cross was about to be 'well and truly put on the map,' quoth he. By one Ronald McDonald no less. Emaciated local citizens would 'no longer have to wait till they get to Dublin to tuck into their favourite burger and fries . . .'

On Friday afternoons now, if you close your eyes you'll hear the big cars from Dublin approaching like herds of buffalo driven across the plains. You'll catch the crunch as the Rovers and the Volvos and, carrying the most pathos, the fleet of all-terrain Jeeps sweep on to gravelled drives. Perfect-skinned people who just need to escape pour into the houses where they've had their ISDN lines and satellite dishes installed. They come to walk and to eat and to buy indigenous gewgaws in shops with names like Touched by your Presents or The Gifthorse.

You can tell their houses from a hundred yards away. Timmy Boyle's neighbours and friends are the O'Reilly-Hamiltons. Their interior walls have been treated to the finest paints from Farrow and Ball and the soft glow of designer lamps and the occasional glimpse of the O'Reilly-Hamiltons ferrying glasses of red wine about as something simple cooks on the hob, speak firmly of their tasteful immersion into country ways. They have ferreted through Dublin antique shops and auction houses for artefacts of designer rusticity. In the driveway a greeting line of clipped yews stand with their feet in stout black tureens rescued from a demised institution of some sort. I have often thought to set up a little business selling designer outhouses, for that authentic old-country look.

James O'Reilly-Hamilton is a prematurely retired doctor, a former general practitioner who abandoned a southside patient list somewhere in Dublin, leaving I imagine, the gout to run rampant through the community. I know this little biographical detail because earlier than usual one Friday evening, the fresh-from-the-city O'Reilly-Hamiltons came in here with Timmy Boyle and Maud, all four needful of drink. It was the second time Maud had set foot in the Boomerang, Christmas Day three years ago having been the first. It was she who peered over the counter to find me writhing on the floor behind the bar clutching my side. Something inside me had spontaneously combusted. I haven't been well for some time but the ferocity of this attack took me by surprise, as if suddenly there was a hot ember burning through my torso. When Maud peered over

I was rolling around, sweating freely and holding my side as if to catch the lump of coal which was about to come through my skin and damage the floor.

Maud was insistent upon calling an ambulance. I longed for the intervention of experts myself but my fear of ever owing a thing to Timmy Boyle overcame me when he pulled his little mobile phone out. I roared it back into his pocket. To my surprise none of them pressed the issue. I assured O'Reilly-Hamilton who had come around the bar and whose hands were all over me now that I was used to being curled foetally on the floor.

'Well. I'm a doctor,' he said, 'and a man shouldn't be used to this.'

I gasped and wriggled and moaned for a further ten minutes which made quite a theatre for the folks. Finally I could sit up with my back to the soft drinks fridge.

'Well then, you poor man,' said O'Reilly-Hamilton finally, 'what are you suffering from?'

Ah. On Saturday afternoons the O'Reilly-Hamiltons and sometimes the Boyles put on their North Face windcheaters, set their security alarms and go to walk the trails in the woods wherein they nod to all the other weekending bipeds and endure good-humoured walker gridlock at the bottom of Claw Hill. They gasp from collective angina attacks halfway up the Claw and at the top Joyce O'Reilly-Hamilton commits a selection of her most profound thoughts to a commonplace book which she carries a little too ostentatiously. While she has her moments of conspicuous contemplation he wonders aloud why they don't pack the whole Dublin thing in and move the whole darn kit and caboodle here.

Then they come back down the hill and argue that they

have in every way been up a mountain. They make evening trough at little restaurants in the town and tell acne-spangled young waitresses exactly what they've been doing all afternoon. They ask if they mightn't have the name of the chef so they can tell him or her that this, this is as good as anything they can have in Dublin. From habit they eat quickly, like pigs with trains to catch. These stuffed Portobello mushrooms would be twice the price in Dublin you know. Twice the price. And all natural.

And of course we poor boobs love it. Without speaking a word about it to each other we have mounted a pageant with which to honour the money, to usher it in and store it up and gaze at it worshipfully. Suddenly we are all obliging parodies of ourselves, kitted out in Magee tweeds and knee-length Barbours and there is a new orthodoxy. Why yes, you know this *is* better than any meal ever eaten in any major city anywhere and why yes, we *do* have the best of both worlds here and how very wise we have all been to opt for the enchanting *quality* of these fabulous lives we live, because it *is* a choice, it *is* a trade-off. It is.

And we have committees to monitor our quaintness levels. There's the usual Tidy Town fascists and the Tops of the Town loons of course. There's the CyberFriendly Group who have a name for being stand-offish. We have both a Small Businesses Association and a Business Houses Group. We live to comply with the wishes of the Tourism Cooperative who overlap in aspiration and personnel with both the The Buildings and Architecture Commission (no less!) and The Local History Society who offer periodic lectures which mark and celebrate the monochrome past from which we have all escaped. We exhibit our literacy by means of, not one, not two, but four Reading Groups one of which now descends on my back lounge for weekly orgies of parsing and interpretation. And of course it is unwise to laugh behind the exquisitely sensitive backs of members of the Poetry Society. Weekly tributaries flowing from 'local poets' are allowed pour into a corner of *The Herald*'s letters' page and one wouldn't want one's old-fashioned views to be the subject of some withering pieces of doggerel. No Sir.

I wondered while clinging to the floor under the academically detached gaze of the Boyles and the O'Reilly-Hamiltons and whoever else was peering over the bar counter at the time how my passing (which seemed imminent) would be marked in *The Herald*. Most prominently, no doubt, by news of an auction to be held freeing my estate of the premises and fittings which have been my life. There would be an eyewitness account of my death from Timmy Boyle. 'Boomerang Man Gone. Not Coming Back Either Says Boyle.'

And there it will be, five paragraphs on how colourful local publican, bachelor, shuffled off his mortal coil while bathed in the heavenly light cast by a fridge full of West Coast Coolers. At the moment of death the shadow of the didgeridoo passed over his face. The event was witnessed, no, attended, no, graced by Jaycees kingpin Tim Boyle (as *The Herald* calls him). Mr Boyle intends to mount an annual pageant to commemorate the event.

The Jaycees! Crowning it all, the gaily coloured golf umbrella sheltering us from the hard rain of ordinariness here in Judes Cross is the Junior Chamber of Commerce or to give them the sexier title which the members prefer, The Jaycees.

Timmy Boyle is the chairman of Judes Cross Jaycees and as such his celebrity is so radiant that mere mortals are advised not to stare at him without benefit of special eyewear. He is the centre of all this renewal, the hub, as he would say himself, of the cartwheel from which all our commercial spokes radiate. As a hub he froths and effervesces with ideas by which we can up our quaintness quotient. Under Timmy Boyle's hubship the town is going after some fugitive market. Going after the Yanks. Going after the Golf Crowd. Going after the Anglers. Going after the Families. Going after the Leisure Set. Going after the Krauts. Elliot Ness was idle by comparison.

We are all expected to play our part. Last spring Boyle sent a man to me whom I know to be not just a professional type but a hardcore golfer, a man whom I'm sure couldn't hold a tune in a bucket. He said he'd come to check that it would be okay to use the back room on Thursdays for sessions. These to be held during summer months, and pitched at unwary visitors.

'This comes from the Jaycees,' he said significantly.

'The Jaycees. Did they keep the Tremeloes out of number one years ago?' I said. 'Whatever happened to them?'

'Hmmm?'

'What sort of a session?' I said.

'You know,' he said, 'a sesh-ooon, as they say in the Irish. Some craic.'

Seshoons are the least part of our endemic craic problem. Our social diary is dotted with weekend festivals and themed weekends and steam-engine rallies and gymkhanas and harvest celebrations. And still there is no peace. We must reinvent ourselves annually.

Last summer the Jaycee stormtroopers conducted a major plebiscite among us locals and 'our frequent visitors' seeking suggestions for a monument 'which might capture the character of our town and become a focal point for tourism'.

A subversive notion coursed through the imaginations of the conscientious objectors and the disaffected drinking crowd and I personally wrote 127 letters helping to ensure a landslide victory for the establishment of a permanent flame at a site which would be the Tomb of the Unknown Hustler.

A chiding editorial followed in *The Herald* but face it, this is an old town with its mouth open, its hand out and drool all down its chin.

Yes the good times have worked us over quite thoroughly. A staunchly hideous church now stands like a huge chunk of Toblerone behind Dwyer's supermarket and the town hall, which a casual visitor might presume to be the realization of the winning design in a competition held among the village idiots of the region, sits like a shoebox at the top of the square. Every building that hasn't got the mandatory stone or wood frontage has been face-lifted with plastic and poor spellings. The letter *C* got run out of town when we weren't looking. Laid off from Klassy Kuts. Let go from Koffee 'n' Kookies. Given its kards from Klothes 4 Kiddies.

Money is eating away at the town like the canker down in my gut. Which reminds me of this year's big production, Timmy Boyle's new wheeze (if that isn't an inappropriate description under the circumstances), which is to make the town smoke free. We are going after the Americans who are apparently repulsed by the phlegm-flecked coughing seshoons we stage for their entertainment in our smoggy little bars. According to *The Herald* we have already garnered considerable favourable publicity 'across the big pond' for our efforts to become the world's first smoke free, alpine fresh, drizzle soaked holiday destination.

Maybe it's just me and whatever has been eating my

insides. When I told O'Reilly-Hamilton that the attacks were familiar to me but not yet diagnosed or even considered by a qualified medic he and Boyle cut up rough about taking me to the hospital. They called Lorraine, asked her to come in an hour early and by fifteen minutes past six O'Reilly-Hamilton was introducing himself at casualty down at the General and Boyle was jackdawing into my ear.

'Foolish man Sheeds,' he said, 'you're a foolish, foolish man. Didn't think you'd be so silly with your health.'

His voice reminded me to make a phone call. I called Lorraine, made sure she threw out the two half-full glasses of lager under the front bar counter. Just in case.

You see for three years now, since that Christmas morning when Maud's porcelain beauty was lit for a moment by the sun, I have had the same little routine. When the last lunchtime people leave it is almost three o'clock and young Lorraine takes her break while I load glasses and dirty plates into their stainless steel washers. Then I shine the bar till I can smell nothing but stale beer, old smoke and forest pine. Lorraine has kids and she works a split shift which suits her fine and suits me too. From eleven to three she's here and then she comes back at seven and stays till eleven and although she's young and has some notions there's never been a cross word between us.

Anyway that's how we work it. Lorraine goes away to her other life in the afternoon and when I have the counter polished and all the barrels checked I get to cleaning out the black-plastic slops trays from under the cold steel taps that line the bar like centurions with their liveried shields. We have four taps for stout and the slops from these I pour into the sink. It's the flat amber slops from the lager taps that I'm interested in. I pour these into a glass and rinse each tray as

I go. When I'm done I usually have a pint glass full of pellucid lager slops. Some Harp, some Furstenburg, some Carlsberg and some Fosters. If I feel like it I'll toss the Smithwicks Ale in there too. This I carry through the back lounge and out the back door to the small ledge at the back of the boiler house. Even in winter when my feet crunch the frost on the ground as I cross the yard I know it will be warm as a glasshouse in there. Then I come back in and have my cup of tea and a wrapped chocolate biscuit which I take from the small selection we keep behind the bar.

At half past four I go back to the boiler house again and I remove the slops which I left in there the previous day. When I open the door and the light falls on the surface it will be filled with little dead flies and other minute debris. It looks like the white water around the *Titanic* thirty seconds after she went down. We keep a clean house here but with the warmth and the sweetness back in the boiler house I'm as good as guaranteed that the surface of yesterday's lager slops will be a beery mass grave, filled with anything between fifty and one hundred of these tiny black flies. I'm never disappointed. If only everything in life were so reliable.

It takes me less than a minute to separate the little flies from their last resting place. It's interesting work. I take a Kleenex tissue and trawl it slowly across the surface of the stale beer a few times and that takes care of most of them, they come out like sheeny oil on a dipstick. The remainder I fish out with the blade of my penknife. Then I hold my right hand above the glass and squeeze the tissue between my thumb and forefinger so no droplets of nourishment will be wasted. Finally I take the glass and pour its contents into two separate and gleaming pint glasses which I have brought out with me. When each is about one third full I bear them back to the front bar and stick them under the counter. That's all.

At thirty-five minutes past five every day my friend Mr Timmy Boyle will come through the door looking like a German holiday-maker who thinks this is the most authentic little drinking place he has ever seen. He will swiftly consume two pints before heading for his tea and his evening of business. I wait for the first swishing sight of him and then I reach for one of my slops glasses. This I stick under the Furstenburg tap. By the time Boyle has his belly against the bar I have his foaming pint of lager in front of him.

'All yours,' I say.

'Smart man Sheeds,' he says, 'I think we'll keep you.'

Every evening the same. Sometimes he adds that he's thirsty for Fursty. Who cares? But I smile at him and watch him wander to his table, a large galoot in a Louis Copeland three piece just about to guzzle my *soup du jour.*

What did I hope for. Dysentery? Weil's Disease? Gutrot? Beriberi? Tetter? I don't know. I entertained all sorts of ideas. That a passing rat might urinate into the brew, that an exotic tsetsie fly might stray into the boiler house thirsty for stale lager, that the accretion of all that insect essence might result in the Jaycee kingpin metamorphosing into a Kafkaesque fly. Mostly I just enjoyed watching Timmy Boyle drink up his couple of pints before hitting the road. Mostly I enjoyed knowing what he didn't know.

What is there to hope for anyway?

'I don't usually do this stuff on the first date,' I said to the nurse.

'Well I'll be gentle,' she said, 'and maybe you'll get to like it.'

And she slathered my white little skillet-gut with jelly and ran the ultrasound over it, eyes never leaving the monochrome flickering of the monitor.

'Anything?' I said as she handed me a wodge of green tissue to wipe my gut with.

'What were you hoping for?' she said.

'Nothing, I suppose. Anything.'

'Your doctor will be told,' she said.

Boyle's big head inserted itself between the curtains.

'Long more?'

I shrugged.

'Not long Mr Boyle,' she said brightly as if Boyle had come to offer Michelin Stars. 'Just the last test. We have to examine Peter's back passage for obstruction. Just in case.'

And she patted my shoulders as if I were a simpleton brought in by Boyle as a corporal act of mercy. He withdrew his head. 'Call a vet, Jim,' I heard him say as he walked away across the casualty floor, back to his chum.

'Thanks for that,' I said but she was already absently fiddling with fresh rubber gloves.

That was two weeks since. All afternoon now I've felt the pressure here in my breast pocket, the perfect pregnant weight of the box caulked in cellophane, ready to deliver that perfect fresh tobacco smell. Twenty Major. There's another world waiting in every unwrapped box of twenty. Who knew this could be so much fun? Why has the government been keeping this from me? No denying it, the angular heft of a full box of smokes in your palm or in your breast pocket is worth its weight in anticipation. Twenty Major, the indispensable paraphernalia of modern sin.

Boyle will be arriving soon. *The Herald* is here and

County Sound Radio have set up a little desk in the Outback. There is a rumour running through the Jaycees that national television have instructed a crew to produce a curiosity piece for their country bumpkins news round-up. The crew hasn't materialized but O'Reilly-Hamilton is here, solicitous after my health, wondering if I haven't had my results yet. Not yet, I lie. O'Reilly-Hamilton is here to dress up the gimmick and will be making a speech on the public health aspects of Judes Cross No Smoking Year which begins officially today, 26 January. I sort of like O'Reilly-Hamilton and wish he wasn't here for this.

Boyle's arrival is a little coup. A camera crew reverses in the door in front of him, illuminating him with lights, holding a sound boom like a small didgeridoo over his head. His pallor suggests make-up has been applied. He is superb. Affecting not to notice the hubbub he strides straight towards me, alive with that incurable robust energy of his. I slap his regular brew up on the counter and as the camera flicks from Boyle's face to mine we go through the ritual of our usual little exchange. Then I pat my pocket absent-mindedly and fish out my little surprise. I have Boyle's interest as I set about opening my cigarettes, reluctantly disturbing their enclosed perfection by scraping my thumbnail under the cellophane seal. My delinquency is an infant thing however and despite myself I fold the cellophane and slip it into my breast pocket. Then I lift the gold foil which I roll into a ball and self-consciously drop kick into the space behind the bar. I can tidy it later. Everything is quiet.

I can tell by the faces that they think this is part of the show, that Boyle and myself have cooked up a little morality play which we are now staging for the benefit of a national audience. But, you know, I have been genuinely waylaid by a sudden inexplicable longing to huddle over my own cupped hands as a match flares, to take that first drag and then as my lungs fill up glance up slowly like a top safe-cracker who hears a sound on the stairs. I have been thinking about cigarettes for two weeks now. For the best part of a lifetime I have missed out on the grand informality of giving that takes place between smokers, one smoke offered in sodality to another sinner. Maybe that's the last generosity, I think, yellow-clawed outlaws reaching towards each other with fags and lights, the communion of lit matches and shared haze. So with thumb and forefinger I begin tweezing cigarettes out of my pack and dispatching them out over the counter, hurling them end over end like a crazed knifethrower picking on various customers.

'Here.'

'Here.'

'Here.'

'Go on, the one won't kill ya.'

The great tobacco rebellion is in full swing.

I stab my own cigarette into my mouth and redden it with this new Zippo I bought. The Zippo is a louche rat-pack touch which I regret. The smell of sulphur and the sound of a scratched match are necessary to the moment. Still, a rookie error. I should have Swan Vestas. There was a design classic. Still.

I suck the cigarette and stand gazing at the hand which holds it while the sour smoke burns the roof of my mouth. The weedy photographer from *The Herald* is on his feet now. Boyle is still standing in front of me, eyes narrow. Five seconds. One, two, three, four, five and now it's like I'm whistling with the volume turned down. A stream of grey smoke leaves my lips and disperses only when it makes contact with Boyle's nose. I sense people being drawn towards the bar now, a gathering sensation of horror.

'When did you start with the fags Sheeds?' Boyle asks.

'While back,' I say. 'Missed them you know.'

He looks down at the Major, which I am holding now between thumb and index finger.

'Major,' he says.

'Mmmm, Major,' I say.

'For that small-town taste,' he says. 'Major. Them boys could do you some harm you know Sheeds. I thought you'd be too damn PC for smoking anyway.'

His bonnet has been swarming with this PC for a long time now. Hah. I take another drag, blow the smoke out more quickly this time.

'Well, Timmy, I suppose you don't know everything that you think you know. Life's short. Smoke fast, leave a yellow corpse. That's the new motto in here.'

'Well, you'll be all right there Sheeds, don't worry your good heart,' he says.

'You reckon Timmy?'

'Well, Sheeds, you're not inhaling,' he says. 'Sure you're not?'

This is true. And if it weren't the sudden laughter kills any chance of denial.

'Fuck you big man,' I say.

There is perfect silence and suddenly I feel foolish and adolescent. Boyle's face painted with the solemnity of a man about to hand over a telegram of terse bad news. The camera guy has his free hand in the air hushing the crowd.

'I'm surprised to hear you say that,' Boyle says canting the words with sudden ferocity into the vaulted ceiling of the Boomerang. He steps to one side and turns his back to me momentarily to make sure his audience is with him, 'very surprised. You know I'm as surprised as poor Maud must have been when you popped the question to her and then dropped your hand on her titty thirty years ago.'

There is silence so pure that my heart quiets itself. Stops.

'What's wrong Marlboro Man? You could toast one of your lousy sandwiches on your cheeks right now.'

Stops.

I'm not with him. I'm gone. I am a young man whose shameful drink-bitten father owns a tatty bar outside the town but I have sideburns which suit me and a happy future if I learn to stick with things. I'm a young man with his new girl, walking the hassocked field on the far shoulder of Claw Hill and I'm blown about by impulses and ideas, owned by a springloaded tongue that makes plans quicker than any brain can weigh them. And I have a girl here, who I can make laugh, a perfect russet-haired girl who I have dreamed of for half a decade. We have plans. We are going to go to New York City next summer. I'll smoke weed and drink fecklessly and we'll work two jobs apiece. I am in love, that is what I am. First. Last. Everything. I am young and in love and could fly off this hill without wings. Suddenly I am asking if we shouldn't be more than what we are here today, if we should-n't fly off this hill together, if there isn't a lovely perfection to our symmetry, a diamond flawlessness that demands that we preserve it always and, surprised, she moves in to kiss me. We shuffle our hands in a momentary blur of movement her right reaching with girlish tenderness for my cheek, her thumb kneading the flesh beneath my eye while my right hand confusingly comes to rest on the plump, jumpered drumlin of her left breast, turning it experimentally at first then, anxiously, ardently as if it were a giant radio dial on a ship and I were Mayday, Mayday, Mayday. And suddenly I am just that, Mayday, and all that stands in front of me is a pair of brown and startled eyes filling up for me to drown in.

Stops.

The channel switches and now my side is hurting me, burning and the silence hangs like the cigarette smoke. I'm due to speak a line. The show demands it.

'You know Tim,' I say, 'there's a brown envelope sitting in the back kitchen these two days now and I hope the news it has for me is nothing but bad. That's real life Timmy.'

'It's a gallstone, you fool,' says Peter O'Reilly-Hamilton in his low, crisp voice.

I drop my Major into Boyle's Furstenburg, where it dies with a snake's hiss.

Joseph O'Neill

Ponchos

When William Mason made a daily habit of taking a seat at the far end of the dark, tunnel-like interior of the Starlight Restaurant, he was thankful that his parents had called him William because William abbreviated to *Bill*, and *Bill*, he believed, was a name to stand a fellow in good stead at the Starlight, a 24-hour diner that served men with no-shit, no-flies-on-him names such as Frank and Steve and Champ. But for all the Starlight regulars cared, William discovered, he may as well have been called Mavis. None spoke to him, not even after nine months of spending five mornings a week on one of the half-dozen revolving counter-stools bolted fast to the ground like every other stick of Starlight furniture, as if (William reflected as he entered the establishment one January day) the diner were afloat at sea and not grounded in Manhattan, New York. No sooner had William conceived this notion than he was dissatisfied with it; and so, as he joined the other solo breakfasters at the counter, he devised a more elaborate nautical conception of the Starlight: as a dockside inn frequented by men waiting for their ships to come in, waiting even in the knowledge that for every tattered skiff of fulfilment that entered the haven there set forth a fleet laden with new if-onlys, why-oh-whys and where-is-she-nows.

Ruminations of this kind were typical of William Mason, a man so compulsively prone to extravaganzas of figurative self-absorption that his wife had only the day before accused him of 'living in a fucking private joke landscape'.

'Joke landscape?' William said, frowning as he thought about the conceit.

It was at this moment that Elisa Ramirez threw in the direction of her husband's head the 'Happy Days at the Century of Progress, Chicago' cocktail shaker.

The cocktail shaker was a multiply commemorative article. Manufactured as a souvenir of the 1934 Chicago Exhibition, it now functioned as a relic of Elisa's graduate student days at Columbia University, when, applying Prownian close-reading techniques, she had unpacked the shaker's socio-historical content with the same ferocity and magical skill with which (in William's trope) she conjured rabbits of relational transgressions from the top hat of her husband's ostensibly blameless conduct. Elisa's contention (she'd explained all those years ago to William, a fellow-student on the point of abandoning a Ph.D. thesis entitled *Prufrock, Pale Ramon, and the Predicaments of Presumption*) was that the shaker embodied a false promise of leisure and escape. How could the carefree realm of the aperitif, with its happy hour and drinks parasols, its egg whites and angostura and maraschino cherries and Curaçao, its mud in your eye and its bottoms up – how, in the Great Depression, could it represent anything other than a dream-world for the vast majority of Americans? Elisa suggested that this Cloudcuckoolandishness was captured by the movie-within-the-movie in Woody Allen's *The Purple Rose of Cairo*, in which the character played by the character played by Jeff Daniels – an archaeologist on the brink of a 'madcap Manhattan weekend' – repeatedly proclaims his intention to consume a cocktail which, in the end, he never gets around to drinking. Elisa invited William to her place in West Harlem to watch the movie and see for himself what she was driving at. The young academics took in the bittersweet comedy while mixing eye-openers. Following recipes engraved on the shaker, they sampled an Old-Fashioned, a Manhattan, an Alexander, a Gin Rickey, a Tom Collins, a Bronx, a Dry Martini, a Palm Beach, a Clover Club and, finally and aptly, a Between The Sheets. This intoxicating carnal ritual – noggin and snoggin', as William was pleased to put it – survived, with diminishing vitality, for two years. By the time five years (two matrimonial) had passed, the cocktail shaker no longer saw active service. Propped against a pile of cookbooks and gathering a coat of congealed dust and cooking fumes and cat's hair, it functioned purely (at least in William's mind) as a totem expressive of the couple's enduring commitment, through cooped-up, dust-bombed Brooklyn years, to each other and the idea of the Great Love.

Therefore, even as he ducked the whizzing missile, William was alive to the profane dimensions of what was happening; and his first thought was to check on the damage suffered by the cocktail shaker, which had bounced off a wall with a hollow crash.

'Fuck the shaker!' Elisa shouted clairvoyantly. 'This is not about a fucking shaker!'

William straightened with a submissive air. She was right, of course. But he could not refrain from noting that the vessel had collected a dent at the spot bearing the recipe for a Dubonnet (½ gin, ½ Dubonnet, 1 orange bitters), or from allowing the incident to take shape in his mind as roughly representational of the problem confronting the couple. The emptiness of the hurled object, the unhappiness of its trajectory, the fruitlessness of its terminus: he could not help sensing that these elements were invested with the properties of an analogy for the couple's unsuccessful attempts, these last two years, to produce a child.

Then William saw that Elisa was weeping, and, detecting an unspoken invitation, he approached his wife and held her and waited for the storm to pass.

For this was how William apprehended episodes of this kind: as akin to the rains that fell daily on an otherwise sunny and pleasant place. The fertility treatments, he decided, had given Elisa a distinctly tropical temperament – which was funny, since he himself was (albeit in a non-climatic sense) tropistic. '*Tristes tropiques*,' he whispered into Elisa's hair.

But the following morning, even as he took pleasure from the recollection of this phrase, he could not help feeling that his grasp of the situation, however figurally attractive, was shaky; and on his way into the city he was pained afresh by the grievous resignation with which Elisa, after she'd untangled him from her, had turned to prepare dinner (soup with scallops). Precisely how, William wondered as he emerged from the subway and leaped over a freezing kerbside pool, should he take her remark about his private joke landscape? After all, William ventured to himself, the alternative was to dwell upon the bare heath of literalism; the alternative was Howl, Howl, Howl. Could she not see this?

Had she no idea of how badly he needed distraction from life's glaring futility?

As often happened when his thoughts touched on this last issue, there entered William's mind the image of the fish roundabout of the San Francisco municipal aquarium, which he'd once visited with Elisa's sister and her kids. The roundabout consisted of an elevated circular tank of seawater in which pelagic creatures from San Francisco Bay sped in an anticlockwise direction. William had stood silently in the darkness of the viewing area as large and small swimmers orbited him – flying, was his impression – in celestial-blue water. Gangs of Pacific mackerel and yellowtail jack came around again and again and again. A solitary sting ray flapped clumsily into the one-knot headcurrent, looking harassed and out of place. No sharks, William noted. He contemplated the rush of fish from a metaphysical perspective. These circuiteers were incapable of seeing, let alone comprehending, the non-aquatic dimension in which he stood. Ignorant of the nature and limits of their element, cluelessly and helplessly circumfluent, they travelled hopefully onward, for the entertainment of unimaginable extraneous beings, without the slightest prospect of progress of illumination or salvation. William filled with despair. The fish roundabout, it was clear, was an unimprovable metaphor of the human condition.

This revelation authorized and indeed compelled William to abandon his artistic activities, which is to say, his nocturnal attempts to write poems. As a poet, he was solely animated by mankind's relationship to the spatial and temporal infinities; and for William it followed that, having stumbled on a physical object that constituted the last word on these themes, silence was the only intellectually honest course of action open to him. William toyed briefly with the idea of constructing a fish roundabout of his own and displaying it as an artistic installation, but he lacked the vocational urge and desperation for fame that were necessary to realize this idea. Released from ambitions of high art, William applied himself more contentedly to his work as a copy editor for Blue Funk Books, an imprint whose authors he sometimes characterized, when drunk and exclusively self-amusing, as 'flies feeding on the steaming excreta of Foucault, Barthes, and Lacan'. Blue Funk Books' premises were in a building on West 23rd Street. A hundred yards away, on the west side of Eighth Avenue, was the Starlight Restaurant.

'Menu?' said George, the man behind the counter.

'Toasted muffin, extra jelly, decaf black,' William said heavily.

Every day George asked William the same question and every day William gave the same answer. What, William wondered, would have to happen for George to ask 'Usual?', the question he addressed to other repetitious eaters? William looked down the counter at three members of this class. Two stools away was a commercial artist in his forties, named Johnny, who had painted the near-photographic depiction of Ted Williams that hung in a corner of the Starlight. Beyond Johnny was a septuagenarian in a New York Mets jacket – Donnie – and beyond Donnie another old-timer whom William knew only as the magician. A thin, desperate-looking man – William was reminded of the dying Charles Schulz – the magician always carried a pack of cards in a holster attached to his belt. William had seen him do tricks only once. Afterwards, somebody had asked him how he did it and he'd replied, with noticeable bitterness, 'Hard work and practice.'

William removed a copy of the *New York Times* from his otherwise empty computer bag. As he leafed through the newspaper, he listened in on the conversation between the men at the counter. Donnie and George were mumbling to each other about odds: Donnie was a bookie and George (who thirty-three years ago had abandoned his post as a border guard for the Bulgarian army and defected across the Greek frontier) liked to bet. Johnny, meanwhile, was delivering the angry, pause-filled monologue that invariably accompanied his reading of the *New York Post*, a harangue typically directed at one or more of Hillary Clinton, Bill Clinton, Latrell Sprewell, Alec Baldwin, Sean 'Puffy' Combs/'P. Diddy', Osama bin Laden, Saddam Hussein and Tom Daschle, personages who day after day popped up in the pages of that newspaper like infuriating fairground targets. William did not hold Johnny's tiresome pronouncements against him because Johnny could be entertaining to an eavesdropper, albeit often in a disgustingly frank and self-pitying way. For example, it was Johnny who'd propounded the monkey test: if a woman's enthusiasm for sex was exceeded by her enthusiasm for seeking out a man's pimples, blackheads, overlong mole-hairs, dangerous-looking freckles and pluckable grey hairs – for, in Johnny's words, 'picking at you like a fucking monkey' – then it was over. 'You know what I'm talking about, right?' Johnny said to an interlocutor who was not William. 'She won't give you a blow job, but she'll pinch and squeeze shit out of the back of your neck for hours. Well, that's when I know we've reached the end of the road.' Suppressing a query that had surfaced in his mind – what if one's wife had no recreational interest in either personal grooming or sex? – William instead recalled a test he himself had once devised: the Ibsen challenge, as he'd called it. If a romantically meaningful other could not name a play by Ibsen, or at least display some familiarity with the Ibsen phenomenon, that was that. William knew himself or cared very little about Ibsen, but the unexpectedly fierce dismay he'd once been caused by a redhead's complete ignorance of the literary giant, whose name had randomly come up in conversation, had taught him something important about himself: he could never fully respect a woman who was clueless about the father of modern drama. It therefore behoved all parties, he concluded, to dispose of the issue in the early part of any relationship.

Elisa, of course, had known all about Henrik Ibsen. His birthplace, she was able to inform William (who had casually brought up, ostensibly *apropos* James Joyce, the subject of *When We Dead Awaken*), was Skien, the small Norwegian town whose name was related to the old Norse noun that gave us 'ski'. It was at this moment that William felt within himself an immaterial chute-like movement. He was, he understood, falling in love.

By the time William had finished with the sports section and the toasted muffin, his neighbours had started an animated discussion. They were talking about the sudden appearance on their TV screens of a free pornography channel. Donnie had been the first guy to pick up the rogue broadcast, and he'd tipped off Johnny and the magician about it a few days earlier.

It made William uneasy to hear old men chortling about dirty movies.

Evidently, this also bothered Johnny. He asked, 'What the fuck's the matter with you guys? How old are you, seventy, seventy-five? And you're still beating off to this shit?'

Donnie wiggled his fist with an expression of contentment. This made him and the magician laugh.

'Let me ask you something,' Johnny said. 'You still thinking about women like you used to, say, thirty years ago? They still driving you nuts?'

The magician, a discreet man, raised his eyebrows mysteriously.

Donnie said, 'It don't go away.'

'Oh boy,' Johnny said, 'that's just terrific.' He had a drooping, greying moustache, thinning black hair and a colourless, shadow-stained face that put William in mind of an old shirt. Johnny pushed aside his plate and sat back on his stool in order to run his thumbs along the inside of his waistband and release pressure from his gut. This gesture, William knew, signalled the imminent airing of one of his theories. 'Now what do you think about this,' Johnny said. 'You got women's rights, okay? Women suffer because they're exploited like sex objects. okay, so we're okay with that.' Johnny smiled by way of concession. 'But here's what I want to know: what about men's rights? That's right, men's rights. We're the ones they're bombing with the sex. We're the ones being targeted here. It's all aimed at us. You can't take the fucking subway or take a walk down the street or listen to a song on the radio without having something or somebody titillating you, pushing tits in your face or showing some ass.' Johnny clawed at the air with one hand. 'Scratch, scratch, scratch. Corporations, magazines, TV stations, billboards, newspapers, womankind – they're all in on it, they've all got us simmering. And we're helpless, because we're not in control of our responses. I'm talking millions of years of evolution here. We're programmed like fucking dogs.' By now, Johnny's speech had assumed the fluency of outrage.

'What's happening, of course, is that somebody's making money. Did you ask for porn on your TV? No. But guess what, it's there anyway. Can you not watch it? Of course you can't. You're a man. I don't care if you're the frigging Pope, you were born to jerk off. You know what I'm saying? They're taking our natural instincts and they're twisting them for profit. We're the victims here. The billion-dollar Viagra industry, the billion-dollar porn industry? That's our fucking billion dollars.'

Donnie, winking at the magician, said, 'Help! Save me from my hard-on!'

This annoyed Johnny. He said, 'Would you just listen for once, you goddam felon? Just once?'

Donnie, who did not like to be reminded of his past, took an offended sip of camomile tea. Johnny kept pressing him, 'Can't you just admit that I may have a point? Am I so off-base on this one?'

'You don't fuck around,' Donnie said bluntly. 'You fuck around and you get caught, you know what you got coming to you.'

'This isn't about me and Daleen – although, as a matter of fact, now that you mention it, as a matter of fact she didn't make any allowance for the fact that I'm a man. She gave me no leeway at all. One strike and I was out. This is what I'm talking about. Women don't have the slightest fucking idea of what it's like for men, on a biological level. It's part of the conspiracy of silence, it's all about political correctness: nobody talks about the struggle we go through every fucking day. Nobody gives us any credit for that. That's right,' Johnny said emphatically. 'We should get credit for all the women we don't sleep with.'

The magician and Donnie started laughing. 'Yeah,' Donnie

said, 'I'm just fighting them off. I'm a real hero. I should get the Purple Heart.'

Johnny crumpled his napkin in disgust. 'What's the point in discussing anything with you people. You're just – I'm wasting my fucking breath here.'

It was at this moment that Johnny swung around on his stool and spoke for the first time to William Mason. Johnny said, 'So how about it, bud? Are you with me on this one?'

For a second, William was too surprised to respond. Then he said, 'Yes, I think you've got a point.'

'Oh yeah?' Johnny said.

'I have a friend,' William said deliberately, 'who's an artist – a painter. There isn't anyone with a greater appreciation and understanding of art than my friend.'

Johnny said, 'I hear you, buddy. I'm an artist myself.'

'Anyhow, he once told me something that I've always remembered. In a museum, he said, you could be contemplating the most entrancing painting imaginable – a Vermeer, say, or a Picasso or Van Gogh – but as soon as an attractive woman enters the room, she's the spectacle, and the Vermeer is just a bunch of colour and paper. She doesn't have to be beautiful; she just has to be desirable.'

William sensed from his companions' silence that acquaintance with this insight had not produced in them, as it had in him, a small aesthetic revolution. 'The simple fact,' he explained, 'is that no work of art can compete with the feelings triggered by the mere sight of a woman.'

Johnny said, a little abruptly, 'So you're saying I'm right. You're saying that men are programmed to suffer.'

'Well, yes, I guess so,' William said.

And it was true, William admitted to himself, that in springtime he was mugged by spasms of longing caused by the appearance of certain women walking down the street. But William could in all honesty commend himself for the fact that, post-Elisa, such involuntary physiological reactions had never turned into temptation. This achievement, William believed, rested on the notion of the Great Love with which he had, almost from the beginning, consciously – and, so far as he was aware, reciprocally – mythified his relationship with Elisa Ramirez. The myth, formalized in due course by matrimonial vows, meant that any threat or adversity – even death, William could sometimes bring himself to think – could be withstood by a wilfully romantic adjustment of perception. Like Islam or Marxism, the Great Love was an all-embracing narrative that, as William pictured it, rooted fast commitment's tree against the wind and rain of erosive time and the odd lightning bolt of third-party allure. On this last score, William was helped by two items of empirical self-knowledge: first, that he would take little pleasure in an isolated or treacherous sexual encounter; second, that nothing liberated and excited him more 'in bed' – William had always found the metonym hilarious – than the profound familiarity and consent that, all being well, a faithful marriage stimulated. But, he was forced to acknowledge, not all was well on this score. For nearly two years, his and Elisa's lovemaking had been marred by reproductive effort. The problem was not simply the interference of thermometers, ovulation charts, copulation schedules, ejaculatory precautions; the problem, according to William, was the calamitous purposiveness of the sexual act. To be any good, sex, like art, had first and foremost to be a self-pleasuring exploration.

But when he'd revealed this satisfying formalist correspondence to Elisa – she was in the bathroom, getting ready to head off to Hunter College, where she worked as a history professor – she'd snapped 'What?' with a pure revulsion that William had never imagined possible. The small moment injured and bewildered him. For weeks he compulsively visualized Elisa's loveless expression and stung himself with the contempt in her voice. He saw himself as she had at that moment: tedious, pedantic – 'You mean finicky,' was the normal Masonic response to people who accused him of being this – and physically unwholesome. William, a tall, blond man with baggy jowls, a whitening moustache-slash-goatee and baggy eyes – Gucci eyes, Elisa had once joked – had always assumed that, absent clear evidence to the contrary, he was repellent to women. Now, for the first time, he applied this assumption in relation to Elisa; and his self-loathing became so acute that one weekend, when Elisa was back in San Francisco visiting her parents, he lay down on a mirror and manoeuvred his face and jowls into positions that yielded grotesque reflections which, William painfully noted, resembled the flattened and squashed visages of Francis Bacon's subjects. William's torment had other symptoms. In Elisa's company he found himself very tired and, to her obvious irritation, oddly hard of hearing. He also found himself almost incapable of sexual arousal. Hampered by a strong sense that his wife was, in substance, submitting to fleshly trespass, her naked body – that of a small, boyish, dark-haired woman – was emptied of erotic significance; and it was only with a great deal of eye-shutting and gritty concentration that he was able to fulfil his monthly coital responsibilities.

After about three months, William began to regain his old sense of perspective. He saw that he'd been irrational, depressed and, he was pretty sure, the victim of some random chemical glitch. He did not speak to Elisa about what he'd been through; and she, who during his gloom had also been subdued and preoccupied, did not throw him any further looks of detestation.

It was around this time – this was back in the fall – that the couple decided to consult a world-famous fertility specialist named Dr Nico Hildenberg, whose services happened to be covered by Elisa's insurance policy. Dr Hildenberg, a languid, well-groomed man in his early forties, ran a clinic on the Upper East Side and, William felt, bore an inappropriate resemblance to the golfer David Duval. Hildenberg processed hundreds of patients at a time in furtherance of a vast research project, and immediately after examining Elisa he ordered a regime of tests and treatments that exposed her to gynaecological peering and scraping, to never-ending 'blood work', and – just to think of it made William angry and loving – to injecting herself, every day of the first fortnight of each menstrual cycle, with figure-bloating and mood-disturbing hormones.

William's role, meanwhile, was to produce semen samples from time to time. One such appointment, William was reminded by Johnny's speech about the sexual victimization of men, was scheduled for later that week. The prospect made William feel dreadful.

William dreaded, first of all, walking into the building, which announced itself, in huge lettering posted on its front elevation, as THE SAMUEL P. SCHLOSSBERG CLINIC FOR REPRODUCTIVE DIFFICULTY. This mode of public humiliation, William had noticed, seemed to be common in Yorkville, where medical facilities adopted designations that, in trumpeting their benefactors' generosity, were disastrously specific and loud about their patients'

CONDITIONS OF THE SKIN or COMMUNICABLE DISEASES or need for SURGICAL ENHANCEMENT. William dreaded the waiting room full of barren couples, too, but most of all he dreaded the semen production area, where a sadness of masturbators – William's collective noun – waited in the corridor for the signal to proceed, as breezily as possible, to the masturbation room. The room contained a washbasin, handwipes, soap, lubricant, a pile of tattered porn magazines, a video-TV set, and a leather-covered chair that seemed to have been removed from the club class section of an aeroplane. On entering for the first time, William was confused by the expectations suggested by these facilities. (Was the chair *de rigueur*? Should he watch the videos? What was the significance of the lubricant?) He was also troubled by the perennial question of time: if he emerged from the room after a minute or two, he would be marked down as a premature ejaculator and erotic pubescent; if he lingered much longer, he would be suspected of enjoying himself. Setting aside these uncertainties, William dropped his trousers and set about his task, aided not by the available pornography but by imagining Elisa in historic or fantastical situations of ardour. (That was the most exciting fantasy: the fantasy of himself as an object of desire.) Then, just as he reached the point of ejaculation, he realized that he was unsure about exactly what to do with the receptacle he was holding; and, fumbling urgently, he watched in horror as almost all of his semen – three days' worth, as per the 'abstinence instructions' – spat into the disastrously downward-tilting glass tube and then flowed out, on to his leg. For a minute or so, William slumped on the leather chair in a state of anguish. A whole month of injections and drugs and anxious expectations had been put to waste by his blunder. Opening his eyes, he glanced again at the tube and its negligible fluid contents. 'Oh, William,' he said.

Baking with self-reproach, William fastened his belt and placed the near-useless sample into a compartment in the wall. Overcoming an impulse to emigrate forthwith to a distant island – Micronesian scenes actually flashed through his mind – he wretchedly presented himself to a female laboratory worker; and it was decided, after a short, shameful discussion, that William would try to produce a second sample in an hour and a half or so, after he'd 'relaxed'.

William collected Elisa from the waiting room and took her to a restaurant across the street from the clinic to eat breakfast and tell her the bad news.

Elisa, to his amazement, laughed. 'Oh, Will, you're so clumsy. I should have guessed this would happen.' Then she said, 'Well, it's not the end of the world. You'll go back in there and do it again, this time properly, and everything will be just fine.'

William said, 'The quality won't be the same.' He added, 'I'm not sure that it's going to be that easy. I don't know if I can make it happen.'

'Oh, sure you can,' Elisa said. She reached over, and William felt the small, warm shock of her grip on his hand. He shook his head glumly. 'It's no fun in there, Elisa. I'm not sure I can face it again.'

Elisa got up from her seat across the booth and sat down next to her husband. 'Why don't I go in there with you?' she whispered. 'Let me help you.'

William said, 'No way. Absolutely not. No.'

'Why not?' Elisa said. As she stroked his inner thigh, William was reminded of her astonishing libidinousness during their first months together. It was almost incredible to him, now, that one night in SoHo she'd fallen to her knees on the wet cobbles and he'd been forced, out of embarrassment and fear of arrest, to restrain her from undoing his zipper. 'I'm sure it happens a lot,' Elisa said as she tugged at his ear-lobe with her teeth. 'Nobody's going to mind. Besides, I'd like to be there. It'll make it special.'

He saw that she was offering to bring into the world a romantically sustaining event. He said, 'No. I can't do that. Stop. Stop that, Elisa.'

Not noticing her husband's anger, she persisted in kneading his thigh with a stout, freckled hand. 'I said stop,' he hissed. He grabbed her wrist and returned her arm to her side.

'OK, fine,' Elisa said. She smiled courageously, and William decided not to say what was on his mind – that this show of passion was too late, and wrong, and certainly fraudulent, that she had at some forgotten moment forfeited some right he couldn't immediately identify. 'I'll take care of it on my own,' he said, picking up the menu. 'Don't worry about it.'

An hour or so later, William returned to the clinic and, embroiled in a video of lesbian sex and with no thought of Elisa, successfully produced a sample.

William noticed that the conversation at the Starlight counter had picked up again. Now Johnny was telling a story of something he'd seen in a restaurant in New Haven, Connecticut, which was Johnny's home town. 'So this guy came crashing into the restaurant with blood all over him. He just came barging in through the door and started falling against the chairs and tables. Everybody started laughing. They thought it was a stunt, a student joke. They thought he was clowning around with ketchup. His so-called blood was dripping everywhere. It was falling on my shoes, in my beer, in my girlfriend's coffee. Then he fell to the ground, and I noticed that he had this gash in his neck, a long, thin-lipped kind of gash, like a mouth.' Johnny shook his head. 'It was just awful. Meanwhile, get this: everybody kept on laughing. This poor son of a bitch was lying there in a pool of blood – you ever seen a pool of human blood? – this poor bastard was fighting for his life, and all he could hear was fucking laughter.'

'What happened to him?' George asked.

'I assume he died, George,' Johnny said solemnly.

'You assume?' George said.

'Well, I didn't want to get mixed up in it,' Johnny said. 'I took off pretty much there and then.'

There was a short silence, and then the magician spoke up. 'That's strange,' he said. 'That reminds me of something that happened to me nearly fifty years ago now. It was almost exactly the same thing. At that time I lived in Newark. The only reason I'd go into the city was to go on a date. In fact, I always took my dates to the city, to show them the sights, maybe catch a movie. New York was kind of a confusing place for me, because I couldn't remember which landmark I'd shown to which girl.' The magician chuckled. 'Anyhow, one day I take this girl to a fancy place near Times Square. This was a girl called Ruby Silverman. We'd been seeing each other for a while, and as a matter of fact I took her to this restaurant to break up with her.'

'You're going to finish with her in a restaurant?' Johnny said.

'Well, maybe not in the restaurant, but certainly on that date,' the magician said. 'I figure I'm going to do it with class, because I like this girl a lot and she deserves to be treated right. So we're eating and she says to me suddenly, Stanley, are you going to marry me? And I say, I can't say yes, so you'll have to take that as a no.'

'Pretty smooth,' Donnie said.

'Ruby Silverman,' the magician said. 'Jesus, I sometimes wonder what became of her.'

Johnny said, 'So what happened?'

'Well, sitting next to us is a black man who's having dinner with his two grown-up daughters. He's a kind of a heavy-set guy in his fifties. Fat. He's wearing a suit – this meal is obviously some kind of occasion – and he has a napkin around his neck so that the spaghetti sauce won't stain his shirt. Can you believe I remember that napkin? Right at that moment, right as I'm telling Ruby that it's not going to work out, I hear this shuffling noise. I look around and I see he's having a heart attack. His face is swollen and he's kind of tilted over the table, very still, frozen. But his daughters are just eating their food. They're just eating as if nothing has happened. They seem annoyed that their father is having a heart attack. They wish he'd stop having a heart attack and stop embarrassing them.'

How alone we are! William thought with anguish. He remembered how Elisa and he had gone their separate ways after that meal across the street from the clinic – he back to the masturbation facility, she to work. She had walked away down the street with her back turned to him. Rain fell and she held aloft a dark umbrella. She wore her tasselled leather poncho, and all that occurred to William, as he sat in the Starlight, was that she had been cloaked in a kind of pluvial poncho, too, what with the umbrella canopy and the tassels of rain hanging from the tips of the umbrella spokes.

JOHN MACKENNA

Maps

And thou shalt go to thy fathers in peace.
Genesis 15:15

i

I had two fathers and this is some part of his story.

ii

There's a particular kind of window you find in institutions. For example, there's a tall, elegant window that appears in late nineteenth-century hospitals, all kinds of hospitals, maternity, general, psychiatric. Even the ones my father would have called County Homes. More often than not, the frames of these windows are painted a distinctive shade that hasn't altered in eighty years.

This window is one of those, it has that specific shape and height and depth of sill. It has the same peeling shade of paint, a faded far-off white, smoked to yellow. There's a man sitting in a chair, staring through the old glass of this window, glass that twists the outside world, gnarling trees and denting cars and putting bends in the straightest paths. The man is staring at something beyond the cars, beyond the paths. He's staring at a virtually leafless tree. In the weak shadow of that tree he sees an old man working slowly. The man beneath that tree is my father.

Some days I come up here, climbing the wide stone stairs, just to be away from the others, to get off the ward. And sometimes I take a chair and sit here and watch the old man beneath the tree. Occasionally, as today, there's another old man sitting on the bench across the corridor from this window but he doesn't heed me and he doesn't heed the things I say to my father.

My words go round inside the window like flies, humming and hissing against the things they cannot see.

Our fathers who are in heaven, hallowed be your names.
Your memories come, your will be done in Heaven as it was on Earth.
Give us this day our daily laughter.

And the other words go round outside, like butterflies or paper blowing away, like sounds that haven't found their resting places.

Forgive us our trespasses as we forgive you who trespassed against us.
Lead us not into regret but deliver us from recrimination.
For yours were the lifetimes, the losses and the scant glories,
For ever and ever.
Amen.

iii

My father settled in the hospital. I won't say he was happy, was he ever happy? But he didn't complain. By the time he was brought in he couldn't speak, though I know he always dreaded the thought of coming here. It's the kind of place he never wanted to be. I think he longed to die at home, in his own bed in his own room, the way he always thought he would. The thing is, he almost managed it. If it hadn't been for my calling that afternoon he would have died at home and escaped whatever misery the hospital brought.

But I did call, the same way I called every Saturday afternoon for the last ten years of his life. He always pretended surprise, like he hadn't seen me for months. I called as much for myself as for him. I called for the smell of heat from the range, the sizzle of the kettle, the warmth of the lino in the kitchen, the worn feel of the green paint on the banisters. I called for comfort.

When my mother died, I thought all that would go, that the place would become cold but I was wrong. I'd never realized, until after my mother was gone, how much my father had put into keeping the house the way it was.

But that Saturday, when I went in, I knew there was something wrong. It had nothing to do with the fact that he wasn't sitting at the table, glancing up from his paper with that air of mock astonishment, nor that he didn't answer when I spoke his name. It was the smell, the caustic smell of the kettle boiled dry on the range. I knew, immediately. I went upstairs and checked the two bedrooms, pushed in the bathroom door, expecting to find him slumped against it but the place was empty.

It was a wet Saturday, the end of October. Looking out into the yard, I saw the light in the turf shed. I ran through the rain. And there he was, lying on the ground, turf spilling out of the bucket beside him. He had a kind of crooked, boyish grin on his face. For a moment I was relieved. I thought he was drunk. I thought he'd fallen over drunk and couldn't get up. I grinned back and kneeled to help him but when I saw the curve of the side of his mouth I knew it wasn't a grin, it was the way his face had been frozen by the stroke.

I tried to prop him against the turf but he was a dead weight so I put my coat under his head and ran back through the house and into the Millers next door and asked them to ring for an ambulance. Mrs Miller came back with me and we sat with him till the siren split the street.

I helped to carry him through the house. I sat with him in the ambulance. I stayed the night with him in the hospital. I called at home the following day, to tidy up, but Mrs Miller had already done that. She even had a small fire lit, in case my father came back, as though he ever would.

I sat with him in the hospital every night for a week, until his strength started to return and the agitation began. He didn't know where he was but he knew he wasn't where he wanted to be. He tried to tell me things but I couldn't understand. All I knew was that he wanted to be back in his own room in his own house. It was as if he had a map in his head and someone had rubbed all the roads off it. He knew he was somewhere and he knew he wanted to be somewhere else but he had no idea how to get there. And the more he searched the more confused and agitated he became. Only when the nurses put him in a chair and took him down to physio, did he quieten, in the false belief that he was going home. Worst of all, he cried constantly, the kind of cry you hear from a child who has given up. One of the young nurses came and sat with him and held his hand, as my mother might have done, and the tears still furrowed his face.

It took him months but he found his way back to some kind of physical wellbeing. His mind remained a blank and his voice was silent but he regained a good deal of his strength, enough to allow him out into the gardens of the hospital. And, once he had that independence, he seemed to settle a little better in the place.

The Rake they called him, all the nurses.

You're a rake, Mr Kinsella, they said, in that laughing way young nurses have, that way that makes you think they want to shag you. I was just sorry they weren't saying it to me because it was lost on him. Everything was lost on him. He was in a world of his own. Now and then I tried to talk to him but it was a waste of time. He was out there, ploughing his own furrow. That's why they called him *The Rake*, nothing to do with his collapsed libido, just his obsession with gardening.

He spent his whole time in the hospital grounds. Whatever the season, he was out there, his cap pulled down, the rag of a scarf he'd had for years tied around his neck and a rake in his hand.

Wintertime he hung around the polythene tunnels out the back, like a ghost that had strayed from the morgue. I used to think he'd get on the gardener's wick. The gardener was a young fellow, but I think he genuinely didn't mind. He gave the old boy cigarettes and let him potter around with the seeds and plant stuff for him, though I don't believe they passed two sentences between them in the whole four winters. Come the spring, he was away with it. Out in the garden from early morning, raking the grass after the mower. Into little piles, in a line, and then into one mountain in the middle. He'd get three days work out of one cut.

In summer it was weeds. There wasn't a dandelion that raised its golden head but he dug it out. Everywhere, any weeds at all, and then he'd rake them up, everything except poppies. He'd been the same at home when I was a kid. The garden was as neat as an apron but wherever poppies flowered he left them, don't ask me why. But, autumn was his happiest time. Out from dawn to dusk, raking the leaves. Masses of them all over the place. Building enormous banks before he barrowed them away. I'd drive up and see him out there on the big front lawn with the wind showering the leaves like confetti but it wouldn't matter to him. He'd ignore me. So, I'd stand behind him, watching him work away as methodical as you like, raking and raking till everything was clear.

October, November, up to Christmas. The rake in his hand, he wouldn't give up till he had rounded up every last one.

Was he happy? As much as it's possible to be in the circumstances, I suppose.

iv

There's a strange thing! My father could drive but he never bought a car. I know my mother would have liked a car. She never made a song and dance about it but it was obvious that she'd have enjoyed having one. Occasionally, when there were family funerals at the other end of the country, my father hired a car and drove and she was in her element.

She had a way of stepping in and out of a car that reminded me of the film stars I saw on the Pathé newsreels. It was the same when she got off a train, she'd step down, like that, her hand drifting behind her. She had elegance and grace and I wanted us to have a car, if only to see her climb in and out in style, if only because I believed she was entitled to it.

And it wasn't a question of money, we could well have afforded it. There were only the three of us and, when I was eight, my father was promoted to foreman in the factory. He was well paid. And my mother worked three days a week in the bakery shop.

Can we get a car da?

What would we get a car for?

It'd be nice, for going places.

But, sure, we do go places.

Yeah but we could drive places, on holidays, to matches.

But we never miss a match. Have we ever missed a match that we wanted to go to?

No

See.

And he was right. We never missed a match that Kildare played, winter or summer. If it were in Athy or Newbridge he'd get out his motorbike and off we'd go. If it were somewhere else we'd get a lift or go by train. That was the time when he was mad into football, the eternal optimist. It was the only thing that truly animated him. I'd stand beside him on the embankments and marvel at how a grown man could get so worked up about a game of football. Or, if the place were crowded, I'd sit on his shoulders and hold on for dear life while he forgot I was there.

The names come back to me like it was yesterday, Mick Carolan and Boiler White and Kieran O'Malley, big men in the white jerseys. And my father's voice ringing in the late afternoon, a breathless commentary.

Come on Kildare get stuck in them go on Mick Carolan your ball. Up for it man rise for it now go on go for the point take your point ah for Jaysus sake what are youse doing passing it take your score now you're in trouble now are you satisfied go for him go for him for feck's sake go for him yes that's it that's it yes yes yes ah ref for feck's sake. Did you see that, did you? Did you see the way they took the legs from under him? They should be off the two of them. That was dirty. But what would you expect? Ah Jaysus ref, get yourself a pair of glasses. Them men should be off you're a blind bastard ref. Now he should point this. Steady now steady. Yesssss. Good man that's the answer for them. Now Kildare, face this ball, get it back in around the sticks up for it. Ah feck's sake ref give him a saddle altogether there's no sense in that. Now's the chance now's the chance now ah feck it . . .

And at half-time, he'd politely buy ice cream or chocolate from the hawkers, all mellow and conversational. But as soon as the whistle went for the second half he was off again.

Then home, to the smell of the range in wintertime, to the windows open and the smell of flowers from the yard in summertime.

Often, when we got home, my mother was out and the table was left set for us. Sometimes, she was there, her face flushed, waiting to welcome us home. Always smelling of perfume. Glad to see us. Ready to hear us replay the game over the tea table.

v

It's strange how you can live with people and not notice what's gong on until someone says something or something happens and you come face to face with an inescapable truth, strange how significance passes for banality.

An afternoon, two or three weeks before Christmas, I was sent home from school with a sick stomach and I got back to the house and let myself in. I sat at the range for a while, warming myself, watching the cold and wet steam out of me. Then I went upstairs to get a bundle of comics from under my bed. I heard a noise from my parents' room.

Is that you, mam?

Her voice was quick and high and different.

You go downstairs, I'll be with you in a sec.

I was sitting at the range when she appeared.

What are you doing home?, she asked. But not like she was annoyed or anything.

I was sick.

She brought me into the bathroom and took my temperature. I heard the kitchen door close and then the back gate bang.

The wind, my mother said.

And then she cuddled me on her lap and brought me back to the kitchen and made me an egg flip and told me I was her pet.

Another day, I came home to find the front door bolted.

I must've forgot, my mother said. *Lucky it wasn't your dad, he'd think I was losing my head.*

An evening that Christmastime, my father and myself were on our own in the kitchen, putting up the decorations. I was standing on a chair, he was holding a box of baubles.

Only for you.

What, da?

Only for you, I'd be at the bottom of the river wouldn't I?

Don't say that, da.

It's true.

Don't be talking like that.

We'll go to matches again, won't we?

Yeah. We will.

And see the Lily Whites?

Yeah.

Only for you, only for you.

I was almost twelve then. You don't expect your father to change, to become a stranger when you're that age. But I started noticing things. He'd come home late, slightly drunk. It had never taken very much to get him drunk. Two or three small ones and he was on his way.

But there were other things, more shocking to a child. We'd be sitting at the dinner table and I'd look over and see tears running down his face, for no reason. And then I'd look at my mother, expecting her to say or do something, but she'd just continue with her meal. That frightened me, the ordinariness of it.

What age was my father then? No more than in his late forties, the same age I am now. And then we missed a couple of football matches, league matches. He'd go off to Mass on the Sunday morning, he always did the door collection at early Mass, but he wouldn't come home till two or three in the afternoon and, when he did, he'd go upstairs and I wouldn't see him for the rest of the day. Sometimes, my mother sent me to play with my cousins and sometimes she just went off for the afternoon herself. But nothing was said.

Whenever he stayed out late, my mother took me into their bed so that when he came in he'd have to sleep in my room. He never kicked up about that. Just did it. I liked being in their bed. It was warm and safe in there. And there was something else, a suggestion of excitement, my mother's perfume, the shape of her body against her nightdress, a possibility that frightened and intrigued.

And then my mother disappeared. My father took time off work. He collected me from school. He had dinner ready for me every day. I asked him where my mother was.

Away, for a couple of weeks.

When will she be back?

Soon.

This week?

Soon.

We went to a match that Sunday. Kildare were playing Offaly. It was April. We stood on the embankment in Athy and watched the game. My father was silent through the whole thing. I had some sense that his silence had to do with my mother's absence.

When we get home, will mam be there?

I don't think so, not today.

When?

Soon.

One afternoon late the following week, she was there to meet me at the gates of the school. She looked thinner than she had been but she was smiling. That Friday I was left in my cousin's house and my father and herself drove off in a hired car but I didn't mind because I knew she'd be coming back.

Things were never the same after that. I was old enough to recognize the changes. My father and I went back to our football but neither of us had an appetite for the game. And things were changing at home. It was as though my mother's coming back had altered my father, hardened him. He didn't cry any more but neither did he laugh very often. It was like he was punishing my mother for returning and punishing himself for having her there. That was when my first father died. He left us gradually, slowly, evolving into the man who would replace him.

vi

My father was the gardener, I was the poet and my mother was what, our audience? She was adamant that I was going to be a writer, convinced that I'd immortalize her. And I believed her because her faith was flawless.

You'll tell my story, won't you?

I will.

Not all of it, you'll know the bits to leave out.

Yes.

That's my man.

But things have a way of turning sour. My new father was erratic and unreliable. His bonnet swarmed with bees.

I remember one early summer evening, I was listening to a woman reading a poem on the BBC. I was fifteen then and I wanted my mother to hear that poem because I knew she'd like it. But she was out shopping so I scribbled down the gist of it.

It was a piece the woman had written for her boyfriend who'd been killed when his aeroplane blew up. She dreamed, time after time, that she'd go out to the garden shed and find him curled up in a corner. In the dream, he fell from the plane and landed in the shed and she found him there, stunned but alive. And she brought him into the kitchen and they sat at the table and drank tea and said nothing, just sat there, amazed at the miracle, glad to be alive, happy just to be together.

My mother smiled when I told her about the poem. I knew she was listening closely, I knew by the way she'd stopped eating, by the way her head was turned, by the way she had to swallow hard to keep from crying.

And then my father had his say.

That's nonsense.

What is?

That bloody story. Tripe.

It's only a story.

Stories like that do nothing but milk people. The world is full of people telling stories. And what good do they do? Pretending to people, taking advantage of them, making them think things'll be all right when there's not an earthly chance of it. It's all about codding people to line someone's pocket, bloodsuckers, the lot of them.

And he was off, ranting as he did when anyone died in town.

It's tripe, the same tripe as the rest of it. Memoriam cards, verses, flowers, dreams, tripe, the whole bloody lot of it. Soft soap for soft heads.

He finished and stood up and stormed out of the house. I heard him take the spade from the tool shed. My mother and myself sat at the table listening, listening to the sound of digging from the garden. It was like listening to a gravedigger at work.

And do you think a story like that might come true?

Maybe, I said. *It might.*

The thing was, my father knew then, even though I didn't, that my mother had only months to live. But that didn't stop him, he couldn't leave an open door in case some hope sneaked into our lives.

But, strangest of all, right to the end, she kept trying to bring him back into the picture, as if she felt some guilt. Sometimes he'd come straight home from work and we'd have our tea and he'd go out in the garden and, when it got dark, he'd come in and we'd sit down and have our supper together in front of the telly. My mother would sit beside him on the couch and I'd look at them out of the corner of my eye, thinking once, maybe once, he'd hold her hand but he never did.

In the last few weeks, she'd be there in the evenings, in the kitchen, ironing clothes that she knew she'd never wear again, ironing our shirts, the shirts we'd wear at her funeral. And afterwards she'd sit with me and tell me how much it meant to her to know that my father and I would get on together.

I wanted to ask her why she didn't tell him that. There was no point in saying it to me. She had to get him to listen, too. But he wasn't coming home those evenings, instead he was hiding in some pub, running away, even before she was gone.

You'll get along, won't you, the pair of you?

We will.

You'll do your best to make it work?

Yeah, I will, I will do my best. We'll be all right, don't talk about it.

You've always been closer to me. Maybe he knows.

Stop talking like that.

And then, come nine or half nine, she'd go upstairs and I'd hear her twisting and turning. And later on I'd climb the stairs myself and I'd lie in the dusk, wanting to go to her, to hold her, to kiss away her pain and I'd think about the other fellows my age, out on their bikes around the town, at the pictures with girls. I wanted to do ordinary things with her, go places with her, sit in the shadowy picture-house. I wanted time with her and I wanted time for her.

I'd wake at half eleven or twelve and hear him coming in the gate.

One night, about a week before my mother died, my father got so drunk he came in through the wrong gate, into the Kellys' next door, and Mickey Kelly had to bring him home. My mother standing in the kitchen, thin as a whip in her dressing gown, and me and Mickey Kelly helping my father through the door.

The holy family. Him lying in the kitchen. My mother twisting and turning in bed. Me sweating in the dark.

The following Saturday, the doctor came to the house three times. In the end, he called the ambulance and she was taken to hospital. She died that night. We came back home and found she'd left our clothes washed and ironed and ready and two brown loaves and an apple tart baked in the oven.

vii

I remember him standing at my mother's grave. Standing there as straight as a rod and everyone coming up and going through the usual stuff.

Sorry for your troubles.

Thanks. Thanks.

All those things that people feel obliged to say.

She was a lovely woman.

Indeed.

All the clichés trotted out like ponies.

God bless her, she went quick.

She did.

And he listened to them. And threw in a few of his own.

It was a relief for her in the end, a sweet release.

Of course, of course it was.

And people gave him Mass cards and he thanked them.

That's very thoughtful of you.

Why wouldn't we?

And the wreaths piled up around the grave.

You're too good, too good.

Not at all.

And I thought of us at home. Her and him and me and the way he wouldn't give an inch. But there was worse to come.

He tried it on with me the following week when the letters came from the companies flogging memoriam cards. Did he think I didn't remember?

Isn't that a nice card? The few words are nice. I think your mammy would have liked that. And we could put the photograph of her from Maureen's wedding. That's a lovely photograph. What do you think?

I think you're a cunt. That's what I think.

He just stood there looking at me, saying nothing, and then he went out and started working in the garden. We didn't talk again for three weeks. He got on with it, ordered the memoriam cards, got them back, sat each night addressing envelopes until every card and letter had been acknowledged. And then he went on the batter. Went on a total tear. A couple of evenings, when I was coming home from school, I met him in the street, paralytic.

That's your ould fella, isn't it? Hey, Kinsella that's your ould fella, scuttered. Are you not going to bring him home? I'll give you a hand to carry him if you like.

Or he wouldn't come home till all hours. I didn't care. I'd lock the door and he'd sleep outside.

Or I'd find him unconscious in the kitchen when I came back from playing pool, sitting there, propped up, snoring his head off.

Or I'd come down in the morning and find a pool of vomit on the floor.

But the worst times were when he was only half pissed.

Where were you?

Out.

I know you were out. Don't be fucking smart with me. Where were you?

Playing pool.

There's some bastards hanging around that pool hall. I don't want you associating with them. You hear me? Do you hear me?

They're only lads from the school.

I know who they are. You don't have to tell me who they are. I know their seed, breed and generation. I don't need you telling me. I knew them and their fathers before ever you were heard of and I know what they're like. So you keep clear of them. You get home here by eight. You've enough to be doing.

And I did, to spite him, to show him I could do what he couldn't. I was home every night by eight. And sometimes he was there, in the garden, and sometimes he wasn't but I was always in on time. Lying awake, thinking about her, missing her, missing the warmth of her body, waiting for him to appear. Hoping he was at the bottom of the canal. Hoping someone had done him in. Hoping God had leaned down and squashed the life out of him. Knowing He hadn't because there was no God to do that.

And then one night I almost did it myself.

I heard him stumbling in the door, listened to him pounding around the kitchen and, finally, heard his snores. I lay in bed. I couldn't sleep. Eventually, I sneaked downstairs. I needn't have worried. He was stretched out on the couch, out cold.

I got his razor from the bathroom and went to where he was lying. The air around him had a stale, beery smell. I bent over him and looked at his face, puffy and blotched and smiling. I put the razor against his throat and started to cut but all I got was a narrow stripe of blood, a little trickle from side to side. He went on breathing and the blood blotted and then it stopped and I knew I couldn't cut him deeply enough to kill him. So I left him with a thin line of blackening blood from ear to ear and put the razor in the bathroom and went back and watched him sleeping. I was glad he wasn't dead because I didn't want him to have that freedom.

He never mentioned the cut on his throat, the same as he never mentioned so many things. He just went on drinking all that summer and through the following Christmas. He even let the garden go. He'd still go out and weed the flowers and stuff but he didn't sow anything.

I got on with school. He'd come to the parent-teacher meetings all spruced up, all concerned about how I was doing or wasn't doing. And he'd talk to the teachers and they'd tell him how I'd gone downhill since my mother's death and then he'd arrive home full of zeal.

You've brains to burn boy. Use them.

Hah.

Don't you hah me. You're sitting there in school, the teachers tell me, doing shag all. There was a time not too long ago when you'd be coming in here evening after evening full of poetry and I couldn't get you to stop it, even when your mother was dying.

I didn't know she was dying.

Well, you know now and it all seems to have stopped doesn't it? I don't hear any more poems about aeroplanes now, do I?

Sometime the following spring he started back on the garden. He'd go out maybe two nights a week for a drink but it got less and less. And then he'd only go out once or twice a month and he'd come back home after two or three pints. I think he drank himself through the pain of my mother's death. I've tried it since but it doesn't work for me.

viii

I faced him down, finally. It was after my daughter's funeral.

I used to envy other fellows, seeing them in the pubs with their fathers. But that day, a fogged up, grey day in November, he came back to the hotel. We had a meal, my girlfriend and her parents and her sister and my father and me.

After the meal, when the rest of them had left, we sat in the hotel and I faced him down. I suppose the funeral brought it all back, my mother dying and everything. It was there again. It was raw.

The thing is not to let this get to you, not to give up.

What the fuck are you talking about?

I'm talking about the baby dying, not to let it get to you.

The way you didn't let my mother's death get to you? The way you went on like there was nothing wrong with here even when the woman could hardly stand up? Is that what you mean? The way you didn't give up for her sake.

I gave up a long time before that.

Not good enough, not good enough for what you put my mother through.

She wasn't just your mother, she was my wife, too. You know nothing about it. You weren't even born then. It was your mother kept me afloat, pushed me into not letting people see how I felt. It got to a stage where I could laugh anything off, anything. And do you know why? Because your mother said I could.

What are you talking about?

I'm talking about things long before you were around, things when there was her and me, just her and me.

Did I spoil it for you?

That's not what I meant! You know, when your mother got sick, I wanted her to fight, the way she'd fought for me. But she wouldn't. She gave up on herself. She slid into the arms of death. It took her eight years but it was a slide all the way. I didn't want to lose her but she wouldn't fight. I tried to help her, to make her fight, I couldn't fight for her, could I? I tried to coax her. Then I tried making a jeer of death and the stuff that went with it. Nothing worked.

That's not the way I remember it.

There's a lot you don't remember, a lot you never knew.

I remember all the shit when she was dying. You know, I'm sorry you turned up here today. Now, excuse me.

ix

A long time later, years after my mother, his wife, was gone, I started visiting him again. He may have thought it was because I wanted some kind of reconciliation. Or he may have thought I did it for his sake but, in truth, it was for me. I needed the comfort of the house, I needed the reassurance I felt each time I stepped down into the kitchen.

One of the first weekends I came and stayed, we went out for a drink and talked football and nonsense.

Do you want another?

No, I'm grand with this.

Right. Right.

I was thinking, you should bring the young lads with you the next time Kildare are playing, we could all go. Bring them down for the day, give them an interest in the game.

Yeah, I might.

Might was never a good fellow.

I'll try.

Just do it. It's only a match.

It's not as easy as that.

Why not?

You know, things are rough enough, at home, not great.

Since when?

Four, five months.

You never said.

It might work out.

Of course it'll work out. These things have to, you have to make it, the pair of you, for the kids, no question about it. It has to be made to work out. We worked our way through problems, your mother and me. Course we did. You can't walk away from things like that.

This is a bit more difficult, you know.

We had our troubles. We didn't always get on well. We had our arguments, same as everyone. It took me a long while to see that there has to be give and take. You mightn't remember but one time your mother left for a couple of weeks. And that was all about little or nothing. Because I wanted her to give up working in the bakery and she wanted to put the money towards a car. I was wrong, I saw that and she went on with the job. And she saw that a car wasn't the be-all and end-all of life. You go off and patch this thing up, the pair of you. Head off for a week together. That's what your mother and me did. We left you in Stella's. You probably don't remember. We talked and we saw the folly of fighting about a three-day job and a car. We saw what we were in danger of losing. So, you'll do that?

Yeah, I'll do that.

Good man. Now, we'll have another drink. And I'm buying.

And that was that, out of sight, out of mind. Did he really think my mother left him because of the car and that sad job in the bakery? Was he naive enough to believe that?

He had chosen to forget all the rest?

He was sixty-eight years old then. My mother was twenty years dead. Where was the point in reminding him? And where was the point in rooting about for the truth?

x

Afternoons at the hospital were strange, him raking out there without a word out of him. Me sitting at the window, alone, trying to get myself to talk, telling myself this was it, this was the ideal opportunity.

You can say anything you like, he'll never know, he won't understand and you can get everything off your chest. Just go and do it!

I had wanted to tell him these things, back when we could communicate, but all we ever talked was the bull shit of football. And I'd outgrown that long before he imagined. I'd lost interest in standing in the freezing cold and the rain watching second-rate players. The heroes were gone by then, Mick Carolan and the rest of them. I wanted to point out that if he'd shown half the passion at home that he showed at matches, things might have been easier for him.

But I couldn't because he didn't know the half of it. He didn't know what was going on. Oh, I don't doubt he had his suspicions about the closing door and the banging of the back gate and the strangeness in her voice and the flush on her face and the sharp smell of perfume. But there were other things and where was the point in telling him? He wouldn't hear and I wouldn't speak.

xi

The last time I saw my father he was lying dead, curled up in a pile of leaves. He'd gone missing the evening before. It was early November and he'd been raking his leaves into mounds around the hospital garden.

That morning there was a pure-white fog coming in off the river. The nurses arriving for the night shift the previous evening had found his overalls folded neatly on a bench, with his boots on top. We searched the grounds and the bank of the river and the boiler room and the polythene tunnels but there was nothing.

The following morning, just after eight, the gardener found him under a mound of leaves he'd raked the week before.

I could imagine him, in the dusk after five o'clock, leaving his clothes where they'd be found. I could picture him slowly crossing the open lawn that drops gently to a stand of trees and bedding down for the night in that heap of fallen leaves, easing himself into them like an old animal.

Snug as a bug in a rug, he used to say when he put me to bed. And there he was, his old body wrapped in rusty leaves that gave some colour to his death pale skin. Snug as a bug in a rug.

xii

What was it, old man, that really broke you? Back then, what was it that changed you from one father into another? Was it all those intimations? Was it her running away? I have no idea.

There's a lot you don't remember, a lot you never knew.

But there are other things I do know, things I want you to know, even now that you're dead.

In some fugitive hotel room in Donegal she decided to come home, but not because of you. Rather she was faced with the fact that she had to come back to me.

I remember that Christmas when I was on the chair and you were talking about the river, you were clinging to me. She did the same; she clung to me, too. I was her hope and her ambition. You were just the outward appearance.

I don't say this to hurt you, just to let you know. You have the right to know that neither of us really loved you. In spite of everything, in spite of all the football matches and all the sadness inside you and that compulsion to cling to me, my only thought was for the freshness of her skin.

Perhaps we both loved the same things in her but I was in love with her long after you'd given up. You must have seen that you had no hope of coming between us. Was that the trouble?

Had you known all the facts, would you have gone into the river, as you threatened? The fact that we camouflaged it all as a game to be played on the nights when you were missing, on the wintry afternoons when only the light of the range from the living room followed us tentatively up the stairs.

Even when she was dying, I wanted to go to her, to hold her, to lie beside her, skin to skin, not just for me, for her as well. Yes, I wanted you to take her hand but only because that would offer her some consolation, lull her into thinking things between you were all right. Most of all, I wanted to be the poet she dreamed of because, even then, I knew the absolutions poets have.

I shouldn't be saying this out loud, should I? I shouldn't be breaking faith with her.

But I am.

And not to hurt you more than you hurt or were hurt, simply to explain, to clarify, to apologize if an apology is needed, to take responsibility. We all must take responsibility – you betrayed each other in so many ways and I've betrayed you both.

xiii

Time to go back down, to leave the fragile old man who sits on his bench across the corridor. Time to get back to the ward, to wave goodbye to that other old man in the shadow of the tree, the man who goes on raking without ever lifting his head. Why does he never lift his head? I wonder, sometimes, about that. But, more often than not, I think about her, her and me together.

Am I happy? As much as it's possible to be in the circumstances, I suppose.

Molly McCloskey

A Nuclear Adam and Eve

I fell in love with Nina when she was ten and I was nine and she was just another negligible presence in our world. I used to watch her from the docks at the lake that summer, playing with her brothers. The boys, all teenagers, were tanned and supple and looked as though they'd dropped out of the sky. Some celestial tropics where people dozed in hammocks, swam in see-through seas and sat scantily clad around fires at night. Later, when I was old enough to think about such things, I wondered how they'd all emerged from such unpromising beginnings.

Their father looked like a marine – an officer rather than an enlisted man – a buzz cut and weathered features, disciplined and distant and largely humourless. He had one of those firm middle-aged bodies you could still picture scaling walls and shimmying up rope ladders and perpetrating a single-minded, patriotic violence. Their mother was cordial but also stiff. She regarded everything and everyone with a reluctant sort of irony. She had good bone structure and smooth translucent skin, that receding, haughty quality that in another culture, and on another woman, could've been beautiful. But you got the idea she'd put such childish things away.

The family home was dustless and eerily still. I felt muffled when inside of it, either because we spoke softly there, or because the house swallowed up in its sunny gloom all of our girlish energy, making it seem trivial and embarrassing. Heavy crystal vases graced the mantle, the polished teak furniture shone, and the cream-coloured sofas were spotless, their pillows plumped. It was like a roped-off exhibit of a dead president's quarters. There, among these delicate human constructions, Nina's brothers looked unnaturally constrained, as though they really had descended from a realm of violent passions and pleasures on a grand scale.

But at the lake they came alive. Mermen streaming through the green, slithering up from the deep to hoist themselves agilely on to the dock. They would lie on the warm boards to dry, chests heaving, black hair glistening in the sun, their laughter bouncing off the skies. And Nina beside them, their perfect diminutive complement, issuing from them as naturally as an echo or a wake. They would rise her atop their shoulders or ferry her on their backs out to the perimeter of logs or coax her off the diving board when she faltered (knees bent, hands joined in an arrow above her head), and all the while I watched her. Wanting, more than anything, to be her.

Our brothers introduced us, one late afternoon near the end of summer. (I had a brother too, though he was a gangly, pale being whose disappearance I prayed for daily.) The sun was dropping behind the trees – the Douglas firs that ringed the lake, imperious as in a fairy tale and looking capable of mutinous or oracular speech. Ben and I were gathering our towels and sneakers when I saw Nina and her brother walking towards us.

'What's your sister's name?' her brother said to Ben, without preliminaries.

'Jane,' Ben said.

Her brother looked from me to Nina and back again. 'This is Nina,' he said. 'You two'll be in the same school next year.'

'See,' Ben said, as though I had earlier contradicted this fact. 'You should get to know each other.'

I glanced at her, expecting her to laugh or sneer or at the very least roll her eyes in derision. Instead, she did something I still find startling, something I thought only ever happened in storybooks, or among children even younger than ourselves, in other times and places maybe, but not in our town and not in the twentieth century. She took my hand.

⋆

In a way, we raised her. My parents were technicolour. They threw parties out the back in summer, off-handed, reeling affairs. My father mixed drinks at a wet bar – planks positioned atop two small tables on the lawn – and Nina and I would weave between the dancers, delivering his cargo. My father was laid-back but funny, and very likeable, the kind of guy who these days might be employed running holiday pub crawls in the Caribbean but who, back then, succumbed rather good-naturedly to marriage and family and a little harmless DIY. My mother took life more seriously, at least in its ethical dimension; she regarded moral rectitude as a spectator sport and herself as God's appointed cheerleader.

She used to bring home strays (what Nina referred to as my mother's 'outreach programme') – single mothers, people who were raising handicapped children or nursing incontinent parents, the young mailman whose wife had died of a cerebral haemorrhage at the age of twenty-seven, the woman behind the checkout at our local Safeway who was working her way through community college. On our small back porch in summer, my mother hosted Sunday dinners for these individuals she had befriended out of admiration, the kind of people who in years to come would star in two-minute slots on the *CBS News,* the unsung heroes of our world.

'She's an inspiration to us all,' Nina would say, mimicking my mother, who could be counted on to say that to at least one of her guests at least once every Sunday.

Nina kept an eye out for candidates, sad cases my mother might've overlooked, and though it seemed, initially, that she was exhibiting a nascent sense of irony, I realized later that something in her meant it. She liked the weirdness of it all, it's true, the talk-show feel of my mother's gatherings and guessing who the guests would be and what hilarious adult secrets they'd let slip. But she also genuinely liked the idea of a makeshift family, people coming together voluntarily for the provision of mutual comfort. She looked at them like they were sad and lovable animals, three-legged dogs making their bathetic way through the world.

Tim, the mailman, was our favourite. We felt an intimacy with him for his having handled our letters, for the fact that he wore shorts while working and never crossed the threshold of our front doors, suggesting a vague discretion that appealed to our budding if rather goofy sense of the erotic. We felt proprietary towards him, or protective, because of his bandy legs and his unmanly occupation. Masculine to us was the pre-posthumous JFK – someone distant and omnipotent and world-famous – or else something more amorphous, the clack of helmets and the collective grunt that drifted from the football field, from the dozens of boys padded to the point of indistinguishability.

Nina wrote me a note, addressed the envelope to my place at the table – *third from the back door* – drew a coloured stamp with a profile of my brother, who just then was drooped morosely over his dinner, and made Tim deliver it to me at the table. We howled with delight, as though he were a performing animal, a monkey using silverware.

Being a mailman still had that Norman Rockwell quality to it. The Unabomber hadn't happened yet, or the anthrax scare, or even the spate of shootings by post office employees that gave rise to the term 'going postal'. Being a mailman didn't yet mean being caught in the crossfire of American madness. If Nina and I were twelve today and Tim came to dinner, we would gaze on him bashfully, reverently, the way we once did policemen. But back then all we felt was a near-sexual thrill in spying him out of context, as he attempted to assume the complexities of a three-dimensional character, drinking wine and talking about SALT II. The modesty of his long pants striking us, paradoxically, as obscene.

Even our parents weren't exactly real to us. They were cardboard cutouts somebody'd placed in our path, to hinder or amuse us and remind us of what we wouldn't in a million years turn into. About the only thing that was real to us was us. (Later, when our high school history teacher informed us of the 'invention' of adolescence in the mid-twentieth century, we felt undermined and a little resentful, like characters in a futuristic novel who discover they've been cooked up in a Petri dish.) We couldn't help it, we saw a marvellous absurdity in everything; life was one big wink in our direction and we responded in kind.

We made a cult figure of a Polish émigré who did hair commercials on television and couldn't pronounce her Rs. We pasted pictures of her in our lockers and for months greeted one another by saying, 'I am Whula Lalenska', and erupting into uncalled-for laughter, already displaying the appetite for meaninglessness that would come to mark our generation. We tormented our math teacher who had broken her leg and thus forfeited whatever small claim she'd had on being taken seriously. She came to school wearing pants with one leg cut out and managed to ambulate by swinging her casted limb around in a half circle as she went, beads of sweat gathering above her upper lip. We even got a job and, for a while, that was funny too. We worked at a small drive-in hamburger place. While I shuffled around lazily, Nina nursed unformulated notions of working-class decency and somewhere in between we learned to syphon the gas off the armies of whipped cream cans assembled in the walk-in fridge. While the whipped cream drooled lewdly from its nozzles, we squeaked and giggled our way through the off-peak hours, charmed by the versatility of nitrous oxide.

Was she beautiful? I'd like to say no, or not exactly. I'd like to say something from the core of her shone and that that was what they saw and wanted. I'd like to say her soul made her desirable because it was life-hungry and tragic, and that promiscuity, after all, is a form of generosity. In fact, all those things are true, but she was beautiful too, which meant that none of them really mattered.

Nina lost her balance. A disequilibrium engendered by too much adoration. (We thrive, apparently, when receiving a reasonable amount of love from a moderate number of people who have adequate cause; anything less or more requires a superhuman grace.) But her downfall was so determined that it bore a strange resemblance to knowledge: an acceptance of what needed to be done and the fact of oneself as having been singled out by destiny to do it. The way I imagine the great dancers must feel, the composers, the saints, or anybody who's a conduit for something rare and unearthly.

★

There's a peace that comes from dozens of strangers mulling silently over the same idea. You can feel it in grocery stores. A singleness of purpose that results in a certain collective and hypnotic energy. It's why I believe in flying yogis and group prayer and naff candlelight memorial services. There's a melancholy too, though. A sort of, so this is what it's all amounted to: a lot of people alone under fluorescent lights, a grotesquerie of choice.

As in an airport, elastic bands stretched between metal poles channel us in a slow slalom towards the checkout counters. Sometimes children press down on the bands or even sit on them, causing the poles to tip over and creating an almighty clutter, which in turn gives rise to a certain nervous goodwill. Because a defensiveness takes hold of us in line. Maybe it's our sudden closeness, maybe it's the winos; the booze is sold from a counter the far side of all this somnolent order and they have to pass in front of us to reach it. They shuffle in and out while we watch, with gloomy concentration, like neutral observers at a needle exchange.

You can spot the single men by their telltale meals-for-one. You could loiter in the no man's land between one sliding door and the other, where baskets are stacked and dogs wait shivering and a photo booth operates, and prey on them like they were runaways in a railway station. Because men alone are such sad beasts. They have a way of looking like they don't deserve their lives.

And then there are the little old ladies, with their slight humpbacks, their raincoats and headscarves and their bright modern athletic shoes. They look heroic and unsentimental. Their bodies are bent into unusual shapes as though God is already wadding them up. And I feel like apologizing to these women, for the assault they've undergone, for the exponential increase of everything unpleasant. They take small steps and peer closely at any item they're considering. They can't afford the breezy distraction the rest of us exhibit, the thinking of twelve things at once as we acquire our next meal.

Because you see a lot of that here, daydreaming. A slight vacancy in people's eyes, something that tells you none of this is quite sufficient. They're thinking about last night or what's become of someone they knew years ago and have suddenly remembered, or maybe they're thinking about the child or the children in their lives. You catch their eyes and without meaning to, they smile, and you become the accidental beneficiary of their daydreams.

And then I think of Nina, in a clapboard house with a dog and a love seat under low skies thousands of miles from here and a husband who lets her know he doesn't give a damn about the past. Because today is all they have. Today is the only day worth living.

He told me once, when I called them after he'd gotten

out of rehab, that there was a particular power in AA rooms. 'It comes from everybody thinking the same thing at once,' he said. Now, sometimes when I'm in a grocery store, in the midst of that involuntary harmony, I remember him saying that and then, by extension, I remember her. I never asked him what it was that everyone was thinking.

We visited him in rehab, Nina and I. Before they were married and before I moved away. He was wearing a sky-blue cotton sweat suit that looked somehow like baby wear. We were early and when we arrived they were all jogging around a cinder track, the men in one direction and the women in another.

'What's that about?' I asked. 'The opposite directions thing.'

'I don't know,' she said, her eyes fixed on the track.

'Seems like it would be more distracting. Like telling people not to think about sex.'

'Or not to think about whatever,' she said.

He spotted us and waved and she smiled and leaned forward and gave a big wave back, as though she were seeing him off on some heroic undertaking, a Nepalese trek or a parachute jump for charity. It surprised me. Here he was, her man, her lover, her de facto fiancé, the guy who not so many years ago had put her back together again. The one, too, who'd tongued champagne off her breasts and made mulled wine for her in a log cabin while the snow fell and the sap oozed from burning logs like a life-juice. Who'd taken her out in a canoe on Lake Clear to toast his near unbearable love for her, the bottle of yellowy-white wine wedged between his feet, another suspended by twine over the side of the boat, chilling.

Of that day, she'd said simply: 'I've never been happier.'

And here he was, hapless and uncool, looking weirdly in sync with his companions as they went round in another lap of what could've been a conga line at the dreg-ends of a wedding or an interminable event at the Special Olympics. They were all in the same bedraggled state of shock, brought on by the demands of physical exercise in an abruptly unmediated world, and I looked at Nina and wondered had life as we knew it taken everything we had. Or at least the things we needed to keep us one step ahead of farce. I was thinking about the end of heroes and the indignity of self-help and the emasculation of modern man, and I was beginning to find the whole scene a little bit depressing.

And then I looked at her and knew: she loves him. And I was sad and envious and all my grandiose investigations vanished in irrelevance.

Nina's job was to tell Jimmy exactly how his drinking had hurt her. Jimmy's job was to sit there and take it. It was my job to support Nina, to drive her here and remind her that this wasn't just wanton cruelty on her part.

I sat in the waiting area, reading 12-step literature and picturing Jimmy up against a wall and Nina throwing daggers at him. Not meanly, but more like it was their secret: the whole sexy, intimate, potentially lethal act. I opened to a page that read:

> *The sad failures which plague our lives today are not the results of chance. We earned them. They are the payoff for a thousand drunken yesterdays. They are the costly ruins upon which we can build new, happy, sober lives.*

A thousand drunken yesterdays. I liked that. It rendered Jimmy's life poetic. It gave it a deep blue glow of nostalgia that seemed to cover a lot of what was gone and over with for all of us. I sat there and thought: that's my offering to Jimmy, that I'll remember his life like that, like a pageant of incredible yesterdays, beautiful ruins crumbling in the twilight.

I wasn't supposed to be thinking this. It was also my job to be part of the 'social network' that would improve Jimmy's chances of staying dry once he got out, and romanticizing his downfall was not high on the list of the ways I could be helpful. So it was just for me, this one. Because he'd been the life of the party and he was trying hard now, in his earnestness and his sad blue jumpsuit.

Booze had hacked away at him like he was undergrowth until he was just a small and unprotected core and she didn't want to be in there, doing this to him.

'All this kicking someone when they're down,' she said, 'I don't know.'

'It's probably good to get things out on the table,' I said.

'He really wasn't nasty, he was just sad in the end. He'd look up at me from the sofa and I'd know he was too paranoid to leave the house. To even sit up. But he was never violent and he didn't run around and he didn't even yell. He just went from someone who was lots of fun to someone who was drunk and lost.'

'Well,' I said lamely, 'it must've been pretty hard living with him sometimes.' I was supposed to be priming her for the task ahead.

'Oh, I just feel shitty,' she said. 'Shitty going in there and being so negative.'

'I know, I know,' I said, 'but you've got to.'

I had no idea whether she had to or not. What did I know about tough love? And what did they do with people who couldn't get anyone to vouch for their awfulness? I guessed that in rehab, that was the lowest of the low. It made clear how underpopulated your life had become.

★

She had her landscapes, her languages, her physical inflections. She had big dark eyes and black hair and a way of looking over her shoulder at you as she turned to walk away, like something you'd learn in a B-list charm school. I see her on a blanket, this is years ago, on the golf course at the far end of our town, stretched out under the stars and not alone. In the background there's a soundtrack of sprinklers, the rhythmic flick of their metal wrists like tiny fly fishermen casting in the darkness. She is looking for something and it isn't love. She's had a lot of that and I don't believe she used sex to get any more; that's an overrated theory in any case. She is looking for something else, something like what Jimmy was looking for beyond the high itself. A power to match her own, maybe, or a place where there were no more questions. And it's their past misguidedness, I sometimes think, that binds them.

Boys didn't go after her. You hung on the periphery and waited, biding your time till she woke to your particular charms. You made your adolescent anxiety look like laconic irony. You did whatever you dimly perceived was necessary to acquire the persona she seemed partial to: a louche jadedness, a redeemable core, a hint of some vague potential, as of star power. The nascent lover in you stirred and even if you never succeeded, however briefly, in making her love you, eventually it hardly mattered. Because she became a myth we owned collectively. She was like a book so many people have read you begin to think you have too and you know parts of it and how they make you feel and you have your opinions which you're not afraid to share.

She wasn't tacky. She wasn't 'loose' in the 1950s too-much-tits and a cloud of shame kind of way. Of course her stock declined; even Nina couldn't give cliché the slip. A desperation crept in and she required adulation from ever murkier quarters. I had the awful feeling I was watching her devour people. But she was never reduced to a rite of passage (Nina was tragic rather than pathetic) and she never suffered the fate she might've in my mother's day: groped by so many hands until she became, paradoxically, an untouchable.

Instead, she was the embodiment of everything we were learning, or learning to leave behind. The plundering of innocence and innocence's way of desiring its own defilement. She grew up faster and more furiously than the rest of us and we lived, vicariously, her corruption. Sensing somehow that it was just a more dramatic version of the modest initiations and small losses of certainty we seemed daily to undergo. She picked people up and put them down again, like they were so many curios on a conveyor belt, teaching us the lesson of our own expendability. And how who we were in life would depend largely on how we were loved.

⋆

Jimmy doesn't talk to her much about the booze.

'It scares her,' he says. 'Nina, Nina I talk to about the non-booze. The new life. Living in the solution.'

I think of Jimmy on a staircase, twelve steps, and Nina at the top like he's a baby learning how to crawl.

'You can tell me,' I say, 'you can say anything to me, you know that.'

We've imagined each other, of course. It's part of the package, part of the landscape of adulthood and the few things you're not supposed to think about but do: suicide, and sex with the people who belong to someone you love and are loyal to. I used to look at grown-ups when I was a kid and think – in the kind of thought that is formless but there, all vapours and potential, the pre-big bang consciousness of childhood – that there was a logic to the romantic lives of adults. That they ran smoothly and efficiently like a small office in which everybody knows their job and is happy with it. I thought that people married each other because it had been arranged in some department of heaven and that it was simply a matter of sifting through the hopefuls who presented themselves to you like they were auditioning for your show.

I'm far away, and Jimmy feels me safely on the other side of a vast, unnavigable deep. He sees me at Christmas and sometimes in the summer when we hold our affection between us and turn it this way and that, as though it is an item of undetermined value we chanced upon in passing. And we're not sure whether to feel sheepish, or dangerously clever. But this kind of thing can easily amount to nothing. It's just a place our minds go when they're lonely and unfocused.

'It's funny,' he says. 'The things you miss are not necessarily what you would've guessed. I miss red wine with red meat. I miss the way a crystal tumbler feels in my hand, the weight of it, and the way tonic lets off little sparks that land on your wrist. I don't miss getting drunk,' he says, 'or *just* getting drunk. I miss a whole context.'

'Jimmy,' I say, 'is this wise?'

He tells me that a lot of people get divorced when they quit drinking. Marriages that lurch along for years like a three-legged race only to founder in the cold clear light of day and somebody's newfound dignity.

'I think of it as Step 13,' he says, and I don't know where he's going with this.

'Well, Jimmy, you're changing all the time.'

I have read the literature, I have spoken to someone at work who's the same as Jimmy. I may be living on another continent, I may think thoughts I shouldn't, but I take my job as part of Jimmy's social network seriously.

'Don't panic if you're going through a rough spot with Nina. Because you're changing all the time.'

'I'm not suggesting that,' he says, 'that things are bad. Things are not bad. It's just interesting to consider. From a psychological standpoint. Like who *are* these people that when you suddenly wake up you have to get away from them? What have they been doing to you all this time, the time you were out of it? It reminds me of my dog.'

'Yeah?'

'Yeah. The way I used to feel about my dog when I was a kid. I used to think: Supposing my dog suddenly could talk, I don't want him to be able to say that I ever, even once, mistreated him because he couldn't answer back.'

'You thought that?'

'It was my first idea of justice,' he says.

'It was a good start.'

'There's a guy I know who said he'd hit bottom when he found himself washing his hands in Germany. I loved that.'

'So tell me,' I say.

'He was involved in a mess, a love triangle, sleeping with some guy's wife and pretending he wasn't. So they invite him to their house in Germany, the husband thinking he's a friend, you know. But the husband is also a shrink and he asks him: Why are you washing your hands so much? *Vie are you vashink your hants*? And the guy says: It's humid, my hands get sticky. Which is actually true. The next day the husband comes home from work early and this guy and the wife are in the kitchen. Just making lunch, drinking wine, not doing anything, but completely naked. The guy was so shocked he started to wash his hands.'

I picture the scene. Two naked people and a plate of knockwurst between them. 'So the husband was right,' I say. 'It was guilt.'

'If you ever find yourself in Germany,' Jimmy says, '*vashink your hants . . .*'

I wondered what it was like, hearing all those stories. I wondered was it like being a kid again. I imagined them all in a church basement, a clutch of ex-drunks sitting cross-legged on the floor, their eyes wide, their necks craned. Childish astonishment. Like this is their reward for finding their way out of the wood: an afterlife of bedtime stories.

She talks about him like he's a story. 'When you fall in love,' Nina says, 'it's like you've agreed to believe the story of someone. Not agreed, that's wrong, you just do believe. And then they do something unforgivable or they start keeping secrets or maybe your own attention just wanders. They become someone else in your eyes and you don't believe it any more. The story hasn't really changed. It's you, you've changed, you've decided it isn't true.'

The night of their wedding, I drove back from the coast to my hotel in Portland, up 6 until I hit the Sunset Highway, the chute that takes you past the zoo and through the last leftovers of forest before dumping you back into the city. Houses appear high up on the right, nestled into the West Hills like a biopsy of San Francisco, and there are pedestrians and traffic lights and the bars and businesses sprout up. And it's all so sudden it's as though your whole world has been shaken out like salt.

All along the way I didn't think much about them, I thought instead about the night rides as a child, coming home from somewhere, encapsulated in the back-seat dark, the murmur of voices from the front, the highway lights puncturing the blackness at intervals, and the marvel of it all.

The world is larger now – it is itself, really – but it feels more like the great flat thing they used to dream it was, and I think if I drive far enough I'll drive off the edge because I'm held by nothing. Long ago, it was like living in a warm blue globe, a perfect circle of yes and no and there-but-no-further-than: the Perrys' property line, the Big Bear supermarket on the corner, the creek at the end of our street that marked the dead end, on the other side of which was a concrete bedlam of rubble and construction. Now there is just an on-and-on quality and when I'm in the car at night and see the lights from the highway and think of the world just dropping off, there's the cheap temptation to feel sold out. It's not that I don't believe the story any more. It's that there never was a story.

It comes back, though. The next day, at 30,000 feet, in a trust so ignorant, an ignorance so complete, it can only recall childhood. When you don't even have concepts for where you are or the kind of peril you're in, and everything is bite-sized and you're reduced to doing what you're told. It's a night flight, and when I wake in the morning I see beneath me the dull cloud mass and then, lower again, the fields, jade-coloured now in the rain, and the black dots that might be beasts or bales of hay. When the pilot touches down, it's to rapturous applause.

Within an hour, I have re-entered the earth's weather. The biblical import of a prolonged and heavy rain. Something comic too, though, in the flooded streets and the puddles, an invitation to some harmless disorder, as though children have been put in charge of the world. We scurry through the downpour under our umbrellas and I imagine us from above, our thousand coloured domes a fabulous shifting mosaic.

When we were young we bought Navajo dream catchers at the Saturday market in Portland and hung them on our bedroom walls, our first act of ethnic tourism. I thought of dreams as huge and shapeless things, vaporous abstractions, and I pictured those webbed devices sucking in our dreams at night-time and a netherworld beyond where every one of them lived on, in a dizzying cross-pollination of narratives. We used to lie side by side in the dark and tell each other stories, about ourselves or things we hoped would happen, and our rooms, I was sure, contained a thousand versions of us. I imagined an infrared light that would enable all the beings we'd ever evoked to be seen, tiny – because they were only thoughts – and covering every available surface and some of them just floating.

Now, I think of everything we didn't know and the future, from the vantage point of then, appears instead an impossibly empty space, Andean in its sweep, a cool white plain waiting to receive us. And the vastness of our ignorance seems beautiful.

★

Somebody coined them the Graffiti Wars, though that makes them sound more playful than they were. It also suggests that

Nina fought back, which she didn't, but then maybe the wars being fought were between different boys, or groups of boys, who were competing over her defacement. Because that's how it seemed to me, as though they were writing all over her.

It was early spring. Our time together was winding down. The previous day we'd been on a field trip to the coast, our whole senior biology class studying crustaceans in the tide pools that were sunk into the moonscape of rocks. It was bright and windy and the colours were piercing, the kind of day that makes the sky appear textured and the mountains two-dimensional. That hallucinatory beauty that gives rise first to elation and then to melancholy.

They were standing by the rocks in the cold sunshine, Nina and the Mormon boy, peering at something he held in his palm. Their heads – hers dark, Michael's light – were touching. With his preternatural cleanliness and near-white blondness, he looked like what all of us might've been once, before we came to earth and assumed our shapes of imperfection.

It was a kind of paradise, that day, and I remember it because it was the day before the graffiti started and Nina lost her innocence. She still had it up to then, because innocence isn't really about what you have or haven't done. It's to do with knowing what people are capable of and understanding that the world wasn't created for your protection.

The next morning we were walking to school, exchanging misinformation about Mormons.

'They go around in pairs with suits on,' Nina was saying. 'I've seen them at my grandmother's.'

'Isn't that Jehovah's Witnesses?'

'Mormons, too. It's called a mission.'

'To convert people?'

'No, it's just for, I don't know, maybe,' she said. 'It's for before they settle down and have kids, I think. They can have more than one wife, you know.'

'That's illegal,' I said.

'Not if you're a Mormon.'

'He told you this?'

'Yep.'

'A kid and four wives,' I said.

I pictured the harems of Utah, Michael in his grass-stained football pants reclining on a massive pillow, a throng of cheerleader-wives draped around the room in silks or carrying dishes of steaming things or sewing his clothes under a dim bulb. A cross between a seraglio and the Industrial Revolution.

'Why are they always blond?' I said.

'Because they only marry each other.'

'Then you get birth defects.'

'Not if they're enough of you.'

We were nearing the corner where we would turn into the driveway of the school when she stopped in front of the large green sign that marked the turn. She was looking up at the sign the way you would if you were lost, and I was looking at it without seeing what had been scrawled on it, because graffiti is like wallpaper unless it's about you. And then I heard her say 'bastard' under her breath and she started walking again.

We rounded the corner and continued up the long wide driveway that would take us past the football field on the left and the woodshop on the right, through the parking lot and beyond the swimming pool and up to the front doors, which were propped open now because it was spring. For the last eight years we had walked to school together, first to the middle school and then to here. I had by then begun to feel nostalgic for us and I admit I was enjoying the solemnity of that particular moment – of the silence, and the loyalty or discretion I fancied I was showing her by not breaking it. I felt oddly detached, as though I had stepped back and were watching God make memories. And I thought, this is what the world is like – big grave feelings and meaningful silences – and it seemed a deep, dramatic place I couldn't wait to enter.

And then I saw that it was everywhere. On the sign that said Staff Parking and on one of the wooden benches outside the front door, on the sidewalk, on the wall of the swimming pool, even on the grass, which ran in strips along the side of the drive.

★

Before we acquired a consciousness of ourselves in historical time, as occupying a particular era distinct from other eras, we harboured the illusion that the world had been ticking over, more or less the same, back into some formless past that stretched roughly to the invention of the automobile. We had seen old photos of carriages, horses standing dejectedly in streets devoid of cars, and that was a past we could respect. Anything more recent was just time waiting for us to be born.

In our own lives, of course, there were increments, points of demarcation on either side of which the befores and afters of our childhood resided. The man in the woods might've been the first such point. We were eleven when he started skulking about and though neither of us ever saw him, he taught us something about time. That it went forward in a more serious fashion than we had realized and that with its passing we would learn new and sometimes unpleasant things, things we'd rather not have known.

His appearance galvanized the town. Meetings were held in various locations. Police circulars slipped under our doors. The parents' association devised a phone tree in case anybody spotted anything peculiar. Nothing had so united the adult population since the proposed four-lane highway, whose progress through those same woods they'd successfully halted. Now, a few people referred to this, suggesting it had been a mistake. As though by standing in the way of technology's advance, we'd brought this menace on ourselves. It sounds strange, I know, but back then ordinary people didn't think about things like CO_2. We took our fridges to the dump and it was something of a day out for the kids. We abandoned them there in all their sad ungainliness, their doors hanging off their hinges, or flung open with such vehemence it made them look like opera stars launching into arias.

Perhaps because my sole experience of the adult male body had been photographs I'd seen in my mother's *Hellenic Art*, I pictured the man a classical statue. Unmoving, and passive in his nudity (though his modus operandi was one of fleeing, and he 'exposed himself' only to the extent of flashing). I imagined one arm lopped off at the bicep, his quadriceps swollen with latent strength, a penis comically small in proportion to all that licentious muscle. In his eyes there was a hurt of sorts, something coy but inappropriate, the look of someone who'd had sex too young and lost the hang of other languages. I saw a round generous buttock, the toes of one foot turned delicately under, a head ringed by a wreath of laurel.

Years later, when they arrested Mr Heath, the owner of our local bicycle shop, for feeling up a boy in the back of his showroom, he confessed – in the sweaty blubbering way we've come to associate with unmasked paedophiles – to having been 'the man in the woods' all those years ago. The Greek, the beginning of our time.

Nina called me from outside Portland where she was living.

'It's here in the paper,' she said, and read the whole thing out to me.

'Mr Heath,' I said. 'Wow.' I remembered him. He was standing in the bike shop with a small-town grin on his face and WD40 streaked his coveralls.

'Didn't your mother have him to dinner one night?' Nina asked.

'Did she? God, I don't remember. Probably.'

She laughed a little, though sadly.

'I'll have to ask her,' I said. 'Though I'd hate to tell her that one of her guests turned out to be a child molester. In fact, I don't think I would tell her.'

'There'd be no point,' Nina agreed.

'She always asks about you,' I said.

'Is she still walking dogs?'

My mother had moved away by then. After my father died, she went north to where she had a sister, in the suburbs of Seattle. When I visited her we sometimes took a ferry to Vashon or Bainbridge Island and at night we'd look across the sound and see the lights up and down the shoreline, the houseboats bobbing in all their toylike and inoffensive luxury.

At first, my mother'd volunteered at an animal shelter and then she started her own business walking dogs and looking after people's pets while they were away. A few times she'd gone back and 'disappeared' pets who weren't being properly cared for. She gave them to friends and, once, kept one for herself.

'You can't do that,' I told her. 'That's illegal, that's kidnapping. Sooner or later someone's going to detect a pattern. And anyway, you're probably breaking children's hearts.'

'Oh no,' she said, 'I'd never do that. We're talking about a guy who's hooked on heroin and can't look after his cat. That sort of thing.'

'Maybe that cat was the only comfort he had,' I said.

'I thought of that,' she said. 'And I'm trying to help him. I drive him to his methadone and I bring him hot meals and I'm here when he needs me. I like this guy. But there's no reason the cat has to be miserable too.'

Her brand of interventionism exasperated me, but I admired it at the same time. There was nothing abstract about her goodness; it was customized and it was locally administered and she was kind to the people in her path. And I thought she was one of the few individuals I'd ever known who was both genuinely happy and keenly aware of suffering.

'Yeah,' I said to Nina, 'she's still walking dogs.'

'I keep meaning to go up there and visit her. Me and Jimmy should go. Would she mind that, if I brought Jimmy?'

'Of course not. She loves Jimmy.'

'Yeah, we should do that.'

'You should,' I said.

'We will,' she said, and I could feel her enthusiasm already waning.

After we hung up, I sat in the kitchen and drank a beer and noticed that the skin on my fingers had grown waxy and stretched, like it was a part of me forging ahead into old age, cutting a swathe through the years to make them safe for the rest of me. I pushed the beer bottle around the table and wondered what Nina was doing now and how she felt. And I thought about goofy Mr Heath and the beautiful Hellenic nude and how the truth is always somewhere in between.

If we were incapable of imagining a past that didn't include us, neither did it occur to us that there was a future beyond our own lifespans. We looked at the world on a map and considered the contours and the colours of its nations something final and decided on, and we assumed that this ultimate incarnation had been arrived at because it made a self-evident sense. We saw ourselves as living at the End of History and we'd never even heard the term.

In science class, we were confronted with a timeline on which a space the size of our thumbnails equalled 60 million years and we had no idea how to take such information seriously. We learned about glaciation in the Pleistocene epoch, the flourishing of marine invertebrates during the Ordovician period, the first fish arriving in the Silurian, amphibians in the Devonian. And it was all as inconceivable to us as our parents' childhoods. No more, no less.

We had a science teacher who talked about the earth in terms other than utility, and he awakened in us a rather theatrical environmentalism.

We did a project on evolution. At the edge of the pond behind Nina's house, in a moment of epoch-straddling nostalgia, we stood beside the small shrine we'd built to all the species that had been here and gone, all the old friends who'd made today possible. We'd seen tadpoles there from time to time and their resemblance to cartoon sperm and their shape-shifting over the course of a single short lifetime had rendered them symbols of evolution and imbued the pond with a biological sanctity. Nina was inordinately touched by the idea of extinction and I, in turn, was moved by her emotion.

We said a little prayer in honour of the dead. We held a Green Mass.

'By Order of the Tadpole,' I began.

'Be serious.'

It was December and the trees were bare and the grass was stiff and hoary under our feet. The sky a metallic grey we were used to. Nina hummed quietly beside me.

'We give thanks to the many phyla who have contributed to our being here today.'

On a large flipchart, we sketched a number of extinct animals in coloured magic markers – plesiosaurs, ichthyosaurs, trilobites – and stood at the front of the class paying tribute to them as though we were accepting an Oscar. It didn't matter that we weren't direct descendants; it was all part of the great pudding, the behind-the-scenes bonanza of creation. This was long before the teaching of origins controversy arose, and nobody even blinked when we announced that evolution was the number one example of God's patience.

I liked the ice ages. I imagined the vast stillness of the tundra, the absolute silence of snow, its occasional stirring by wind the only sign of movement for millennia. A world of nothing but blue and white.

Standing beside Nina's pond, I said, 'We bow before the earth and we thank it for having us.'

'We thank the snows for melting,' Nina added, and lowered her head a degree in respect and was silent.

I wanted to undo population. I imagined the imperiousness of an ice age, its sweeping dismissal of all the life forms waiting in the wings. But also, its weakness, its Achilles heel, its monstrous blinding terrain evaporating in the unseen warmth. I felt the whole earth waiting for a signal to awake, as though under hypnosis or in a fairy tale. I thought of every single spring on record compressed into the lone, just audible (or maybe deafening) crack that signaled the beginning of the end. The onset of a spring we're still living in.

We had our own ice ages, which arrived with an annual precision, swooped and then departed, an atavism of the earth itself. The electricity went and there was a terrible tightness to the air and the world outside our windows looked a like a place we couldn't breathe in. There was no school for a week and Nina stayed with us and we went round in our nightgowns and my mother's fake fur coats. We put on make-up out of boredom and huddled in front of the fire, our faces painted, our lives askew, pretending we were Russian royalty on the skids like in a movie we must've inadvertently seen.

When the electricity came back, we went round flicking the switches just for fun and felt for a moment a kind of ersatz wonder at it all. By the time the rains returned we were ready to be ourselves again, and when the streets were once more streaming and the soaked earth squelched under our feet, the week we'd spent drawn up to the fire was like a vague prehistory.

★

About two weeks after that initial flurry (which the janitors had worked overtime to remove all traces of), it appeared again. This time, though, it wasn't blatant but rather in the form of oblique one-liners, tucked away like Easter eggs. On the base of the drinking fountain down near the track, inside the wooden shed where the crew oars and the tennis nets were kept, on the rusted recycling cylinders that languished in the far corner of a dusty lot in the outback of the school's grounds.

Revelations, insults, mysterious allusions. References to an article of clothing, the colour of her lipstick, a particular cul-de-sac not far from her home. A brand name, a nick-name, a pet name, an out-and-out slur. Or just words devoid of context – *your recurring dream* or *your blue notebook* – innocuous enough but for the circumstances. There was the licence plate number of somebody's car. There were frag-ments of what appeared to be dialogue.

In one case, there was simply a date: *3 November, 1979.*

Her name was never mentioned, not that first morning and not in any subsequent waves (whoever they were, they were disciplined), and this refusal to name her in a way made the whole thing worse, as though so much about Nina went without saying. It meant that a kind of conversation had been taking place about her for some time, a subtext that consisted of all the knowledge of her that, together, boys had managed to amass.

Which is not to say that all of it was true, that each scribbled slander or suggestion had an actual correlative in the real world. Who knew? But the encodedness of it allowed us to assign any image we wanted to the words, until our minds were awash with her, and fantasies commingled freely with the truth. (In the end, they could've written anything; our imaginations had been stoked to the point where we'd have grafted a story on to an ellipsis.) The way it was drip-fed to us meant that a certain thrill inevitably attached itself to the discovery of every cryptic snippet. And then the whole thing became weirdly detached from her, or almost, as though it were a game and Nina simply the board on which the game was being played.

She didn't talk about it, not even to me. And nobody, as far as I knew, would talk about it to her. I thought at first that the teachers might take her aside, but what could they say? They knew, of course, that it was about her (by virtue of that mysteriously permeable membrane that allowed information to pass between students and teachers), but they didn't want to make things worse by letting her know they knew. They did attempt some behind-the-scenes detective work which, not surprisingly, came to nothing. It was like trying to address 'the litter problem'. This thing was everywhere and nowhere and it moved, even as we spoke about it, blew around in the wind like rumours or garbage.

My mother heard about it at the supermarket one day from somebody else's mother and, not surprisingly, she determined to take action. But despite her evening homily on the virtues of communication and her vow to take Nina aside and bolster her resolve in the face of 'these pimply cowardly fuckers', ultimately, even she couldn't broach the subject. Instead, she treated Nina with a respect that went beyond anything I'd seen visited on her Sunday dinner guests. It was serious and watchful, managing somehow to bestow a dignity on Nina and turn her suffering into something grand and deep and adult.

As abruptly as it began, it ended, a couple of weeks before summer vacation. We knew it was over because they told us. On the grey door to the gym, through which every single student had to pass each day on the way to PE class, was written *The End*, as though announcing the close of a bed-time story. And that was it. In the short time we had left at school, no copycat artists emerged. The *schadenfreude* had abated and the catharsis had been achieved and the appetite for scandal sated.

And still, she said nothing. I think she adopted the strategy of pretending the whole thing had nothing to do with her. Or maybe she was just keeping it together long enough to get out of town and fall apart in private. She left early for college, mid-July, saying she wanted to get settled. She wrote me frantically happy letters about the new world of northern California – the spectacular coastline and the mind-blowing weed and how wonderful life is when every person you meet is a stranger.

She cracked in October, and it was Jimmy who called me. He was a graduate student working part-time in the school psychiatrist's office while getting his Master's in social work.

'She told me everything,' he said.

'She told *you*?'

'She wouldn't speak to the doctor.'

'But she told you.'

'That kind of free-floating attack is worse,' he said. 'When you don't know who to blame you blame everyone. And that's an impossible way to live.'

I could hear in his voice that he liked her.

He used to make up scenes when they were courting. He took her up to Longview once and parked so they could see the nuclear power plant on the other side of the river. He said imagine there's been a catastrophic fallout and we're the last non-toxic humans left alive. It's all down to us, baby, we're a nuclear Adam and Eve.

She hesitated. Too much responsibility, she said.

Hey, he said, with my genes and your chromosomes, we could make . . . what?

A beautiful species together.

Another time he took her to Summer Lake on the far side of the Cascades to show her the sand dunes that were nowhere near any sea.

Pretend we're in Arabia, he said. These dunes are Arabia and everything else is an oasis. A little reverse psychology on nature's part.

Nina closed her eyes. OK, she said, Arabia it is.

She saw camels, in all their regal ungainliness, cresting the brow of a hill, the sand deep and soft and their long legs buckling. She saw blue pools and carriages encrusted with jewels. There was plant life of an impossible red and there were fabrics that flapped in the breeze and when she opened her eyes she saw Jimmy, like love itself beside her.

I see ads for lost schoolmates on my internet home page.

Do you recognize these people?

There is a row of photographs, obviously taken from yearbooks. Faces looking poised for disillusionment, an innocence just asking to be profaned. Like the photos you see of people who've gone missing. They're always smiling, and it's worse when the people are found and their faces are still dotted around the place, still smiling, their eyes accusing us of a certain belatedness.

If you have any information about these people, please e-mail us (e.g. married name, husband's full name, parents' name, profession, who their best friends were, etc). If deceased, please so indicate.

I look at the names – these ordinary people who've grown interesting enough to disappear. I imagine them in the sub-Sahara or Buenos Aires, or working for *Médecins Sans Frontières* and too serious and busy to be bothered about such nonsense.

Nina is alive and well and living in the north-west corner of America. But when I think about her it's as though she's posthumous. Jimmy too, for some reason. What is it that's dead? Before she launched herself into the wide world, we had our halcyon days. Before anybody turned on her or anything got ugly. We lived in the airtightness of each other's affection.

Now I look at her and feel a fragmentation, but it's mostly my own. Because what I see when I look at her is a life that is greater than the sum of its parts. That's cohered.

One summer, when we were both home from college and she was getting ready to go back to California and I was going back to New York, we were sitting in the dark on the docks and I was thinking about her parents, about that weird formality of theirs, which in a way I'd always liked. It added order to our lives and made me believe that whatever else happened or wherever we went, we were tethered to something limiting and solid. And then I thought about how, once, everything had seemed necessary and inevitable and how that was what I missed about our lives. They had changed by then and were opening up to too many possibilities, most of which we would never be equal to. But how a long time ago, the worlds we knew were limited to one, and if we were equal to that then there was nothing to feel insufficient in the face of. I wanted her to take my hand the way she once had, to be the centre of a world I knew she wasn't any more. I wanted to touch her, by way of comfort, but it seemed like a gesture and, anyway, belated.

Mary Morrissy

Gracefully, Not Too Fast

FIAEVI SJ XLI HSK!

This is how the world appears to the illiterate

Ruth stands under the legend she has just written on the blackboard. It is an infants' classroom so that even though there are only five adults in the room it seems crowded because their outsized limbs are squeezed between the yellow tubular arms of the child-sized chairs or squashed impossibly under the low tables. There are drawings pasted on to the walls, abstract splotches or keenly symmetrical houses. In the grandly announced Play Corner there is a raised sandpit where upturned buckets – saucily showing off their crenellated bottoms – jostle with jauntily anchored spades. Above the coat hooks, which line three walls of the room, the letters of the alphabet are drawn on large white cards with an accompanying illustration. A is for apple, B is for book.

Ruth could have had the pick of any of the rooms in the school but Senior Infants is a deliberate choice. It reduces her students. They don't *fit* here; they are too big. Depending on their own experience, they will either be swamped by nostalgia or – and this is Ruth's hope – will relive some of the terror of the infant's first day of school, the bawling distress, the inexplicable abandonment.

It is a winter's evening. A hangover of slush is banked on the sills of the high schoolhouse windows, spookily irradiated by the sulphurous glow of the street lights. It is wintry within too. The ancient radiators are only tepid and everyone, including Ruth, is wearing an overcoat. Next door there's the busy homeliness of Experimenting with Watercolours, festive clinking of brushes in jars clouded with spools of Prussian Blue and Burnt Sienna; in Room 2B the plaintive chorus of Basic Italian – *che una banca qui vicino?* But here it is silent, and uncomfortable.

Ruth surveys her latest group. She prides herself on being able to read them. There is a young man, about nineteen or so Ruth surmises, unfortunate carroty hair partnered with a painterly pallor. (Jasper Carrott, she thinks, but only as a mnemonic device.) A plump woman with a sculpted chestnut tint perm, large clip-on earrings like bulbous saucers and a soft, weak chin, sits at the very front, her hands clasped together like a diva. Beside her is a fresh-faced woman in her thirties, a mother of young children, Ruth guesses, armed with a notebook. Her ash-blonde hair is cropped for practicality's sake, but stylish too. There is the ghost of a package-holiday tan on her face. A placid, moon-faced girl with fair ropey plaits (like a figure on a Swiss barometer, Ruth thinks) peering over granny glasses sits tentatively in the middle row three seats back. She will be zealous and shy, Ruth decides, probably a reader at Mass, a frequent volunteer at the offertory procession. An elderly man sits at the back of the class. He has the ravaged looks of a drinker. Beneath the false bloom of those ruddy cheeks lurks a pasty-faced, malnourished invalid suffering from a terminal loss of appetite. He has thinning hair half-heartedly spread over his pate and the unkempt air of a widower or a late divorcee; he has not been touched for a long time. This is Ruth's raw material, the blind leading the unlettered.

Ruth Coppinger was a bit of a prodigy. (In retrospect that sounded like a qualification but out of the mouths of maiden aunts it had been coolly admiring. *A bit of a prodigy*.) She was sent to the college of music for piano lessons when she was seven. At eight she was attending singing lessons. By the age of ten she had performed on the radio. Hers was a precocious talent. Her father was immensely proud of her. When she looked back on those early years she remembered little joy in performing; but she savoured his quiet, enormous pride in her. It was his form of love. At great expense she was sent to Mr Edwin Calthorp for singing lessons. She remembered the first time her mother led her up the overhung path to his house. The garden was kept rather than cherished. (It was a time before garden centres.) The house was in what was later to be dubbed the Jewish quarter, when the school at the corner of Mr Calthorp's street was converted into loft apartments and the dingy little bakery became a place of pilgrimage for atheists to buy pastries on a Sunday morning. But back then it was merely a huddle of worthy red-brick streets backing on to the canal. A sign on Mr Calthorp's gate showed a line drawing of a fierce-looking Alsatian and a warning which read Beware of the Dog.

'Oooh,' Ruth's mother said. 'I hope he's tied up.'

She was terrified of dogs. Once on her way to the shops, she had stood for a whole hour at their gate, paralysed with fear, because the dachshund across the road had ambushed her. The silly little sausage dog had plonked himself at the kerb within a few feet of her and launched a barrage of barking. Ruth had come home from school and found her, clutching her shopping basket white-knuckled, pleading weakly with the dog to go away. Ruth had sent him running with one well-aimed swipe of her foot.

The heavy, brown front door was opened by Mr Calthorp's mother. She was a knotty little woman, red-handed as if she had been interrupted in the middle of bleaching. Her grey hair was scraped into a bun. She wore a navy housecoat, sprigged with white.

'Yes?'

'We've come for Ruth's lesson,' her mother said tentatively.

'And you are?'

'Mrs Coppinger, Mrs Alice Coppinger.'

Mrs Calthorp looked at her stonily.

'We spoke on the phone,' Ruth's mother went on, 'remember?'

Ruth blushed at her mother's querulousness. It was a tone her mother used when she was trying to be masterful but it came out prickly and aggrieved.

'You'd better come in,' Mrs Calthorp said. She would always be like that treating the pupils who came to the house as if they were a vague annoyance, as if her beloved son had more important things to be doing.

They stepped into a linoed hallway. Mrs Calthorp showed them into the front parlour. This was a brown room, tobacco-coloured wallpaper, a large foxed mirror over the mantel, a brass urn housing an asparagus fern eclipsing the empty fire grate. A couple of respectable but lumpy-looking armchairs crouched together around the hearth rug defying occupation. Ranged around the wainscotted walls were several other upright chairs, refugees from a dining-room suite upholstered in worn but well-polished leather, but equally forbidding. The door was closed on them and they were left alone.

'It's like a doctor's waiting room,' Ruth's mother whispered, 'except there aren't even magazines.'

Several minutes passed. Mrs Calthorp reappeared.

'You can come up now,' she said, adding meaningfully, 'To the music room.'

They followed her up the carpeted stairs, a red fleur-de-lys pattern, to a return and then up another flight. Straight ahead of them a door stood ajar. Mrs Calthorp gestured to them to enter. Ruth's mother, expecting her to follow, marched in boldly, then turned around only to find the door being closed behind them as Mrs Calthorp melted away into the varnished landing. This was an airier room than the one below, with two sash windows looking out on to the street, and pale fern-patterned wallpaper. A baby grand piano dominated the centre of the room. Along the wall by the door there was a glass cabinet stuffed with sheet music and loitering by one of the windows a couple of music stands, slightly askew like windswept women holding on to their hats. Another asparagus fern stood on a small nest of tables in front of the far window. Weak flames spluttered in the high-built fireplace. Mr Calthorp, who had been sitting at the piano, bowed between the jaws of the opened lid, stood up stiffly and made his way laboriously across the room, fingering the hip curve of the piano as he inched his way forward. He was a tall, thin man, balding on top but there were tufts of tawny hair curling around his ears. The late evening sunlight formed a halo effect around his head, giving him an angelic air as he approached. He was dressed formally like a bank clerk, in a three-piece suit, pin-striped, carefully pressed. He did not meet their gaze, his eyes demurely down-turned, intent on the floor, it seemed. It was only when he drew level with them and stretched out his hand with an odd jerky movement, that he opened them. They were a phlegmy colour, milkily ghoulish. Ruth's mother gasped.

'My mother didn't tell you then,' he said, smiling faintly, as he sought out Mrs Coppinger's hand. 'That I'm blind.'

He clasped both of Mrs Coppinger's hands in his like a priest offering condolences.

'And where is little Ruth?' he asked freeing one of his hands and threading his fingers through the air in search of her head. Ruth's mother hurriedly pushed her into position.

'Ah there,' he said, smiling again. 'So, young lady, let's hear you sing.' He took her by the hand and they moved at Mr Calthorp's stately pace back to the yawning piano.

Mrs Coppinger stood, gloves in hand, watching their procession uncertainly.

'That will be all, Mrs Coppinger,' Mr Calthorp said when he and Ruth had reached the piano and he had eased himself down on to the padded stool. 'We'll call you when we're done.'

Suddenly as if on some unspoken cue, Mrs Calthorp materialized at the door and ushered Ruth's mother out.

Mr Calthorp did have a dog, not a harnessed guide dog – nor the ruthless Alsatian the sign on the gate suggested – but a small white Scottie which sat on his lap. Whenever he made for the piano it scuttled away and sank into a small basket by the fireplace.

'Meet Mimi,' he said. 'She sits in on all my lessons. If she doesn't like what she hears, she howls. It's Mimi who decides whether you stay or go.'

'Well?' Ruth's mother demanded when the first class was over and they were safely out on the street. She had spent the half-hour lesson standing in the unwelcoming front parlour, afraid to sit down. 'Without even so much as the offer of a cup of tea,' she added.

The waiting had sharpened her air of complaint.

'Well?'

'Oh, we just did some scales, and arpeggios.'

'And?'

'Strong voice, he said, range needs work.'

'Motivation,' Ruth says loudly. It is the first word she speaks and it sounds – as it is intended to – like a reprimand. 'Why are we here?'

Ruth already knows the answers. Guilt masquerading as a social conscience, a love of books, a social activity that gets you out in the evenings, do-gooding.

'Why indeed,' smirking Jasper Carrott says under his breath.

'I just can't imagine what it would be like not being able to read,' offers the Swiss *Mädchen*.

'Anyone else?' Ruth asks.

'Books have been such a comfort to me . . .' the permed matron declares. 'Mrs Turnbull,' she adds helpfully, 'Mrs Daphne Turnbull.' She turns awkwardly in her chair to appeal to the other students in the class. 'Especially since my husband passed away. And I always wanted to do charity work . . .'

'Well, Mrs Turnbull,' Ruth interrupts. 'Let me remind you that literacy is not a matter of charity; it's a right.'

After the first couple of weeks her mother stopped coming with her – it was only a short bus ride away – and so the singing classes became for Ruth a time apart, a little oasis away from her mother's twitchy unease, her deep undertow of unworthiness. She treasured the cloistered quietness of those journeys to Mr Calthorp's and the joyless discipline of the lesson itself. It was hard work and Mr Calthorp was not very patient.

'No, no, no,' he would cry banging down his hands on the keys in the middle of a song. 'Flat, flat, flat. Can't you hear it?'

When he shouted like that, Mrs Calthorp would wind her head around the door.

'Everything all right in here?' she would ask looking gimlet-eyed at Ruth, as if it was she who was causing the commotion.

He usually ignored the interruption.

'It's like this. Bah bah bah, bah – bah.' He hummed rather tunelessly himself, Ruth thought. She would watch him when he was in a rage like this, his bleached pupils turned searchingly heavenward. She wondered what he saw when his eyes were open. Was it the same darkness as she saw with her eyes closed? Or was it different? But she didn't ask. Since that first day with her mother, no mention of his blindness had been made. And after a while she simply forgot about it. And yet, and yet it made a difference. Expressions would flit across his face, irritation a lot of the time, a dark cloud of impatience settling on his brow, but other emotions too that she found harder to read. A sort of rapture if he were pleased, a secretive kind of joy. And of course, his blindness protected *her*. She could pull faces whenever she liked. Frequently, when he made her go over a particular phrase again and again, she would stick her tongue out at him. Her timing was poor and he would make her sing unaccompanied, using the metronome. She would watch him fumbling with the menacing pendulum – how she hated it, ticking back and forth, back and forth, full of leaden reproach – and she would deliberately shift position knowing that this confused him. Suddenly he would look up and with a strange kind of lostness ask: 'Where are you? Where have you gone?'

Mimi hated the metronome too. She would dive off Mr Calthorp's lap and burrow into her basket, yowling painfully. Frequently she made such a racket that he would turn the metronome off and Mimi would scramble back on to his lap. It was the only time Ruth liked Mimi. She was envious of the little mutt, who nestled on Mr Calthorp's knees. He fondled her, stroking her thick tight curls. Sometimes he would bury his face in her coat and make growling doggy sounds and Ruth would look away, embarrassed. That was the thing about blind people; everything about them was visible.

Ruth wanted desperately to please him, because, she supposed, he was so hard to please. His lofty name (a Prod, I'll be bound, her father had said) and his blindness gave him a kind of unapproachable nobility which unnerved her, though his manner, his jovial avuncular style belied this. It was not that she didn't know how to wheedle affection. When her father came in from work in the evenings she would climb aboard his sprawled but tense limbs as he slumped in the armchair in front of the television. She would drape her arms slyly around his neck and cradle her head against the rough skin of his neck. Beneath his white Bri-nylon shirt she could hear the steady thump of his heart. And she would wait for his jaded indifference to give way, for him to throw one arm lazily across her knees and prop her elbow up with the other and snuggle into the hollow of the armchair until both of them were snoozily comfortable. Meanwhile, lying on their stomachs on the carpet watching TV, Barry and John would greet him with a casual 'Hi Dad' before turning their attention back to the screen.

'Boys,' he would say as he sank into the slovenly cushions.

She envied and admired this easy, male shorthand. She had to work harder, she knew.

But she couldn't cajole Mr Calthorp. The only way with him was to be the best little singer she could be. Early on she had some success – highly commended for her rendition of *Where E'er You Walk* at the Father Mathew Feis (under tens), the spot on the radio programme, *Young People at the microphone* – and now we have Ruth Coppinger to sing *The Harp That Once*. But it wasn't enough. Ruth always worried that Mr Calthorp had brighter pupils than her, more ambitious, more musical, prettier. Though why should pretty make a difference – he couldn't see, after all.

The more musical, more ambitious and prettier pupil did exist, though. She materialized one spring evening.

'Come in, come in, Ruth,' Mr Calthorp said, somehow sensing her hesitation when she entered the music room and found the interloper standing by the piano. A stunned twilight threw faint shadows on the busy wallpaper. 'I want you to meet another one of my star pupils, this is Bridget. Shake hands, you two.'

Neither of them made a move. Bridget was very pretty, taller than Ruth by a head, with glossy dark hair and eyes that seemed jet back. But she was wearing a tacky-looking school uniform. The skirt dipped at the front and there was a piece of the hem hanging. The collar of her shirt was dingy and frayed; her tie was not real, but one of those fake ones on a piece of elastic. And there was, frankly, a smell from her. A smell of dampness as if her clothes had not been properly aired, and as if she bathed in cold water. Her fingernails were bitten and not very clean. Ruth knew that look from the tinker women who called to the door with their broad ravaged faces and creased palms, leathery women with swaddled children. But she wasn't sure if the look came from being a tinker or just being poor. The girl smiled bashfully showing a crooked set of teeth.

'Howrya,' she said.

'Now, I thought,' Mr Calthorp said, 'that it would be good to get my two brightest pupils together for a spot of duets. Wouldn't that be fun? Two voices better than one, and all that!'

He obviously doesn't know, Ruth thought. He has no idea how poor she is. Ruth's experience of poor people was limited. Sometimes it seemed that *they* were poor – when it came to the singing lessons they certainly were. Her father indulged in jocular grumbling about the cost of indulging 'notions' – and Mr Calthorp fell into this category. But then when they passed beggars on the street, it was undeniable that they, the Coppingers, were better off. Ruth's mother would pull her roughly by the arm if she even so much as halted at an outstretched hand, or listened to the pious lament of their woes. Mrs Coppinger said it was wrong to give them anything because it only encouraged them. They only used it for drink anyway. Poverty was something to be feared – not for what the poor in their rage might do to you – but for its perilous proximity. As if it might be infectious.

Ruth suspected that somehow this girl had got in under false pretences. That she had duped Mr Calthorp in some way. That she had taken advantage because he was blind. Ruth, however, had been brought up to be polite so she said hello in an icy bright voice.

Every second week, Bridget came to Ruth's lesson and they practised together. She had a clear high voice which relegated Ruth to singing descant.

'Your strength, Ruth,' Mr Calthorp said, though Ruth saw it differently. She was the background, the plodding undertone to Bridget's soprano. Ruth was going to theory classes at the college of music so she could read notation but Bridget relied on her ear. She spoke about music in a totally different way.

'That bit in the middle, where it goes up, like going upstairs,' she would say in her flat, hard accent, so at odds with her singing voice.

'The bridge,' Ruth would offer.

'There's a watery piece towards the end, like the bath tap dripping.'

The run of semiquavers, Ruth thought.

'Well,' Bridget added, 'like our bath tap. Drips something rotten and there's a big green stain on the bath from it.'

So, Ruth thought, they do have running water.

'She's so instinctive,' Mr Calthorp would say admiringly of Bridget, 'such a feel for the music, and perfect pitch with it.'

He often talked about her to Ruth. At first she didn't mind; in fact, she was quite flattered. It gave her a pre-eminence; it was *some* kind of recognition.

'I hope you don't mind sharing your class, Ruth, but Bridget hasn't had all the advantages you've had. And it's good training, for choral work in the future.' Ruth was lucky, he said, she had a voice that blended. Ruth heard the message loud and clear – her future as a bit player in a choir.

She didn't tell her parents about Bridget. She suspected they wouldn't approve. Her mother would only go round to Mr Calthorp's and protest vociferously, helplessly. Her father would say they weren't a registered charity. She knew too that being compliant about Bridget's presence was one way to please Mr Calthorp. Maybe the joint lessons wouldn't last, maybe they'd just enter a few competitions and then it would be over. In the meantime, she was pleasant if off-hand with Bridget. She noted assiduously any further signs of impoverishment, and there were plenty. Bridget never had her own sheet music, for one, nor did she have a music case whereas Ruth considered her slim leather wallet with the chrome handle as proof of the seriousness of her vocation. Bridget didn't press for friendship either. She seemed nervous to Ruth, or was it shifty? Her crooked smile was placatory and sometimes when Mr Calthorp was losing his rag – as Bridget called it – she would throw her eyes to heaven in a comradely fashion. But Ruth treated such overtures with disdain. It was all right for her to pull faces right under Mr Calthorp's nose, but the two of them doing it would have smacked of collaboration. And betrayal.

For Bridget singing seemed effortless. She never had to look at the music, she just took a deep breath and out it came, pitch-perfect, sweet, tuneful, whereas Ruth, stuck with the more sombre line, felt she had to struggle to be heard. Sometimes she was distracted by the beauty of the melody line, though in truth it was Bridget's voice that distracted her, so clear, so uncluttered, as if it was the most natural thing in the world to open your mouth and just . . . sing. It wasn't natural for Ruth; it was practice, it was work.

Jasper Carrott puts up his hand.

'If, as you say (Ruth bristles), literacy is a right, then aren't we doing the State's job for them? I mean, these people have been let down by the education system, aren't we just applying plasters here?'

'That's as maybe,' she replies. 'But we're not here to discuss the rights and wrongs of the system, Malachy.' She has scanned the register and decided that he must be Malachy Forde. If she doesn't get to know his name she might end up calling him Jasper to his face.

'But we must look at the bigger picture, surely?'

'Go to the movies,' she says.

'I was just saying . . . there are implications.'

'If it's debating you're after I suggest you try the public speaking class,' Ruth says loudly, hoping to stem this foray into abstraction. 'We're here to be effective teachers, to be of use. You won't find much interest among your pupils in discussing the how and whys of their illiteracy. We're not here to nurse their grievances, we're here to do a job of work. They want to be able to read and write. End of story.'

There's always one, Ruth thinks, a show-off, a waffler.

Mr Calthorp entered them for the McDavitt Cup – girls, singing pairs, under twelves. He sprang this on them after several months of classes together. *The Ash Grove* was the set song. He had the sheet music ready and after their warm-up scales he handed them a copy each. Normally he would give them a new piece at the end of the class and tell them to throw their eye over it for next week. A curious turn of phrase for a blind man. So this was a departure. He played through the piece twice humming along in his grating voice. Ruth watched Bridget. She seemed fidgety; distracted somehow.

'Got it?'

The girls nodded in unison. An old habit. Anyway, there were some silences Mr Calthorp could read.

'Ruth, why don't you start, you can sight-read. Bridget, you'll pick it up, as we go along. Key of G.'

Ruth launched forth. *By yonder green valley where streamlets me-an-der* . . . She muddled through it somehow to the end.

'Good, now let's try it together. You take the tune this time, Bridget, Ruth you try the seconds line.'

Bridget held the tune, of course. But after the first couple of words she resorted to singing la-las while Ruth struggled with the words and the descant.

'Lovely,' Mr Calthorp said. 'This time, Bridget, let's have the words as well.'

Ruth, standing beside Bridget, noticed her hand first. It was trembling. She was holding the sheet in front of her with one hand, while with the finger of the other hand she was tracing the shapes of the letters as if they were in braille, as if by running her fingers over them they would come to life.

'Them's hard words, aren't they?' she said quietly.

'A bit arcane, I'll grant you,' Mr Calthorp said. 'And by the way, note how it is to be sung, Bridget. What does it say above the clef?'

Bridget was a clenched ball of concentration.

'What does it say?' Mr Calthorp repeated.

Bridget shook her head sadly.

She can't read, Ruth realized. It's not that she can't read music. She can't read. Ruth felt a weak swell of triumph. She glanced over at Bridget and caught her eye. There was panic there, a terrible naked fear, a pleading for help. Cover for me, the look said; help, the look said.

'Girls?' Mr Calthorp asked.

Silence.

Ruth and Bridget were locked in that glance, fear meeting refusal. Neither could break it.

'Girls?' Mr Calthorp asked in that lost voice of his as if he weren't sure if they were still there.

Neither of them moved.

'Bridget?'

If he had said Ruth's name, she might have relented. She might have volunteered the words that could have saved Bridget. Four little words. But no, it was Bridget, it would always be Bridget first. So it was really Mr Calthorp who had decided.

'I seem to remember asking a question, Bridget,' Mr Calthorp said in that jolly tone he used when he was uncomfortable. 'Or is nobody bothering with the blind old teacher?'

He tinkered idly at the keys, playing the opening phrase of the melody.

'What on earth's the matter, Bridget? What's the problem here?'

Bridget snuffled noisily, but that was nothing unusual. She seemed to suffer from colds, a permanently running nose.

'Ruth, we seem to have lost Miss Byrnes for the present. Why don't you try it?'

Ruth sang like she never had before, strong and clear, the words perfectly enunciated. She closed her eyes so she wouldn't have to see Bridget standing there, vanquished.

When she opened them again, Bridget had disappeared. She had fled, closing the door silently behind her. Mr Calthorp didn't even realize she was gone.

'Lovely,' Mr Calthorp purred at the end. 'Maybe we'll give you the melody line this time. And why don't you inform Miss Byrnes how this piece should be sung?'

'Gracefully,' Ruth read to the empty room, 'not too fast.'

Ruth pads between the aisles passing out pieces of paper. On each sheet is the musical notion of *Three Blind Mice*.

'To understand the plight of those who cannot read, we must first of all know what it *feels* like,' she says putting on her reading glasses. 'Now, Miss Furlong, isn't it?'

'Marianne,' the plaited born-again Christian says pleasantly.

'Well, Marianne, you'll notice some musical notation on the sheet in front of you. I'd like you to sing the piece of music. It's quite a well-known tune, you probably sang it on your mother's knee, so you shouldn't have any difficulty.'

Marianne paws the paper timidly. There is an uneasy silence in the class coupled with relief that it is she who has been put on the spot.

'I don't read music, actually,' Marianne says smoothly giving what she hopes is an endearingly self-deprecating look. 'You'll have to ask someone else.'

'But I'm asking you, Marianne.'

'I told you, I don't read music.'

'Come on, Marianne, you must make an attempt.'

'But how can I?'

'Everybody's waiting, Miss Furlong.' Ruth takes off her glasses slowly and sets them down deliberately on the table in front of her.

'You mustn't badger me like this. I told you I can't read music. Ask someone else.'

'But I want *you* to do it.'

'But I can't . . .' Marianne wails.

'Exactly, Miss Furlong, my point exactly. Now, how does *that* feel?'

Bridget did not return. Mr Calthorp was baffled.

'I thought I was giving her an opportunity here. She has a God-given talent and I wanted her to make use of that, to better herself.'

He had taken to confiding in Ruth. He would take her hand looking for consolation, reassurance. He was like a man scorned in love. Even Mimi was getting short shrift, pushed impatiently off his lap and sulking now in her basket. Mr Calthorp rubbed Ruth's fingers thoughtfully. He seemed to need her to make sense of it.

'Have you any idea?'

Ruth shrugged, then remembered that Mr Calthorp couldn't see shrugs.

'Maybe her parents couldn't afford it?'

'It wasn't a case of money,' he said sharply. 'It was never a matter of money.'

The mother of two asks a question. Her name is Jean Fleming.

'What should we use for materials? I've got primers at home from my own kids but that'd be insulting, wouldn't it? I wouldn't like to be faced with those Dick can run books at my age. Didn't much care for them even when I was four.'

Ruth smiles. She likes this woman. She *gets* it.

'All that business about Mummy in the kitchen making endless sandwiches. And all Daddy seemed to do was wash the car.'

A titter runs through the classroom.

'I'm glad you raised that,' Ruth says. 'Every pupil is different and often you'll have to adapt to their needs which are often quite specific. It often means making up your material as you go along. Word games, picture cards and the like. You can use the labels on household goods, cereal packets, cans. Everyday stuff.'

'How do they manage?' Jean muses, as if she's thinking aloud, as if she and Ruth are friends chatting over a cup of coffee, trading confidences. She talks wonderingly, her forehead creases quizzically. 'How do they get by? They must be terrified, afraid all the time of being discovered. Always covering up, covering their tracks. I don't think I've ever met anyone who couldn't read. But then, how would I know?'

'I remember the first person I met who couldn't read.' Ruth discovers herself talking, taking up Jean's reflective tone. Stop, stop. 'I remember her name even, Bridget, Bridget Byrnes . . .'

Ruth falters. She has betrayed herself. Keep yourself out of it, she tells her trainee tutors. People don't want to hear how much you love reading, what prompted you to get involved, my first illiterate and all that. This is about them, not you.

'Now where were we?'

It was a sin of omission, a lesser offence. If she had told Mr Calthorp that Bridget couldn't read, what difference would it have made, anyway? He could hardly have given her lessons in that. She had protected Bridget from exposure, by saying nothing. She wondered idly how Bridget had managed to hide it for so long. Someone at home must have been able to read. She must have taken the sheet music home and memorized the words between classes. Sooner or later though, Bridget would have been unmasked. Better that Mr Calthorp thought her ungrateful than for him to know her secret, the shame of that. Bridget's secret was quite safe, stowed away in Ruth's hard, competitive little heart.

All it bought her, in the end, was time. Another year of solo lessons unencumbered by Bridget's better voice, more instinctive feel for the music, her bloody perfect pitch. She remembered the day she arrived for what was to be her last class. She had just turned twelve and Mrs Calthorp showed her into the front parlour. Mr Calthorp came down to fetch her, which was unusual, but instead of climbing the stairs to the music room, he placed a restraining hand on her arm and said:

'Why don't we sit here for a while, Ruth?'

She got to sit – finally – on one of the big armchairs. He perched on the edge of the other one.

'I've been thinking,' he said. The expression on his face was candidly sorrowful, but his glassy eyes seemed blankly evasive. 'About your lessons. And your voice.'

'My voice?'

So here it was; she inhaled deeply.

'Well, often at your age, the voice changes, modulates because of . . .'

Because of breasts and periods was what he wanted to say, she suspected, but couldn't.

'And sometimes it's best not to train the voice during puberty, to let it develop in its own way. Then in a couple of years, if you're still interested we can work with what will be a fine, mature voice, I hope.'

The room was dark, shadowy. It was winter, the clocks had just been turned back. The lights should be turned on, she thought, but the mood was gloomily in tune with Mr Calthorp's mortifying verdict. Somehow, she thought, somehow he has found out.

'But it's been fun, hasn't it?' He said this with a false brightness, the brightness he used to jolly things along.

He was absolutely wrong about that, she thought vehemently. The singing classes had been a lot of things for Ruth Coppinger. But fun, never.

The piano lessons petered out too, though she managed to get as far as Grade 6 before, three years later, she simply gave up. It was not a road to Damascus thing; it was a gradual loss of faith. It wasn't even that she lost interest. It was Mrs Bradley who changed. Mrs Bradley – stout, whiskered, irritable – seemed content to let her play on, faults and all. Once she would have stood over Ruth; drumming time on the lid of the upright, stopping Ruth so often that in an hour-long lesson she would never get through a piece from beginning to end. But latterly she had taken to sitting by the window looking out dreamily over the roofs of the city. She seemed sunk into a kind of trance so that Ruth would have to cough loudly when she had finished to attract her attention. Meanwhile all around them music flourished – the brash din of the college orchestra, the smooth and fluid bow of some bright young violinist, the urgent arpeggios of a soprano yearning towards cadence. Ruth could read the signs – indifference as a prelude to rejection.

'Well,' Ruth says gathering together her papers. 'I hope I haven't put you off completely.'

She's taking bets with herself that Miss Furlong and Mrs Turnbull will not be back next week. It's better this way, to weed out the faint-hearted at the start before they can do any harm.

The students heave themselves out of their miniature traps, and file out. The drinker at the back is the last to leave. Perry is his name. Robert Anthony Perry. The furnishing of a full name gives him away, its titular pretension, its striving self-importance. Anthony is probably his Confirmation name. He pauses at the desk smiling in a gamey way, an old reflex, Ruth imagines, drawing on some ancient source of shabby charm. After-class approaches like this are usually a form of special pleading, a false frankness. Between you and me, the hanger-on is saying, I'm different, not part of the common herd, I'm worthy of your individual attention.

'So what does it mean, then?' He gestures towards the motto on the blackboard.

Ruth has forgotten about it; usually she asks the class to guess at the end, to lighten things up a bit, but something has distracted her with this group.

'Oh that,' she says distractedly hoping to put Mr Perry off. Jean Fleming saves her. She bounces back into the classroom having left her gloves behind.

'Oh, by the way, I meant to ask,' Jean says on her way out. 'Are you the same Miss Coppinger who used to teach at St Ignatius's? My niece went there and spoke so highly of you.'

Jean Fleming is lying. Her niece, Marie, with merciless adolescent judgement, used to call Miss Coppinger a total bitch. Her mother, hushing her, would concede that Miss Coppinger had a reputation for directness, for standing no nonsense. Discipline had certainly never been a problem for her, Jean's sister, Molly, would say. Miss Coppinger could face down a class of unruly boys with the set of her shoulders and the fix of her stare. Molly attributed her fierceness to her size. 'You should see her, Jean,' she used to say, 'she's *tiny*, five foot nothing, mop-top ginger hair like Shirley Temple, or one of those other child stars.' She was a great loss to the school when she went, Molly said. No one was surprised, though, when she moved into Adult Ed; she was always a bit of a crusader, always willing to go the extra mile. Played the piano for all the school operettas and would gladly do Beatles numbers and ragtime during the intervals at concerts and open days though she wasn't even the music teacher.

'Still tickling the ivories, then?' Jean asks brightly.

How little she knows, Ruth thinks. She is furious suddenly. Furious about the years of practice, the tantalizing promise of perfection, all that cruel vocational energy expended. For what? For this – tickling the ivories.

Mr Perry is still standing there. He shuffles his feet conspicuously.

'Oh, I'm sorry,' Jean says, 'I interrupted you.'

'No,' he says switching his gelid attention to Jean, 'I was just asking Miss Coppinger about this.' He points again at the blackboard.

'Yes, what does that mean? I was wondering too, but to tell you the truth, I was a bit afraid to ask.' Jean laughs nervously.

Ruth pushes past both of them. She hits the light switch as she reaches the door. 'Beware of the dog,' she snaps plunging them into darkness.

KEITH RIDGWAY

Grid Work

This sea, it's outrageous. I need to take a break from it. I need good food and a lemon cordial. This sea is making me hungry. It suggests impossibles – an unquenchable appetite for space; an intelligence resting, taking in the sun. I've stared at it for a couple of hours now and my thirst is jagged. I won't take coffee, tea, cola, alcohol – they're all diuretic and prohibited, by me at least. Flying is a combative venture – you need to look after yourself up here, it's always a solo crossing. What they offer in the way of refreshment is, mostly, bad for you. They want, I've been told, to intensify the experience. Get you dehydrated and wired, so that you'll feel you've done something extraordinary. Which you have. My shoes are off and I've lost one of them and I want to put them back on because I think I should go for a walk, but I have to fold myself in quarters in order to reach the missing shoe, or to reach the place where I think it is, which it isn't, of course, so I have to contort my left leg and dislocate my right shoulder and I'm getting the fretted net of the magazine holder imprinted on my forehead and the woman next to me is adopting a disapproving body position – as if leaning away from a height – and my left foot is starting to go numb, and I finally hook a finger into the damn shoe and tug it towards me, and lose it, and get it again, and drag it out into my square metre of visible foot space and I straighten and come upright and get my feet into them, just missing by a couple of muscular milliseconds the onset of a debilitating and scream-inducing cramp. Such as happened to me once on a flight from Dubai to Amsterdam, in my sleep. It very nearly got the plane diverted.

I hate it all. The height, the breadth, the claustrophobic sky. Imagine, just imagine, if you can, what life would be like back there in economy.

This sea though. It is, today, properly, as it is on big maps, oceanic. It's pure blue. I haven't seen a cloud since we cleared the Newfoundland coast. Just the sky blue sky and the sky blue sea, each of them watered down a touch, a little bleached by the sun, so that if I tilt my head at an uncomfortable angle and let my mind wander and if sleep comes brushing at my shoulders, I can get confused and think we've flipped, I can think we're travelling upside down, and that if we try to land we'll be heading instead for the outer layers, the tropos, the stratos, the murderous spheres, that we'll be crushed and sundered on the edge of eternal space. I don't like sleeping on flights any more. The dreams are always bad. The nightmares are close.

I'm seven feet two inches tall. I have been seven feet two inches tall since I was twenty-three. I have never travelled in economy.

I stand up in my shoes and crouch my way along the aisle towards the front bulkhead, keeping my hands in view, making reassuring eye contact with both a steward and a teenage girl who's waiting cross-legged by the toilets. The plane is full, completely, and there's the queasy shuffle of bodies up and down the walkways, and although everyone stares at me, no one is making much noise, just little coughs and mutters and snores, and the low-level crackle of newspapers. Everyone had a 4 or 5 a.m. start for this one.

I had my accountant, Lynn Devoy over at HRCK, I had her work out for me once, from a year's detailed records, employing accepted actuarial and industry standard modelling procedures, the amount of time I will have spent in airplanes and/or airports, and/or getting to and from airplanes and airports, by the time I die, at the projected cut-off age of a man with my social and economic background, assuming a working life that takes me (I like my work) to seventy. The figure was appalling. I mean it was just appalling. I had her redo the sums, telling her that I had flown exactly three times before I was twenty-one, and that my travelling time since then had taken a sharp upwards curvature, peaking at the age of twenty-nine, and levelling out, by the time I was thirty-five, to the current rates. Constant eardrum abuse and germ exchange. With occasional two or three month busy periods, fevers. And sporadic, disorientating, one or two week static gaps when I don't fly anywhere at all whatsoever. The figure came back bigger. I mean. It grew. In hours it's a vast number. It's oceanic. In days it's not really a figure that makes any sense at all. In months you get a feeling that it might add up to a punishment for some terrible crime involving violence or the threat thereof. As years, it's a big number. It's a number of years, which, if applied to a person, would mean that you could actually take this person out to dinner and have a reasonably intelligent conversation with them. You could not legally have sex with them, or employ them, or marry them, or put them in the army, or let them have more than a couple of sips from your wine during their meal. And they might want chips. And you couldn't really leave them at home on their own for very long without getting in trouble with various kinds of authorities. But nevertheless, the number of years I will have spent flying by the time I die amounts to a small, sentient human being.

I walk around the galley, giving a steward who's preparing coffee a bit of a fright, for which I apologize, and I get myself a bottle of water and a plastic container of smoked salmon and micro salad, and I wander back down the other aisle, seeing two people I recognize from somewhere, neither of whom are looking my way, probably because they've seen me already. People can always place me. Everyone remembers me. And where they met me. So I don't really bother to remember much about them, unless I'm actually doing business with them, dealing with them, in which case I remember everything. A guy I met in Singapore last year for example, doing the background on the Mantev deal, whose name was Dan Keller, New York guy, a risk management guy from Layman's, I saw him again last week in Charles De Gaulle, and he saw me coming, and I could see him close an eye and purse his lips and search for my name, and relax then, *got it*, and I went over, and held out my hand, Dan, I said, good to see you, and he gave me a big toothy smile and said, Great to see you too, Tallman, how the hell you been?

Tallman. Too tall man.

I got Lynn, in cooperation with my then PA, Dean Hillings, to work out where I should live. To get the number down. Where should I set up home to make my flight time less of a person and more of a market approach plan, debt schedule, option period. A crude calculation based on the shortest mean distance to everywhere I had been in the previous twelve months indicated Baghdad. A slightly more realistic equation, involving a certain amount of delegation and disengagement, suggested six months in Singapore and six months in Chicago. Dean suggested living, à la Howard Hughes, in an actual airplane, or, failing that, in an apartment inside the main terminal at Schipol.

I manoeuvre myself back into my seat. This sea. It glints and sparkles, like circuitry. It has shapes and lines and patterns – all of them entirely a matter of perspective. See? That one there, that looks like a mouth of diamond teeth – that will not be apparent to anyone else, anywhere. Drop altitude a little and it disappears. Go higher and it fades. Sit in another seat and you'll see a cluster of blades, a tree of nails, pixels, eyes blinking. Even now as I look at it it's gone, chased off by the shadow of the plane. So I see a grid of black fields, charred by the sun, solid and still. I kick off my shoes again. Sip my water. My legs meander down into the dark underneath the man in front of me. I can't eat the salmon. I don't trust it.

I couldn't live in Chicago, or Singapore, so near the water. Bodies of water are called that for a reason. They're the skin of the planet, properly speaking. The bare skin of the globe. And we live in the pockets, the dry containers. I can barely live where I live, with the river tearing a strip off the city just a stone's throw from my windows. When the storms get going and the water rises I tend to find reasons for a trip to

Melbourne, Jakarta, Johannesburg, Dallas. Hong Kong terrifies me, if the truth be told, which is a problem, as I'm there about five times a year, clinging to the hinterland, cracking my head on door frames, slumped in the sobbing corners of express elevators and power showers and steam saunas. I hate Hong Kong.

Dean Hillings was killed in a plane crash in Italy in August '98. He had hitched a lift from Marie Kyle who had been in Rome with us clearing up a real mess involving the now thankfully defunct Jackal Group and the European trading arm of Palmer's. Marie was a senior partner with Korman. She never took a scheduled flight anywhere unless she was long-hauling, which she rarely did. Something happened to her pilot. A stroke or something. The plane went down near Pisa, and all five of them were killed. The pilot, the co-pilot (what was he *doing*?), Marie Kyle, Leonard Farrell and Dean Hillings. He was twenty-six, Dean was. He had a sister who sang at his funeral, beautiful voice, I can't remember her name.

Being this tall is absolute. I cannot be other than this tall. I cannot adapt or compromise or tone it down. It is like the colour of my skin. It's like my sex. None of these things can be altered. I don't fit comfortably into executive jets. I don't like them. They adhere too closely to the shape of my body. They are clingy and restrictive, coffinish. I pass on offers all the time. I have declined since the late 1980s, when I thought that my Lear claustrophobia was beginning to assume noticeable proportions. I did not want to pale and sob and pass out on a Paris to London. I didn't want assorted board members of Aker or IBM Europe or Korman or MTV trying to restrain me as I went for the door, went for the door, went for the door. I'm happy enough in a 747. I can relax, more or less, in a 737. I can manage in a BA146. Just about. They have to give me the front row. Dublin Amsterdam. Edinburgh Brussels. Washington New York. I will not, under any circumstances, fly in a turbo prop. No sir. Never.

The woman with the body attitude is reading a French magazine. I think she's Swiss. Probably. She glances at me, smiles. 'Beautiful weather out there,' she says, in an accent that is very Alpine, which could be from any of, what, six countries? Seven? How does she know I'm an English speaker? She's been peering at the title of my book. I nod, but I have a rule. I don't talk on airplanes. Dean said I should sleep and read only. Read and sleep. Sleep he argued, because you spend a third of your life asleep anyway, so you might as well get most of your flight time done during that third. Reading is the enricher, the added value, the motivational engine. He compiled a list of great works of world literature that I should read at 30,000 feet. So that I could argue that I was doing something which I otherwise would not do, that this was gained time, salvaged from the years – making of my small sentient human a precocious, impressive child. Dean was right. The worst thing I can do, unless I find myself sitting next to somebody astonishing, is to start up some small talk. Imagine all that small talk. The circumnavigation of the globe, many times over, in an endless loop of nonsense about good weather, bad hotels, share prices, legroom, genetics. She went back to her magazine.

I need bigger beds than you. I need bigger cars, bigger shirts, bigger suits, longer ties, higher ceilings. You think these things come cheaply? I have to put up with certain inconveniences. Attention. High visibility. Low humour. I need to stay sober, I need to think about where I'm going, I need to duck. If I am a little stooped, then who can blame me? If I find myself beset by odd anxieties of water and containment and banging my head, then who could honestly deny that it's really no wonder? Top of Dean's book list was *Cyrano de Bergerac.* I liked that a lot.

This sea. It just goes on. There is nothing on it. No ships. No land. I stare down at it. They had no lemon cordial in the galley. I was offered orange juice or bitter lemon mixers. I should bring my own. I should buy an expensive chrome flask and fill it with Robinson's Lemon Barley Water or Belvoir Organic. Should I pre-dilute? Should I pre-dilute or just carry the hard stuff and rely on on-board ice and water? I roll my head, cracking the parts of my neck into place, wondering how long we could keep flying if all the land disappeared. If the world went bare. We would go as long as we could, searching for a scrap of cover, and we would fall eventually, quietly, not bothering with terror I think, and we would briefly tear the skin, and be debris for a while, flotsam, sundered, and gasping we would sink, and sink, and sink, and sink, and drift deep down into the belly of the beast.

I think I am depressed. I think I have been depressed since August '98. I think it's killing me.

*

We landed forty minutes late in the pissing rain, which started suddenly as we crossed north of the islands, coming out of the blue and turning it a sodden heavy grey. Then we waited stationary for twenty minutes for a gate to free up. We were alive though. We had made it. This is a minor miracle. Think of the weight these things have to carry now, these unimaginable things. I mean the extra weight. The pictures. Those bright morning moments. The blue sky, the grid of windows, the orange banners suddenly unfurled, the descent, the descent. On top of the weight they've always carried – people and their items, the multiple connections, their reach; corporate profile, airline safety management, a publicly quoted future, manufacturer orders; fear – of the fatigued rivet, the overheated wiring, the botched door seal, the pilot's mental health, the bomb in the hold. Not just all of that, but the new stuff too. Him. Her. Box cutters. Cell phones. Trainers, high heels. The city of targets. Sudden turns. The countryside of reactors and chemical plants. The offices, the barracks, the parliaments, the tall things of the world. The tall things.

I'm sitting in the back of the car, I'm looking at various pieces of paper, bound, stapled, loose. Figures, mostly. Graph paper, chart. You learn to recognize the shapes after a while, to see the patterns, to evaluate at a glance. The way the thing looks on the page. As you shuffle. An unusual shape is what you're looking for, or certain indicators, mathematical expressions, particular **bold face** references. Within the text you stay sharp for various legal and economic euphemisms. Standard English tends to slip under radar. I have a three o'clock in the city. I have a five o'clock in the city. I have a night at home. I have a 7 a.m. to Madrid. My phone has fielded thirteen messages while I was up there. I deal with them. I sign off three contracts. I fire someone. I decide to cancel Madrid, take the day off, I'm just so fucking tired, I'm tired, I'm tired, but I change my mind when my PA calls and says that Madrid is very nervous, Madrid is close to pulling out, Madrid is twitchy, Madrid needs me. My PA these days is Paula Pearson. She is efficient, she appears to make good judgements, she has a solid grasp of five languages and no sense of humour. She's worked for me for about six months. For Christmas I gave her an MP3 player. She seemed surprised. I don't know why. Perhaps she was surprised that I got her anything at all. But I have always bought Christmas gifts for my PAs. Something decidedly non-work related. The first Christmas with Dean he gave out to me for giving him a briefcase. He said it was unfair to get your PA something that he would then feel obliged to be seen using. He changed it for a new mobile phone. Which I then saw him use every day.

The traffic is snarled in all the usual places. When I get through the paperwork I close my eyes and try to doze off, but I can't. I get the driver, whose name I cannot remember, to put on the radio, but then I get him to turn it off again. I open a window and look at the rain. I close the window. I pick up the paperwork and I go through it again. There are shapes within the shapes – embellishments and flourishes. Fretwork. Psychology. You can see the fear in the minor clauses. You can see the hidden weaknesses. They pay a lot of money to keep that stuff out, but this is a limited language, and I have been using it for years. I can spot the fault lines – where they think they're vulnerable, where they think they're strong. I can see the deals behind the deals. I can sniff out the strategy, the long term positioning, the all but secret pacts. The connections, lines, wires, pulses, contingents, switches, failsafes, fallbacks, defaults, the secondary state, the ancient rules, the lift, wingspan, wind shear, tailspin, the money, honey, the dread, fear, the understandings, fear, the reasons, fear, the system, fear, the grid, fear. The human grid. My work. The net thrown over the world. I fly to all the corners and I make sure the cables are holding, the threads aren't fraying, that the seepage isn't lethal. That's all.

By the time I get to my three o'clock it's ten to four.

*

It's hard not to crouch. Everywhere. I find it difficult to walk down any corridor, in any office building, anywhere in the world, without crouching. Even if there is plenty of space. I have been caught before by light fittings, air conditioning, smoke alarms, the claws of sprinklers. I have bled in the corporate headquarters of Microsoft, Sony, ComItalia, Bayer, Griffin Systems, Motorola and, once, involving stitches, in the office of a trade minister in Singapore. These are embarrassing moments. There have been none lately, though I did bloodlessly stun myself on a bronze limb of sculpture in the atrium of my hotel in Seoul about two weeks ago. Nobody noticed.

Paula calls me at eight thirty with some Madrid updates. They have a situation there. Paula is pretty good at this – she briefs me fully, without pause for consulting of notes or checking of details, for about five minutes, with very little irrelevant information, and leaves me having to ask only two questions, one of which is about my flight. I run a hot bath and soak in it for forty minutes, reading a serial thriller. I watch the ten o'clock news. I check my e-mail. I order some books for delivery to the office. The rain is over. I stand on the balcony and look out at the city and I see all the little lights and all the road lines, and I can make out intersections and the hum of the traffic and the flash of airplanes and the helicopter drones and the dead people, all the dead people, all of the dead, dishonoured by this.

When I sleep I dream that I am in an invisible car with Peter Falk, the man who plays Columbo, and I'm driving and he is in the passenger seat, and he is complaining, eloquently, about the impracticality of our invisible car. About the fact that anywhere we park will look subsequently like a free space. That we will be constantly rear-ended. That we will be sideswiped and rammed, that we will not be seen by pedestrians and will therefore kill quite a few, that we will park our car and then not be able to find it again, that we will lose the thing in a multi-storey and will have to feel and grope in every berth in the hope of coming up against something solid, in the hope of colliding with what it is we need to get home in. And all the time he is talking, I am driving. I'm driving. Forever. I'm driving forever. Stop signs, yield signs, roundabouts, speed bumps, one way systems, off ramps, on ramps, filter left, filter right, zebra crossings, pedestrian lights, traffic lights, caution lights, warning lights, cat's eyes, hard shoulders, soft verges, crash barriers, cones, double white, single white, broken white, cross hatch, cycle lanes, bus lanes, no stopping, no learner drivers, reduce speed NOW.

I wake up thinking of paint. That we need to stop and paint the car. That we can just buy a can of ordinary white paint and a couple of brushes, Jesus Christ, and do a quick paint job on the invisible car, just so we can get home before we're killed. I open my mouth to say this to Peter Falk and realize then that he isn't there. That I'm dreaming. That I was dreaming. That I've stopped dreaming now and that outside my window the city is powering up, the cables are humming, the day is starting, the whole thing is alive. It's alive.

★

It's a 737, and I'm standing at the window of the Diamond Class lounge sipping a lemon cordial and holding a wet handkerchief to my temple, looking out at them load it with luggage and at least two animals, in breathable hard plastic carry cages, dogs or cats or something. I straightened up too quickly coming out of the revolving door. There's a lip of a wall there, just hanging there, an architect's leftover, and I hit it on the rise. It's not bleeding, but there's a graze, on the hairline. Slight swelling. A darkness. There seems to be some debate amongst the baggage handlers regarding the animals. One of them, squatting in the entrance to the hold, is shaking his head and shrugging his shoulders, while two others, one of them carrying the cages in heavily gloved hands, seem to be trying to convince him of something. Maybe there are animal berths in there. Maybe they are all occupied. Maybe he doesn't like these animals, or doesn't trust the cages. Perhaps there are some guidelines involving the feeding and watering of animals in transit which he does not feel are being followed. In any case, he doesn't seem ready to allow them on board. I have a horrible headache.

I would like to see a plane crash. From here. From the window of the Diamond Class lounge. I'd like to see a plane, a large plane, hit the ground, break up, fireball. Along the length of a runway perhaps, or on the grass somewhere, or on the edge of the tree line in the distance. I'd like the visual shock of it. The cascade, the bellow. I'd be curious as to sound. What would we hear do you think? Rumble or roar or bang or nothing? How long before the fire trucks and the ambulances came? How would the people around me react? Would they scream, pray, curse, call loved ones, cancel appointments, reschedule meetings, throw up, order a double, weep, cry, slump? How would I react? Would I react? Would I go pale or blush? Would my headache ease or worsen? Would I be all right? Would I be all right?

I want to get it over with. I really do. I want the break to happen soon. So that I can. So that I can.

'Excuse me?'

It's a man I don't think I know. About thirty, flecked grey, black suit, no tie, white shirt, shoulder bag, smile.

'Yes?'

'I'm sure you don't know me. My name is Sean Lyle.'

'Yes?'

He reddens slightly.

'I was a friend of Dean Hillings.'

'Oh. Right.'

'Yes. Sorry. I just thought, well, I just thought I'd introduce myself. I recognized you, though I wasn't absolutely sure, and I thought I'd come over. I was in college with Dean. I saw you at the funeral. Dean told me about you before that. Obviously before that. He enjoyed working for you a lot. He said you were a very good boss. His death was such a shock. Really was. I still can't believe it sometimes. You know, the way you forget that something like that has happened, as if you could, but you could, I could I mean, and I do, sometimes, I don't know how, and then I remember suddenly. It's still a terrible shock, if you know what I mean. So. There. Well. And how are you?'

'I'm fine, thank you.'

He stares at me, still smiling, his shoulder bag still hanging there. It is unusual for people to approach me like this. I am unapproachable.

'Did you hurt your head?'

'It's fine. It's, you know, I'm used to it.'

'Right. Madrid? Me too. I think it'll be a while though. Can I get you a drink?'

We go and sit at the bar and he buys me another lemon cordial and a coffee for himself. He's very chatty this guy. Turns out he's a lawyer at Russell, on his way to Madrid as back-up to the bad guys. He works out that we're on different sides after about two minutes, but he has manners, he doesn't want to talk about Madrid, he doesn't mention it again, he leaves it alone. He talks about Dean. About how happy he was, enjoying himself, enjoying life. He enjoyed life, he says. He says it twice, and stares at me, big sad smile, no tie. He tells me that Dean really liked working for me, because I was a laugh, I was a lot of fun. He looks at me a little sheepishly as he tells me this, maybe wondering again whether he's got the right guy. I wonder too. I don't want to talk about Dean. I really don't. So we talk about Enron. We talk about Andersen's. We talk about Marconi, M&S, AIB. He knows Europe, next to nothing on the USA, quite a bit of the East, Australasia. I tell him some things. Interesting things. Singapore gossip. Tokyo trouble. He enjoys it when I hint at some links and connections he didn't know about, hadn't seen. I reveal a little bit of the grid. Look at that. See how it works? See the circuitry and the current? See the neurons and the mesh?

'Capitalism,' he said.

I don't know if he was going to say something about capitalism or whether that was just an exclamation, because our flight is called.

'I have a rule,' I say. 'I don't talk on airplanes.'

'OK. Good rule.'

'So. It was nice meeting you.'

Maybe I appear foolish to him. Maybe what I know is common knowledge. Maybe I have no skills other than the mundane efficiency of having done the same thing over and over and over again. Maybe I'm past it. I didn't see Enron coming. I should have and I didn't. Not that it had anything to do with me. Not that I would have been expected to see something like that. Not that I had any special knowledge which might have alerted me to the possibility. But still. I should have known. I should have felt the signals in the plexus. I should have sensed the fear in the engine. The power surge. The excess. Maybe I'm a fool. I have an empty seat beside me. The flight is a third full. I touch a fingertip to the graze on my head. There is a medium size bump. I try to calculate the effect this will have on Madrid.

Half way over the sea, Sean Lyle comes and sits beside me. He hands me a note. It says:

> *Any thoughts on this afternoon? This is cheeky I know, but I thought I'd give it a try. Do you think we can get away with 30% or are the numbers better than they're letting on?*
> *SL*

I actually think this is quite funny. I laugh. I'm about to tell him to get lost, but he hands me a pad and a pen and gives me an indignant look, as if shocked that I would think of saying a word.

> *It* is *bloody cheeky. 30%!!! Anyway, I suspect I'll be having this argument with your seniors later on. You can listen in if you like, might learn something.*

I tear off the page and hand it to him. He smiles at it. Takes the pen. The steward is beside us. Someone is having a half-bottle of Chardonnay. It's seven forty a.m. Sean Lyle accepts a glass of champagne.

Well it was worth a try. Doubt I'll learn very much though. If I do I'll buy you a drink. OK?

I give it a moment, a pause. Then I nod, smile at him. He smiles back, slowly, and returns to his seat. Through the window the small sea rolls past. It is slashed here and there by ferries and trawlers and freight. I think I can see the coast of France in the distance, but my geography is off tilt, I'm not sure. The danger is always the same. You loose your bearings. That you cannot coordinate your position. That the axes are obscured. You're lost.

I move across the grid. I travel. I work. It's a fragile little system. It buckles when I touch it. It snaps when I stand. I imagine taking the pad and pen and writing a few simple words. Bomb. God. Death. Device. An arrangement of horrors. The grammar, the syntax, the spelling, none of that matters. Leave the message in the toilet, by the sink, on an empty seat, on a trolley, anywhere. I imagine what happens next. I assume there are protocols, procedures, plans. Lock the cabin doors, divert. There are emergency call signs. Danger on the network. A shadow on the sea. Incoming. Scramble. Contain.

We land in the heat of Madrid. Sean Lyle waves at me, finds his driver. I find mine. In the car I call Paula. There is something I need done. She hears me out, clarifies two points, hangs up. I relax in the car. I do the paperwork, I kick off my shoes, I check some numbers. I have two preliminary meetings. I have a light lunch. The thing is this. We are so close to chaos. You know? We are so close to collapse.

It's in the air. It's in the fucking air. The whole thing is solid but it hangs by a thread in the air. The only currency worth anything is fear. It holds the grid. It holds the grid. It holds the grid.

By the afternoon, by the time we get going with the main event, Madrid at the table, sea faced, ready to deal with the terror, Sean Lyle is gone. Disappeared. Recalled.

I believe.

I believe in the purity of the market. I believe in the free movement of capital. I believe in deregulation. I believe in the integrity of profit. I believe in the fullness of time that I will die in a shock of twisted metal, structural failure, demolition.

I think I'm depressed. I think it's killing me.

Contributors

Tom Humphries is a sports reporter with *The Irish Times*. He has written several sports books, including *Green Fields: Gaelic Sport in Ireland* (Weidenfeld & Nicolson, 1996) and *Running to Stand Still* (Inpho Publishing), a collaboration with the photographer Patrick Bolger and the athlete Sonia O'Sullivan. His many awards include the Listowel Writers' Week Journalism Award. This is his first short story.

Claire Keegan grew up on a farm in Wicklow. Her collection of stories, *Antarctica*, was published by Faber & Faber in 1999. She has won many awards for her stories including the William Trevor Prize, the Francis MacManus Award and the Martin Healy Prize. *Antarctica* was awarded the Rooney Prize for Irish Literature and the Arts Council's Macauley Fellowship. She is now writing a second collection of stories and a novel. She lives in Co. Monaghan.

John MacKenna was born in Castledermot, Co. Kildare, in 1952. Having taught for six years, he joined RTÉ as a radio producer in 1980. His first non-fiction book, *The Fallen* (Blackstaff, 1992), won the *Irish Times* First Fiction Award. This was followed by a novel, *Clare* (Blackstaff, 1993), based on the life of the poet John Clare. Since then he has published two novels, *The Last Fine Summer* and *A Haunted Heart,* (Picador, 1998 and 1999) and a volume of stories, *A Year of Our Lives* (Picador, 1996). He is currently co-writing a life of the Irish Antarctic explorer, Ernest Shackleton. He lives in Co. Kildare.

Aidan Mathews was born in Dublin in 1956. He studied at University College Dublin, Trinity College Dublin, and at Stanford University where he was a pupil of the philosopher René Girard. He has published three collections of poetry, *Windfalls* (Dolmen, 1977), *Minding Ruth* (The Gallery Press, 1983) and *According to the Small Hours* (Jonathan Cape, 1998); two short story collections, *Adventures in a Bathyscope* (Secker & Warburg, 1988) and *Lipstick on the Host* (Secker & Warburg, 1992), which won Italy's Prix Cavour; and a novel, *Muesli at Midnight* (Secker & Warburg, 1990). He has written several plays, among them *The Diamond Body*, *Exit Entrance*, winner of the Sunday Tribune Theatre Award, and *Communion.*

Molly McCloskey was born in Philadelphia in 1964 and moved to Sligo in 1989. She is the author of *Solomon's Seal* a collection of short stories published by Phoenix House in 1997, and *The Beautiful Changes*, a novella published by Lilliput Press in 2002. Her short stories have won a number of awards, including the Francis MacManus Award. She has worked as a journalist in America and in Ireland. She now lives in Dublin.

Blánaid McKinney was born in Enniskillen, Co. Fermanagh, in 1961. She is a graduate of Queen's University, Belfast. She lived for a time in Aberdeenshire and began writing short stories in 1990. Her first collection, *Big Mouth*, was published by

Phoenix House in 2000. Since 1998 she has lived in London. Her first novel, *The Ledge*, was published by Weidenfeld & Nicholson in 2002.

Mary Morrissy was born in Dublin in 1957. She is the author of three books: *A Lazy Eye* (Jonathan Cape, 1993), a collection of short stories, and two novels, *Mother of Pearl* and *The Pretender* (Jonathan Cape, 1996 and 2000). *Mother of Pearl* was shortlisted for the Whitbread Award and *The Pretender* was nominated for the International Impac Dublin Literary Award 2002. She received a Lannan Award in 1995. She has taught on creative writing programmes at the University of Arkansas and the University of Iowa. She lives in Cork and is currently at work on her third novel.

Éilís Ní Dhuibhne was born in Dublin in 1954. She was educated at University College Dublin, where she studied English, Anglo-Saxon and Irish Folklore. She was awarded a Ph.D. in 1982. Her first short story was published in the *Irish Press* in 1974. Since then she has written four collections of short stories and four novels, five novels for children and other works. She has received many literary awards, including the Stewart Parker Award for Drama, the Butler Award for Prose and the Oireachtas Award for a novel in Irish. Her novel *The Dancers Dancing* (Blackstaff, 1999) was shortlisted for the Orange Prize for Fiction in 2000. Her most recent books are *The Pale Gold of Alaska* (Blackstaff and Headline, 2001) and *Midwife to the Fairies: Selected Short Stories* (Attic Press, 2002).

Joseph O'Neill was born in Cork in 1964 and educated in the Netherlands and at Cambridge University. He is the author of two novels, *This Is the Life* (Faber & Faber, 1991) and *The Breezes* (Faber & Faber, 1995), and of *Blood-Dark Track: A Family History* (Granta Books, 2001), a non-fiction account of the lives of his

Irish and Turkish grandfathers. Joseph O'Neill practised as a barrister in London from 1990–2000. He now lives in New York City. He is currently working on a novel about cricket in New York.

Sean O'Reilly was born in 1969 in Derry, Northern Ireland. He lived abroad for many years, mainly in Scandinavia and Europe, working at a variety of jobs. He has published a book of short stories, *Curfew and Other Stories*, and a novel, *Love and Sleep*, both with Faber & Faber. He currently lives in Ireland where he is writing another novel and a film.

Keith Ridgway is from Dublin. He was born in 1965. His novella *Horses* first appeared in 1997 and was followed in 1998 by his first novel *The Long Falling* (Faber & Faber), which has since been awarded the Prix Femina Étranger and the Prix Premier Roman in France. A collection of short stories, *Standard Time,* was published by Faber & Faber in 2001, when he was awarded the Rooney Prize for Irish Literature. His new novel, *The Parts*, will be published by Faber & Faber in Spring 2003.

Caroline Walsh was born in 1952 and reared in Dublin and Co. Meath. She has been a journalist with *The Irish Times* since the mid-1970s where she worked as a reporter and feature writer before becoming Features Editor and Regional News Editor. She has been Literary Editor of *The Irish Times* since 1999. She is the author of *The Homes of Irish Writers* (Anvil Books, 1982) and has edited two previous collections of short stories: *Modern Irish Stories from The Irish Times* (Irish Times, 1985) and *Virgins and Hyacinths* (Attic Press, 1993).